THE AFRICAN CONTRACT

ARTHUR KERNS

DIVERSIONBOOKS

Also by Arthur Kerns

Hayden Stone Thrillers
The Riviera Contract
The Yemen Contract

Diversion Books
A Division of Diversion Publishing Corp.
443 Park Avenue South, Suite 1004
New York, New York 10016
www.DiversionBooks.com

For more information, email info@diversionbooks.com

Second Diversion Books edition June 2016
Print ISBN: 978-1-62681-302-1
eBook ISBN: 978-1-62681-293-2

PRINCIPAL CHARACTERS

Hayden Stone, former FBI agent, now CIA operative

Sandra Harrington, CIA operative

Dirk Lange, South African intelligence agent

Colonel Gustave Frederick, CIA official

Jacob, Israeli Mossad agent, an old friend of Hayden Stone

Contessav Lucinda Avoscani, love interest of Hayden Stone

Abdul Wahab, terrorist fugitive from France, married to Lady Beatrice

Dawid van Wartt, Afrikaner, blames the West and US for the end of apartheid and his privileged position

Nabeel Asuty, Egyptian terrorist in Freetown, works for Abdul Wahab

Ambassador Marshall Bunting, US ambassador to South Africa, an avid birder

Patience St. John Smythe, former love interest of Hayden Stone, now in a relationship with Marshall Bunting

Dingane, Abdul Wahab's major domo in Cape Town

Jonathan Worthington, amputee victim of the blood diamond war

Charles Fleming, CIA station chief in Pretoria, South Africa

Luke Craig, CIA station chief in Freetown, Sierra Leone

Farley Durrell, Sandra's old boyfriend, a CIA deep cover officer.

M. R. D. Houston, CIA base chief at Cape Town

Bull Rhyton, friend of Van Wartt, former sergeant in South African Army

Elizabeth Kerr, intelligence analyst in Northern Virginia

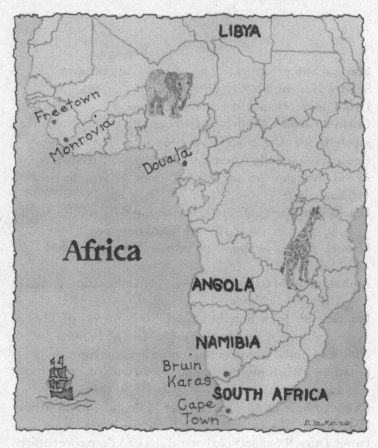

Africa

LIBYA

Freetown
Monrovia
Douala

ANGOLA

NAMIBIA

Bruin
Karas
SOUTH AFRICA
Cape
Town

B. M. Kerns

CHAPTER ONE

BRUIN KARAS, NAMIBIA—AUGUST 2, 2002

Corneliu lay prone on the hard red ground using a thorn bush both for shade and concealment. Almost an hour had passed since he'd seen two men in a small Japanese-made ATV come over the western ridge, maneuvering back and forth to avoid the acacia trees, and approach the abandoned boxcar sitting on the railroad siding. That morning he had been wandering the dry savanna scrubland looking for birds to photograph. Last month Uncle Bull Rhyton had given him an old Nikon F camera with a telescopic lens for his twelfth birthday. Corneliu wanted to send pictures to another uncle up in Windhoek who was compiling a book on birds of the desert.

Now Corneliu used the telescopic lens to watch and photograph the two men. He had good close-ups of their faces. At first they walked around the boxcar and kneeled to inspect under the carriage. The shorter man climbed on top and tried to open the roof hatch. It wouldn't open. Corneliu could have told him that. He and his friend Adam had tried numerous times.

Lying motionless, the sun warmed the back of his bare legs. His father's green commando sweater became uncomfortable, but he dare not make any unnecessary motion to remove it, for fear of being detected. Like a hunter in a stand waiting for his prey to pass by, Corneliu became aware of his surroundings. He watched ants marching in a line; two nervous meerkats made a brief appearance, and a lone antelope tiptoed by. All this while he watched the two men.

From his left Corneliu detected more movement. A stone's throw away a Cape cobra slid across the dirt and dry grass, heading in the direction of the boxcar. It stopped, licked the air with its tongue, and then he continued on. Corneliu pointed his camera and took a picture of the speckled, golden-brown snake. The face of a Cape cobra had freckles like his younger brother. A shadow passed overhead. He looked up and spotted a soaring snake eagle.

From behind him, Corneliu felt a presence, then recognized a familiar scent. Without looking, he knew it was Adam, who seconds later crouched next to him. His dark skin glistened in the sun, brown eyes intent on the two men. "Who them?" he asked.

"Don't know," Corneliu answered. "I think they want to break in."

"Them take that thing from inside. Maybe?"

Corneliu looked at his friend and nodded. "Where have you been? Haven't seen you for a week."

The side door of the boxcar had three heavy padlocks, placed there by Uncle Bull a month ago. That was after he and Adam had broken in. Through the lens Corneliu watched one man, the taller one, go back to the vehicle and pull out a crowbar.

Adam lay flat on the ground. "My mom said your father told her to keep me away from you," Adam said.

Corneliu raised the camera to see what was going on inside the boxcar. He couldn't see anything and squinted his tired eyes. Now that he was older, his father didn't want him to be friends with a Bushman. He'd tolerated it when they were children, but no longer. His father had funny old ways.

"We're friends anyway. Yes?"

"Maybe."

Both men jumped out of the boxcar and moved back to the ATV. The taller man took a black instrument from the seat and held it out toward the open door of the boxcar. Corneliu aimed the camera and snapped the last frame of film. Both men looked at something on the instrument, then climbed into the four-wheeler and drove back toward the ridge from where they had come. The ATV stopped, and Corneliu thought he saw the driver talking into a heavy-looking phone. After a moment they continued on.

As Corneliu and Adam stood and stretched, the snake eagle dropped from the sky, caught the cobra, and lifted it with a slow flapping of wings. The snake dangled and twisted from its talons.

NORTHERN VIRGINIA—SAME DAY

"Ms. Kerr." Elizabeth Kerr's group chief in the National Imagery and Mapping Agency, who for a change wore a coat and tie, rapped on the open door. Next to him stood a tall, thin Asian-American. "The gentleman from the inspector general's office is here for the interview."

Kerr left her computer station, shook the man's soft hand, and offered him a chair. Her group chief left, closing the door behind him. She had learned about the inquiry yesterday afternoon. In her way of thinking, this interview was three months too late. Nevertheless, here it was.

The thin man began the interview by giving his name and showing her a set of credentials. He gave her a condensed version of why he was there. Another US agency that conducted intelligence had registered a complaint against her working group. Vital information in the hands of her agency was not promptly passed over to them. This is where he paused to take a breath.

"The information in question was ... that is, you are the primary source of that information."

"If you're talking about the blip I picked up from Africa three months ago, and that I told my immediate superior about, and that he deemed irrelevant due to other higher priority targets, then yes."

This was almost the last straw for her. Putting up daily with stupid, venal bureaucrats. She had two masters degrees, ten years of experience, and no respect. Worse, she had to commute in Washington, DC, traffic every day, including standing with other workers in the "slug line" in Springfield to hop a ride with a single driver who needed more passengers to get on the HOV lane into the city.

"Did you make your discovery a matter of record?"

"Yes." *Damn right and you know it.*

"We're referring to the memorandum of May 2002 that you filed?"

"And the two subsequent memoranda?"

The man nodded. His demeanor changed. The politeness less visible. "Recount for me what you saw or discovered," he said. "Quite frankly, I'm not all familiar with what you do, or better, how you do it. I don't need to know the details of your job, just what you discovered."

"To put it simply, I saw a blip on the screen. The blip in this instance was an ever-so-slight trace of thermal nuclear energy. A glow. Checking with other measurements and another department, this 'glow' could only be fissionable material." She paused. "I told my boss and he wasn't interested. We had too many things going on with the World Trade Center incident."

"What then?"

"I went on with my other tasks but kept on checking the screen for this blip."

"How often?"

"Daily."

"Did this thing on the screen move at all?"

"No, it didn't, but when the energy measurement increased, I informed my boss and followed up with the second memorandum. Two weeks later."

His eyes widened, and she knew that he had something to chew on. The next question would be why she had waited two weeks to make a written report. She preempted the strike. "Will the other agency, which I presume is the CIA, want to talk with me about this?"

He nodded.

Good. Maybe I can get a job with them.

The man closed his folder. He looked down at the floor. "Your boss tried to lay the blame on you."

"Figures."

"No need to worry." He motioned to get up, and settled

down again. "Have you seen this blip lately?"

"This morning. The signal is growing stronger."

"Where is it, may I ask?"

"In the middle of the Kalahari Desert."

CIA HEADQUARTERS, LANGLEY, VIRGINIA—SAME DAY

Colonel Gustave Frederick walked into his seventh-floor office suite and stopped at his assistant's desk. "Phone John Matterhorn and tell him I'm available anytime this morning."

He shut the door of his private office, poured himself a cup of coffee, and loosened his tie. Standing at the window, he looked out on Langley Forest. This time of year the leaves blocked the view of the Potomac River. The summer haze hung over the trees, signaling another muggy August day in the Washington area.

This morning, the director's briefing had gone well until the subject of Iraq came up. Iraq and Saddam Hussein were in the White House's crosshairs, and the preparation for action was building throughout the Washington establishment. The camp that believed the wise course in the elimination of al Qaeda rested in a protracted campaign in Afghanistan—a policy that Frederick supported—was losing.

This morning Frederick jumped ship. At the meeting the director asked him if he would use his military contacts to assure the agency played a major role in any attack on Iraq. Of course, he agreed with enthusiasm to impress the other senior staff members, but more importantly, it placed him in the eyes of the director as a "team player" and someone who could be relied upon.

He was now in the "inner circle," someone asked by the director to stay around for a few minutes after a meeting. Today, privately, the director asked him to speak with John Matterhorn about a matter in Africa.

Colonel Frederick graduated Harvard and received his draft notice before his acceptance to law school arrived in the mail.

During the Vietnam War, he received his first Bronze Star as a private first class, the second as a lieutenant, and the Silver Star after he had made captain. He had met John in Laos during the war while serving in the special forces.

As a CIA officer John Matterhorn lived in the jungles of Laos and Cambodia running intelligence operations and rescuing downed American flyers. He was good at his work, and Frederick always told John that as a case officer he couldn't help recruiting everyone he met. He recruited Frederick into the CIA.

A half hour later, Matterhorn arrived, and Frederick went to the door to greet him. The man had never attained high rank, but in the agency doors were open to him and opened for him. Short in stature, he looked neat: gray tweed jacket, checkered shirt, and a wool tie. He and his wife were old Directorate of Operations case officers. They had six children: four were in the CIA, one was a general, and the other a Jesuit in Rome assigned to the Curia. A daughter-in-law was a senate staffer, another an FBI agent.

"Gus. Something is going on in Africa."

"Tell me.

"Abdul Wahab, the man we believe responsible for the deaths of two young case officers, is in South Africa."

"So I heard." Three months before, Frederick's team had allowed Wahab to escape from the French Riviera. Since then, he'd been keeping tabs on this terrorist's movements.

"My unit learned that members of a branch of al Qaeda have traveled to Sierra Leone, in western Africa."

"I see."

Matterhorn rubbed his hands together. "We've been getting a lot of chatter on the ether. Something big is going on in the African theatre. We've been so distracted with the Middle East. Our resources and talent are directed there and away from other areas of the world."

"I agree."

"Al Qaeda knows that. The anniversary of the World Trade Center disaster is coming up. These people are fixated on dates and spectacles. Something is in the wind in Africa."

"John. Get to the point?"

"There's a rumor that another agency with satellites picked up a disturbing blip in southern Africa."

"Can you be more specific?"

"A signal that can only come from a form of nuclear device."

Colonel Frederick got up and went to the window. Matterhorn had gone to the director about this intelligence. Had John suggested that he handle the matter? No matter, this information required immediate action. He turned and faced Matterhorn.

"We need to form a task force with office space, personnel, a budget, and so forth. You know the routine. You know the ropes."

Matterhorn stood.

"Come to me with any problems, any issues," Frederick said. "If the agency tracking this nuclear emission isn't cooperative with sharing intelligence, let me know. I'll pull strings. Meantime, I'll send someone to Africa to do a little snooping."

"Let me guess who."

"Who else? Hayden Stone."

CHAPTER TWO

MONROVIA, LIBERIA—AUGUST 6, 2002

The American Embassy's security floodlights cut through the blackness and illuminated the low waves rolling in from the Atlantic Ocean. A muggy wind blew drizzle from the west. Hayden Stone sat with the embassy's security chief, Al Goodman, on the covered deck of the guesthouse after a mediocre dinner at one of the two restaurants still open in Monrovia. The mildew-spotted seat of his chair felt clammy, and he brushed rust off his arm from the metal armrest. Everything in the city appeared damp, old, and murky, like the hulking black rock on which the embassy sat.

From his left, beyond the embassy compound, came a long cry that resembled a wounded animal. The wail accompanied a rhythmic banging on a skin drum that began only minutes after they settled down with cold gin and tonics.

"They're lighting candles on the beach over there," Goodman said. "Mende people praying to a spirit of some kind." He leaned forward, listening hard. "Kélèn drums."

Stone took in the sounds of the rain and the beat of the drums. "The sounds of West Africa," he said. "At night in Ghana, I've been to large gatherings on the beach outside Accra. Drums, bonfires, dances."

"The locals here say it's a way to talk with restless souls. Understandable with all the human carnage this place has seen recently." Goodman sipped his drink. "That beach over there is where former president Doe and his clique were executed by the incoming government."

They were silent for some minutes.

"How long have you been in Liberia?" Stone asked.

Goodman, the embassy's RSO, regional security officer, tilted back in his chair and jiggled the ice in his glass. His eyeglasses sat on his forehead, touching his thin black hair. "Been here for over a year, but this is my third tour. First time I came here, the place was alive. American Firestone Rubber Company had a huge presence outside the city. Voice of America was here. Missionaries traveled back and forth from the interior." He sipped his drink. "Of course, many of you agency folks were about."

"Quite a change."

Goodman chuckled. "Embassy people would drive to Payneville to see the Omega communication tower. Fourteen hundred feet high. Badge of honor if you climbed it."

"Did you?"

"You bet I did."

"See any hope for a rebound here?"

"The country's still in shock from the civil war. The leader of the new government is …" Goodman looked around as if someone might hear him, and gave a dismissive hand gesture.

They stayed quiet for a time, listening to the wails. Two or more drums joined in. The waves pounded as they grew higher, and the lights now brought out traces of transparent green in the gray water. Stone took in the smells of Africa he had forgotten since his last visit—the scent of vegetation breathing at night, smoke from the cooking oils throughout the city, the heavy warmth. He always found it difficult to relax on this continent, but at the same time, it exerted a strong fascination.

Goodman rose from his chair. "Time to go to the airport. Have to meet and greet a visitor on the evening flight in from Paris. It's always a challenge driving here at night. No city electricity. No traffic lights." He tossed the rest of his drink out onto the rocky ground. "Tomorrow, let's try to get in a game of tennis."

"Maybe in the afternoon, when I get back from my appointment."

Stone watched the man descend the two cement block steps from the porch and carefully make his way on the overgrown path to his quarters. Raindrops slipped through the muggy air. Monsoon time.

Goodman appeared to be a decent man, an old Africa hand, but Stone hadn't known him long enough to place him in a friend or foe camp. An undercurrent of animosity existed between foreign service people like Goodman and the CIA, and Stone faced the added problem that many RSOs disliked the FBI. He wondered if Goodman knew he was a former FBI agent now working for the agency.

The embassy assigned Stone a unit in a four-bedroom complex facing the ocean. On entering, he found the room dark and had trouble finding the light switch on the table lamp. The air smelled musty, and he detected another scent he hadn't noticed that afternoon when he had brought in his luggage. A thick, sour ammonia odor.

He undressed, placed his Colt .45 semiautomatic on the nightstand, brushed his teeth, and slipped between the sheets. One benefit of staying in embassy housing in Liberia was the freshly washed and ironed bed linens every night. Still, the cloth felt sticky to the skin.

Overhead, two geckos made their way across the cracked ceiling. He watched their progress in and out of the shadows from the lamplight and hoped they'd dine on the mosquitoes before the insects had a chance to feast on him. The medical unit back at Langley had given him mefloquine tablets, but they were only malaria suppressants, not full protection against the disease. The only things they guaranteed, Stone learned, were weird Technicolor dreams.

He flipped through the book on African birdlife he found in the embassy library, and after occasionally pausing where particularly colorful birds appeared, he became drowsy and dropped the book next to his gun. Yawning, he closed his eyes and debated whether he should turn out the light. Sleep came before making a decision.

A noise woke him. The straight back chair by the door to the toilet had scraped along the floor. Stone remained still. He could see only the top of the chair, where he had draped his trousers. He heard a swish along the floor. The sound approached the end of his bed. As his hand moved for his gun on the side table, the head of a thick, black snake with large scales rose from the foot of his bed. It continued to rise higher and higher.

Stone yanked his feet under him and hugged the headboard. He held the pillow in front of him. His left hand touched his gun, but it and the book tumbled to the floor. Startled, the snake slinked onto his bed and quickly coiled.

"Holy shit!" He jumped out of bed, dashing for the far wall. Once there, he inched toward the door.

The full length of the snake came into view. At least nine feet long, the creature became aggressive. Poised at the edge of the mattress and with open mouth, it hissed loudly. Stone saw that it was about to slide onto the floor in his direction. He ran to the chair and held it out as a shield against the snake.

"Help! For Christ's sake! Help! I got a big-ass snake here!"

The snake dropped to the floor and slithered toward him. Stone looked into the snake's black irises as the head swayed back and forth. It coiled and struck the chair with quick, short strikes, almost knocking it out of Stone's hands. The strength of the creature surprised him. Stone made for the door, but the snake blocked his escape. Striking again, the trousers dropped off the chair, which confused the snake.

"Unlock the door!" a voice shouted from outside.

"Can't get to it!"

The snake showed a fearless display of aggression. Mouth wide, it rose and made a quick nip at Stone's bare legs. Its head touched Stone's calf, but there was no sting, no bite.

The door banged open. The snake backed up, shifted its gaze, and hissed at the figure standing in the doorway.

A familiar woman's voice spoke. "Damn thing's too fast to shoot."

Stone leaped toward the door, eyes on the snake. Another voice, Goodman's, ordered, "Get out. Fast!"

As Stone exited, a marine security guard brushed past and

leveled a short-barreled Remington 870 shotgun at the snake. "Request permission to shoot, sir."

"Permission granted," Goodman barked. "Blow it away."

The lance corporal fired and missed, racked the gun, but before he could fire again the snake disappeared into a ventilation shaft in the wall. The blast from the shotgun had gone through the bathroom door. One of the pellets burst a water pipe.

"Well, Hayden, I see you still manage to find ways to get yourself in harm's way."

Stone turned and recognized CIA officer Sandra Harrington. As usual she looked stylish, in tight khaki shirt and shorts. Barefoot, she had her blonde hair tied back in a ponytail and held a Glock automatic by her side in her left hand.

"Here on holiday?" he asked. So, *she* was the visitor who flew in from Paris.

Her eyes traveled over his body. "Just taking in the sights."

Stone forgot he was naked. He retrieved his trousers from the floor and slipped them on. Local embassy workers arrived, and Goodman gave orders to clean up the room and repair the water leak. The men crept into the room, their eyes on the opening in the wall where the snake was last seen.

Goodman tapped Stone on the shoulder. "That, my friend, is a black mamba. One of the deadliest snakes in Africa. Don't know how it got in here, but the locals do call this place Mamba Point."

"Great." Stone turned to Sandra. "So the boss sent you down from Paris to babysit me."

Before she could respond, Goodman said, "Think we'll move you to the embassy quarters across from the main gate. Ms. Harrington, maybe you should move too."

"The name's Sandra. I don't relish sleeping with a snake in the ventilation system, even though the noted writer Graham Greene slept here." She bent over and picked up Stone's Colt from the floor, sauntered over, and gave him a hug. "Besides, I should stay close to my colleague and keep him out of trouble."

"Welcome to the land of WAWA," Goodman said.

"What?" Sandra frowned.

Stone tried a smile. "An old saying hereabouts. West Africa wins again."

CHAPTER THREE

MONROVIA, LIBERIA—AUGUST 7, 2002

The phone's hollow ring brought Stone out of a hazy sleep. He reached for the receiver, scanning the floor for any unwelcome visitors. After the incident with the black mamba the night before, he had made a thorough check of his new room in the quarters directly across from the embassy. It took time before he allowed himself to close his eyes.

Over the crackling phone line, Sandra Harrington said she was having breakfast at the embassy cafeteria and wanted to know if he was interested in joining her. "Al Goodman will try to be there. After he's handled some employee problem."

Stone agreed, and before replacing the handset, he examined the phone. At least twenty years old, the beige instrument appeared and smelled clean like the rest of the room. He sanitary-wiped it anyway. The room contained the bare necessities: bed, table, a straight back chair evidently borrowed from an embassy office, a shower, and toilet. Over the washbasin, a mirror hung by picture wire. A crack, apparently not recent, ran diagonally right to left. Inserted through the outside wall, an air-conditioning unit hummed, blowing in wet, cool air.

The second-floor window overlooked the backyards of two houses beyond the walls of the embassy compound. The one on the left side balanced a remnant of a corrugated metal roof over its burnt-out shell. The other, directly across, was a three-story Victorian showing a fresh coat of chalky paint. Someone had planted corn in the area between the houses, and banana trees hugged the trunks of immense banyans.

Stone traced his finger along the windowpane and made a line in the condensation with his fingernail. What a difference this world was from the French Riviera. Less than three months ago he had been relaxing in a village along the sea. He had completed a successful assignment for the CIA and now intended to enjoy the Mediterranean ambience. As he sat in his garden, his boss, Colonel Gustave Frederick, phoned and asked if he'd accept an assignment to Africa. He agreed, realizing the trip meant trouble, but that, along with a nice fee, was part of the enticement.

While he waited for his orders, he spent time in Paris visiting Sandra, who was assigned to the CIA station there. He also met with his old FBI colleagues at the American Embassy in Paris, then flew to Los Angeles to visit his two children attending college.

The call from Colonel Gustave Frederick came while tending his vegetable garden in McLean, Virginia. The garden had lain untended since his divorce. Three days later, he was on a plane heading for Monrovia.

He wiped the moisture from his finger. After this last, easy assignment he'd retire for good. Open that café on the beach in Southern California.

Stone found Sandra in the empty cafeteria sipping hot black coffee. She wore a sleeveless blouse and jeans. Over the cup, she eyed him, a twinkle in her green eyes. "I see you're properly dressed this morning."

"Long sleeves and long pants keep the bugs off. Along with prying eyes. What's good on the menu?"

"Fresh fruit and fresh-baked bread."

"Your recommendations are always dependable. I'll have the same. And coffee." Stone gave his order to a short woman who had come from the kitchen. Head drooped, with worried eyes, the woman shuffled away. He saw Sandra studying him. "Bad morning for her?"

"Every day's a bad day for these people," Sandra said. "The ethnic warfare has taken its toll."

Stone knew Sandra as a cool CIA professional. His boss,

Colonel Frederick, had done him a favor sending her down from Paris to assist him. They had worked well together on the anti-terrorist operation three months before in the South of France. He had saved her life in Marseille; she had saved him from the CIA bureaucrats. They were a good team.

Al Goodman entered the cafeteria from the patio area. The sound of the surf followed him in and faded as the door closed. He came to their table, slumped into a chair, and shouted for coffee and a roll. "Awful day already. The roving security patrol found one of our employees dead behind the garage. The doc believes it was snake bite."

"Seems snakes are a problem around here," Stone said.

From the kitchen, the server carried a tray that rattled with the breakfast servings and coffee cups. She placed each item in front of them and gave Goodman a long stare as she trudged back.

"The man who died was her cousin," Goodman said, watching her leave. "He just started work at the embassy last week."

The three picked at their food.

"During the last upheaval, we had thousands of refugees next door on the Greystone compound for over a month," Goodman said. "Little food, little water. All the wildlife disappeared."

"Odd that snakes have returned all of a sudden," Stone said.

Goodman broke his roll in half. "Before he left to go up-country, the COS told me to tell you to stay alert."

A morning meeting with the COS, as the CIA chief of station was known, had been scheduled to discuss Stone's meeting with Jacob, an Israeli Mossad agent. Colonel Frederick had instructed him to contact Jacob, who had some important information to pass on to American intelligence.

"What are your thoughts about your man's death?" Stone asked.

"The doc says the symptoms matched a bite from a black mamba. His initial diagnosis is death from suffocation resulting from paralysis of the respiratory system. Death would have taken about fifteen minutes."

Sandra shivered. "Guess if you're going to handle one of those nasties, you'd better know what you're doing."

Stone found the coffee bitter and thick. Too much and the veins in his head would throb, but a couple of good swallows would get his reasoning in gear. "I'd wager your dead man was bitten by the same snake that paid a visit to my room."

Goodman shrugged in agreement. "The COS said to help you with your meet today. I suppose this is all necessary?"

Stone realized Goodman hadn't been let in on all the details of the meet and was miffed. This was his turf, and he had the right to know what was happening. If Stone got himself killed, he as the security officer would be held responsible. He decided to feed him just enough information to settle him down.

"I'm meeting a guy named Jacob who's an Israeli who deals in diamonds. Travels throughout West Africa from Amsterdam and Tel Aviv. He works for Mossad, but I don't know if he's staff officer or a '*sayan*.' In other words, he helps out when Israeli intelligence needs him."

"The COS told me that."

"He wanted to meet me." Stone paused. "I knew him years ago when I worked in New York City as an FBI agent. This all has something to do with your neighbor next door. Sierra Leone."

"Is Jacob his real name?"

"Probably not," Stone said.

"Trust him?"

"No."

"Why would someone here want to kill you?"

"The snake?"

"It was a message. Obviously, someone doesn't want you to meet your Jacob."

"I agree. But who, I don't know."

"So, you're FBI?"

"Retired. Now I'm with the agency." Stone folded his arms. "You don't like the bureau?"

Goodman looked at Sandra, then back to Stone. "My brother-in-law's an FBI agent. He thinks he's a hot shit."

Stone stayed low in the backseat of the armored Suburban SUV while Goodman drove and Sandra rode shotgun. Four blocks from the embassy compound, the meet, selected by Jacob, was to be in a restaurant. Few people walked the trash-littered streets lining gutted buildings, and Stone expected he and Jacob would be the only patrons.

After two passes around the block, Goodman slowed as they approached the back door of the restaurant and said to Stone, "Check your radio."

Stone keyed his device by depressing the send button. The signal crackled over the car's radio.

"Listen, and don't tell anybody I told you this." Goodman looked at him in the rearview mirror. "If you have to use your gun, don't hesitate. Life's cheap here and yours is cheaper."

Sandra turned around. "We'll be close. Yell if you need help." As the SUV came to a halt, she said, "Out now! Don't stay longer than necessary."

Stone leaped from the car, took three long strides to the door, found it unlocked, and slipped into restaurant and darkness. As he closed the door behind him, he heard the SUV drive off. He slipped the safety off his semiautomatic and inched across the room toward leaking light from behind a door hanging from one hinge.

Footsteps shuffled from the other side, and the door opened slowly. A black man in an ironed white shirt, age forty to sixty with graying hair and red-veined eyes, motioned for him to enter. Dust hung in the air. Even in peaceful days the restaurant couldn't accommodate more than ten customers. The man pointed to a solitary figure across the room wearing a khaki safari jacket, sitting with his back to the wall.

Jacob looked hard at Stone, then shot a glance out the dirty window toward the street.

"You came alone." Jacob said, not so much a question than a statement.

"No."

21

Jacob looked older than the last time Stone had seen him. Thinner, and with a sallow complexion. Stone figured that during Jacob's travels in Africa he had caught a dose of malaria, or maybe dengue fever. Nevertheless, he still broadcasted a defiant look.

He pushed out a wooden chair with his foot. "Have a seat."

"You look good, Jacob." Stone didn't bother to offer a handshake, knowing it wouldn't be returned.

"Cut the bullshit. You have any idea why I wanted to talk with you?"

Stone considered giving him a New York City smart-ass response, but instead answered straight. "My boss said to come here and find out."

"I believe you." Jacob hunched his shoulders and waved to the old man standing by the counter. "A Club beer for my friend."

"It's a bit early for me. I usually wait 'till five. I'll have a glass of water." Stone tried to sense whether Jacob believed he didn't know the reason behind the meet. Knowing this old operative, Stone withheld judgment for the time being.

"They refill plastic water bottles from the town sewer. Hold them up to the light and you can see the bacteria swimming. Beer's the only safe drink in town."

Stone nodded. When the Club beer came, he told the old man to forget the glass. He'd drink from the bottle. "So, what's up?"

"Before we start, who do you work for? I heard you retired."

"I was at home gardening when a friend called. He asked me to take a short trip for him and write a travel story." Stone smiled. "I understand you're here dealing in diamonds."

Jacob's face, his whole countenance, remained motionless. As if on cue, a slight smile appeared. "Diamonds. Yes, I understand you may need one for an engagement ring." He gave his head a little shake. "Since your recent divorce and, of course, your friendship with that contessa in Villefranche."

Stone took a long swig of beer, smiled, and took another swallow. The bastard was good. Jacob's people had made some serious inquiries about him and learned about his marital status—a train wreck—and about his dalliance three months ago with Contessa Lucinda Avoscani. Mossad and Jacob may or may not know about Stone's involvement in the deaths of a number of terrorists along the Côte d'Azur. Chances were they did.

Stone asked, "Why are we here?"

"You're here because the last time I had dealings with your new masters, I met with an unfortunate circumstance." He turned his head and brushed back his hair. Most of his right ear was missing. "With your veterans assigned to Afghanistan, you have some very inexperienced officers working the backwater countries. Mistakes are not forgiven in this region."

Stone stared at the ear and knew Jacob had reason to be pissed at the CIA. He would be, but was Jacob's tradecraft up to snuff? Had he let his guard down?

Remembering Sandra's words about not lingering, he looked at his watch. "We should get to the point."

They looked out the window. Birds, black with white blotches on their breasts, waddled on piles of garbage. The gloom from an overcast sky blended with the deteriorating setting.

Jacob spoke. "There are some disturbing rumors. As you know, many people from the Middle East ply this region. For years, they have come, lived here, and traded goods. Some of these people now trade weapons."

Stone nodded, thinking what he had just heard sounded like some factoid from a news documentary. Anyone who flew on the regional airlines in Africa recognized the Lebanese, Indians, and Israelis sharing the cabin. "And now the jihadists have descended," Stone offered.

"Yes, but this time, a group is here, not to sell, but to purchase."

"Buy what?" Stone asked.

Jacob shrugged with his upper body.

"Let's see, my boss advised that you," Stone pointed, "suggested I travel to Sierra Leone."

Nodding, eyes closed, Jacob pushed a white index card

across the table on which appeared a name, a company, and a telephone number in heavy marker ink. "Memorize," he ordered.

Stone studied the card, looked away, and mentally repeated the words. Pushing it back, he planned to write the information down in code and slip it somewhere secure.

"He is an Afrikaner. You must see him very soon," Jacob said. "He is taking a big risk."

"Understood." Stone watched the man pull back and again look out the window as if looking for someone.

Pulling the radio partially out of his pocket, Stone keyed the transmitter twice, signaling Goodman and Sandra to pick him up. He rose and made his way to the door.

Without looking, Jacob tossed a good-bye.

In the backseat of the SUV, Stone asked if they had detected anything strange while they waited for him. "Nothing," Sandra answered, and added, "You didn't waste any time."

"Got what I wanted." He also learned that, as usual, his boss and mentor back at Langley, Colonel Gustave Frederick, had told him the bare minimum. Even Jacob realized Stone was in the dark, a professional embarrassment as it placed Stone on a lower rung in the operation.

Stone rubbed his forehead. A headache was coming on, not from job stress but from his anti-malaria pills. "When's the next plane to Freetown, Sierra Leone?" he asked Goodman.

"One is scheduled at eight in the morning for Abidjan. From there you can get a connection to Freetown."

Stone touched Sandra's shoulder. "Do you have a pen?"

When she passed it back, he inked in his palm only the telephone number Jacob had given him. He was good at names; still, to be safe, he repeated to himself the name and the company: Dirk Lange, York Export Ltd.

CHAPTER FOUR

MONROVIA, LIBERIA

Above the horizon, through the haze and city smoke, the sun bubbled blood red. Al Goodman had gone to the airport to make arrangements for Stone and Sandra's flight the next day to Freetown. The embassy's cafeteria had closed, leaving the two on their own to find a place for dinner. Sandra suggested they stay in their quarters and combine what snacks they had brought with them.

"Let's try the restaurant Goodman and I went to last night," Stone suggested. "We can borrow that old car sitting on the embassy compound. The restaurant's only a five-minute drive from here."

"Is the food good?"

"Not especially, but it'll be nice to get out."

"At night. In this town?"

"We won't sightsee. Just have a quick meal and head straight back."

Stone began to have second thoughts as he turned the ignition key on the beat-up sedan. The motor struggled, but when he put the shift into first gear, the car moved along somewhat. Driving past the darkened buildings, Sandra showed unease but relaxed when Stone, at the wheel, pointed out the landmarks he recognized from the night before. The streets were deserted. The sun dropped below the horizon, leaving behind a gray glow.

Stone found the restaurant, or what Goodman had called an urban "cook shop," resembling what one would find in the Liberian countryside. It took up the ground floor of a two-story house that hadn't seen a paintbrush since the beginning of the civil turmoil years before. Long strips of black tape zigzagged across the front window, keeping the cracked glass from collapsing.

"This is a restaurant?" Sandra asked.

"Yeah. Goodman said it's one of the two decent ones left in town. They cook outside in the backyard on a stone hearth."

He parked at the entrance so they could keep an eye on the car from inside the restaurant. A group of four casually dressed African males entered the restaurant after eyeing them and their car.

"Hayden, are you carrying your gun?"

"Yes." Stone had his Colt .45 but had brought only one extra magazine. He knew Sandra had her Glock.

They didn't bother locking the car in case they had to make a quick departure from the restaurant. Inside, they met the smells of unfamiliar food. Candles on the three tables along with a kerosene lantern sitting on the bar next to the back door provided light. The city's electrical power was down again.

A middle-aged woman, who Goodman introduced the night before as the owner, directed them to a table next to the window. The four men who had entered before them had taken a table on the other side of the room. Stone and Sandra became objects of curiosity.

"Interesting," Sandra said, looking at the plates and glasses turned over, a napkin placed on top of each plate.

"It's a Liberian custom." Stone overturned his plate and glass. "I suggest having a beer, which will be warm, or better still, the house ginger beer."

The owner said, "You were here last night, sir. With the gentleman from the American Embassy."

"Yes. This is my colleague. What's your special tonight?"

"The special is the only dish tonight. I'll bring it."

"What's it going to be?" Sandra asked Stone, concerned.

"We'll see."

When the meal came, the woman identified the two plates as fufu and jollof rice with shrimp. She placed a small bowl of soup before each of them. "Goat soup," she said. "Another specialty."

"Hope the soup doesn't have too many peppers in it,"

Stone said. It did.

Sandra played with her meal, finding the rice and shrimp acceptable. "Where will you lay over when you return home?"

"Paris."

"You don't want to go back to Nice or Villefranche?" she asked.

"I'm afraid I'm not welcomed on the Riviera. The contessa blames me for shooting up her palace."

"How did you two get together in the first place?"

"Almost twenty years ago, I was a naval officer assigned to the American consulate in Nice. During Christmas season I was invited to attend a local party. I guess you'd call it a dinner dance."

"You were in uniform of course."

Stone put his fork down. The fufu was good, but he questioned the age of the shrimp under the rice. "I was an ensign. It was a fun party. You know, they have this custom in France and Italy where at one of those functions everyone gets up, holds hands, and dances and skips around all the rooms singing loudly. Like being in a conga line. I met Lucinda there that night."

"And?"

"We dated for about a year and then ..."

"Who broke it off?"

Stone shrugged.

"You dumped her."

"My ship left port."

"You were assigned to a diplomatic establishment on land, not on a ship."

Stone played with the rice on his plate. He wondered what Lucinda's reaction would be if he returned to Nice and phoned her. Refuse to see him? Perhaps not.

"Only a few months ago, I planned to live on the Riviera with her. Then everything fell apart."

"Still got that old feeling?"

He laughed. "Funny thing. I don't have a photograph of her, and I can't seem to form a picture of her in my mind."

Sandra closed her eyes.

"No matter how I try, I can't visualize her. I can hold images of strangers in my mind, but not her. Weird, no?"

After pausing, she said, "Same thing happened to me with a boyfriend in high school."

"And?"

"Still can't picture him."

At that Sandra turned her head toward the other patrons, and her expression changed from inquisitive to alarm. It happened fast. Stone saw the local men leave their table and run out the back door. The owner moved behind the bar and began taking the liquor bottles off the shelf.

Like a leopard hearing a branch unexpectedly snap, Stone's reflexes kicked in. His gun came out as he pushed away from the table. His eyes searched the room for adversaries.

Sandra pointed. Outside the dirty window, in the gloom of dusk, a car with its headlights on had parked in front of the restaurant. Four men, not African but Middle Eastern, emerged. Two carried submachine guns.

"Jihadists," Stone said, his Colt out, safety off. "Showtime."

Sandra and Stone jumped from their chairs and raced to the back door. They made it through as two men barged in the front door. The one with the machine gun sprayed the entire room, while the other fired in their direction with his pistol. A young busboy fell, bloody holes in his shirt.

Instinctively, Stone knew the machine gun had to be neutralized first. Using the doorjamb as cover, he squeezed off two rounds into the stomach of the man holding the machine gun. The terrorist clutched his midsection, jerked forward, and fell to the floor, dropping the gun.

Sandra behind Stone, in a crouch, shot the other terrorist with repeated rounds until her Glock emptied. The man, his body splattered with blood, fell backwards. She slapped a fresh magazine into the butt of the gun.

"That was the easy part," Stone said. "The other two outside have to be going around to the back."

"Let's surprise them. We'll go out the front and slip behind them."

"Let's do it."

Passing by the man groaning on the floor clutching his stomach, Stone picked up his machine gun. At the same time, the man pulled out a pistol from inside his coat. Before he could shoot, Sandra fired twice. The man became still.

"Let's move," Stone said, and the two raced out the door.

Outside in the street, they rounded the building and saw the two jihadists entering the back door. Surprised when they saw them, the men turned and opened fire.

Stone and Sandra both knelt on one knee and continued to fire until they emptied their guns. One terrorist tried to stay on his feet but spun in a contorted tumble into a trashcan. The shooting stopped. The two jihadists lay at the doorstep. Still.

As Stone reloaded, Sandra said, "I'm out of ammo."

"Here. Take the machine gun."

Stone checked the bodies lying outside, removing their identification. Large black birds cried overhead. Dogs barked from behind walls.

Inside the restaurant, Stone carefully examined the two dead men on the floor. Again they removed anything identifying their would-be killers.

"You are not going to leave them there?" the owner yelled.

"We'll pull them outside in the street for the police to pick up." Stone said.

"What police?" The owner was angry. "Your embassy has to fix this."

Stone looked around the restaurant. Tables overturned, bullet holes in the walls, broken dishes, food spread on the floor. The glass in the front window had shattered.

"Who will pay me for this?"

Stone walked up to the woman. "Do you take American dollars?"

CHAPTER FIVE

MONROVIA, LIBERIA—AUGUST 8, 2002

The tan Land Cruiser bounced out of a pothole in the two-lane tarred roadway. Hayden Stone sat shotgun and watched the signs to Monrovia's Roberts International Airport pass by. In the backseat, Sandra Harrington held on to the baggage stacked next to her. The thirty-five-mile drive from the embassy took them through endless rows of homes and shacks in varying stages of disrepair. They met only light vehicle traffic, evenly distributed between old diesel trucks belching blue smoke and new military and police SUVs.

During the entire time, Goodman, at the wheel, remained taciturn. The previous night had been spent leading Stone and Sandra through the Liberian legal hurdles consisting of giving statements and signing papers—for Stone, in his alias Finbarr Costanza. The police took the four jihadists' bodies away. Liberian immigration people advised the four deceased's entry papers were "not in order." That helped the American position. Financial recompense slated for the owner of the restaurant further helped matters.

On the phone, the CIA chief of station wished them a safe and mainly speedy departure from his turf. The information on the four thugs would be cabled back to Langley for analysis.

Back in his room, Stone shared his Irish whiskey with Sandra. When finally he slipped between the sheets and closed his eyes, he hoped not to have his usual bizarre dreams that normally followed a gunfight. That night he had none. The whiskey had worked.

• • •

The SUV bounced out of another pothole, shifting luggage in the backseat.

"Sandra and I are scheduled to leave at eight," Stone said. "What are the chances of departing on time?"

"None at all." Goodman blew his horn at a man wandering in the middle of the road. "Once you board, the weather from here to Abidjan is clear. From there to Freetown as well."

People plodded along the side of the road. As for many in undeveloped African countries, travel by foot provided the only means for getting to and from the markets. The women's clothes appeared more somber than Stone remembered. The bright, gay colors were absent. Instead of the light sway in their walk, the people shuffled.

The low-lying airport buildings appeared in the distance as Goodman slowed at a police checkpoint. The pulse always quickened at roadblocks in the third world. Stone knew the rules: be prepared to show your passport, hand over some of the local ragged currency, and at all costs stay in the vehicle. Just hope that one of the young, untrained thugs in a dirty uniform didn't let loose intentionally or unintentionally with his AK-47. Goodman, experienced with the situation, finessed the grinning policemen with their outstretched hands.

At the entrance to the hangar building, Goodman introduced the embassy's expediter, a slender African with airport security badges dangling from his neck. "This fellow will get you through the gate and show you to the lounge—if you can call it that." Goodman extended his hand. "Got business to attend to. Next visit, we'll keep the snakes and bad guys away."

The expediter knew the right people and whisked them through the airport check-in. Goodman had been accurate; the lounge looked unimpressive, consisting of only seven battered chairs in a roped-off area from the main terminal. The plane was scheduled to arrive in an hour, which was only thirty minutes late. Not bad for this region.

Stone and Sandra settled themselves in a corner. She handed him a soda from her backpack. "It still has a chill to it. Damn, the air in this terminal is stuffy."

They sat quietly, watching the throng. No smiles on their faces. Stone witnessed only frowns. No displays of flashy jewelry on the women. No ties on the men.

His mind drifted to the events of the night before. The attack was not a random assault in a city in the throes of anarchy. Foreign jihadists had planned the operation, and he and Sandra were targeted. He knew now that his mission was not a matter of talking with an Israeli contact and going to Sierra Leone to question some South African.

"What's eating you?"

Stone waved off the question.

"You've had that look since this morning," Sandra said. "The one where the creases in your face become hard and those gray eyes lose their sparkle."

Stone moved close to her and whispered, "This mission is not just a stop and shop. As usual, I haven't been told everything. I'm a bull's-eye for some terrorist group and I haven't done squat." He put his finger on her knee. "You were sent down here to help me. Have you been clued in and are holding back on me?"

Sandra's mouth tightened and Stone backed away. He had witnessed what she could do with a quick karate chop.

"I thought we were … closer." Before her eyes moistened, she put on her Italian sunglasses. "You know as much as I know," she mouthed between her teeth.

"Sorry. You're right."

She relaxed. "Do you expect to hear from Colonel Frederick when we reach Sierra Leone? Some response on our contact with Jacob?"

"I'm counting on it. At that time I'll expect more from him about this gig."

"The colonel will give you as much as he thinks necessary," she said.

"Knowing that people want to kill you comes under the heading of necessary."

"Keep in mind Frederick would not have sent you and me here if the mission wasn't important, and he knows from experience you can handle yourself."

She looked over the terminal from behind her sunglasses, still alert after the night's gunfight. If she had a case of the nerves, she didn't show it. Wearing snug jeans and a long-sleeved blouse, a scarf hid much of her blonde hair. Unlike many western women who traveled to Africa, she had the good sense to dress modestly to avoid as much attention as possible.

"How long will you be with me?" he asked.

"As far as I know, a couple of days. Have to get back to Paris." She sighed. "You didn't expect this to be a long trip, did you?"

"The last time Frederick offered a job, he said it would be a lark. Sunning and boating on the Riviera. You know how that ended up."

"So what happened last night can't come as a big surprise." Sandra leaned toward him. "Back in Marseilles, you had some good meals, didn't you? And there was the contessa."

"I still don't think I'm welcomed back there anytime soon."

"Well, you're always welcome in Paris." Sandra's smile had returned.

"Thanks. I may take you up on that." He thought about how she performed during the gunfight. Amazing. Cool and professional ... and the best-looking partner he ever had.

The terminal became energized. Upon hearing a loud scream from jet engines, people rushed toward the doors. The African puddle jumper discharged its passengers, and a uniformed employee directed Stone and Sandra outside onto the tarmac toward the movable stairway set next to the plane's door. The air felt less oppressive outside the terminal.

"What make of aircraft is this?" Stone asked.

"A Yak forty."

He studied the three-engine jet. "Looks like a shrunken Boeing 727."

"Probably a stolen design. A Russian-made Yakovlev forty. Been around since the sixties."

Inside the cabin the air conditioner blew full blast. With all the passengers seated, two men in coveralls slid boxes and crates up the center aisle and stacked them. They worked their way to the rear door, placing cargo as they went, making the aisle impassable. Finished, they yelled something in Russian to the two pilots on the flight deck. One of the pilots slammed the compartment door shut, and the plane lurched forward.

An hour into the flight, the door to the flight deck swung open. The two pilots in white shirts with blue epaulettes were involved in an animated discussion. Balanced upright between their seats was a liquor bottle containing a clear liquid. The pilot on the left picked it up and took a swig.

"Sandra, is that what I think it is?"

"Yep. Good old vodka."

The pilot on the right saw the open door, reached back, and closed it.

Stone shouted in Sandra's ear over the noise of the plane. "This is what I love about Africa. You're always putting up with snakes, disease, gunmen, and drunken pilots."

FREETOWN, SIERRA LEONE

After passing through Abidjan, Côte d'Ivoire, the plane arrived at the Freetown International Airport a little after five in the afternoon. From the plane's window, Stone watched black thunderheads building along the coast. The CIA station had advised that someone would be at the airport to escort them to town. Anyone arriving at the airport and wanting to continue on to Freetown had to cross a wide estuary to reach the city. Only one ferry operated, usually overloaded, and it took someone who knew the ropes to get across with minimum problems.

Descending from the plane, Sandra said, "There's the station chief, Luke Craig."

Standing on the runway, arms folded over his safari shirt, a tall, weary-looking African-American in his late twenties stood wide-legged. At his side an embassy employee with touches of gray in his hair and with access badges suspended on a lanyard around his neck held two blue embassy welcome folders.

Craig introduced himself and then they walked to the terminal. While the local employee took Stone and Sandra's passports and hurried off to passport control to expedite their arrival, Craig removed his sunglasses and directed his attention to Sandra.

As they talked, Sandra's concentration switched to someone across the room in the boarding section of the terminal. Craig was in mid-sentence when she excused herself, saying she had to talk with someone. Both men watched her push through the same door they had entered. Back on the tarmac next to the plane, she intercepted a bearded white man.

It was easy for Stone to interpret her body language—arms akimbo, finger pointing and jabbing the man's chest—and know that her words were rough. The man kept backing away in the direction of the aircraft. Finished, Sandra turned and headed back to the terminal, turning once and presenting her middle finger to the man who rushed up the boarding stairs.

Sandra returned, and before she said anything, Craig moved off to the baggage area.

"What was that all about?" Stone asked.

"That was Farley Durrell. An old partner, business that is—well—a little personal as well." She paused. "The bastard double-crossed me." She glared at Stone. "I don't forgive nor forget."

Stone nodded. *I'll keep that in mind.*

On arrival at the dock, they found the ferry packed with vehicles, but Craig managed to secure one of the last parking slots. The embassy employee guarded the SUV while Craig led the way to the stairs to the upper deck lounge. Finding it jammed with drunken patrons, Craig suggested a spot he knew forward on a covered platform over the bow.

Stone took in the view of Freetown harbor. Using his monocular, he scanned the port across the bay. It hadn't changed over the past five years. Rusty shipwrecks, including a derelict ferry, dotted the water, but the green hills touched by white clouds still provided a pleasant backdrop. Grass and tall trees still reached down to the water's edge. Palm trees here and there broke the monotony. The only harbor traffic consisted of one- or two-man fishing boats, long, thin craft skimming across the water. As his eyes swept the harbor, black thunderheads still engulfed the sky, and he watched rain walk in from the ocean.

Craig went to the bar and returned carrying three bottles of Star beer dripping condensation. "What a bar. I had trouble finding someone to take my money. Drink up. We'll get more."

The beer was cold and wet. Stone thought he had never tasted a better beer to cut through the heat. Fifteen minutes later, when the ferry pushed off from the dock, soot from the two smokestacks rained down on the passengers on the open deck. Where Stone and his companions stood, they were protected from ash as well as from the heavy rain that had begun to fall.

Halfway across the wide bay, Sandra and Craig moved off and spoke in low tones. Stone saw Craig look repeatedly in his direction. Sandra shook her head a number of times. Craig straightened and, with Sandra following, returned. Stone leaned on the wet railing, watching the city grow larger as the ferry steamed ahead.

"We had a short talk," Craig said.

"The beer's very good."

Craig threw a glance at Sandra. "We were talking about you and your reputation for attracting trouble."

"That's why the agency loves me," Stone said.

"Yeah." Craig seemed to regroup. "Game plan is you talk with this South African fellow. Station provides coverage. You make your report, and off you go."

Stone frowned and took the last swig of beer from the bottle. "And you'll take care of the bodies, right?" He studied the label on the beer bottle.

"That's not funny."

"Hayden. Behave," Sandra said. "I just spent ten minutes convincing this guy that you're trustworthy."

Craig fidgeted. "Sierra Leone is not easy duty, Mr. Stone. It's not the South of France."

"I've been here. I know Sierra Leone."

"This morning I read about what happened in Monrovia."

"Gotcha."

Stone looked out at the city. Soft yellow twinkling lights came from the numerous gas and oil lamps. Evidently, electricity still had not returned on a regular basis to Freetown. The South African they were to meet lived somewhere out there in the darkness. What was so important that this man had to tell them?

CHAPTER SIX

FREETOWN, SIERRA LEONE—AUGUST 9, 2002

Hayden Stone caught the coffee mug before it shattered in the kitchen sink. He looked across the room toward Sandra's closed bedroom door. The noise had woken her, which he didn't want. The previous night, he heard her make repeated trips from her bedroom to the bathroom. Obviously, she had caught a West African intestinal bug, part of the travel experience in this part of the world. His turn would come if he stayed too long in Freetown.

The embassy had provided them a well-furnished apartment, quite a step above the Spartan quarters in Monrovia. The fenced, well-maintained, guarded compound accommodated the staff and dependents assigned to the embassy. Back in Monrovia, aside from the skeleton staff, only people on TDY, or temporary duty, visited, and they departed as soon as possible.

In the refrigerator, Stone found milk, yogurt, and local fruit, the makings of a quick breakfast. Opening a blueberry yogurt, he went out onto the second floor balcony to inspect the grounds in the daylight. The morning air coming up from the bay felt fresh. This was the season when one could expect rain almost every day, yet clouds shielded the sun, keeping the temperature down. Only when the sun blazed down from a cloudless sky did the heat drive a person into the shade.

The country had gone through a horrendous civil war since Stone had last visited, and he wondered what he would find when they left the treed suburbs and headed downtown. Here in the bubble provided for the Americans, the world felt safe, with gentle smells, brightly colored flowers, and noisy birds.

From inside, Stone heard something drop on the kitchen

table and knew Sandra was up and about. Back inside, she sat at the table, face buried in her hands.

"Did you hear me make all those trips to the john last night?" She looked up with red eyes. "I caught a bug."

"Intestinal parasite. Could have caught it anywhere. Maybe you should stay here today."

"No way. Got to keep you and Craig on friendly terms; besides, I'll see the post doctor. Hope he's not on a road trip." She looked around the room. "Any crackers here? I can't have coffee or anything that will make me feel worse." She settled on dry cereal.

Stone left her alone to gather herself and went to shower and shave. He assured her he would spend minimal time in the bathroom.

As they waited for the shuttle to take them to the embassy, Stone went over the day's schedule. They would meet with Craig, see what he knew about Dirk Lange, and find out what he had planned as support for his meeting with the South African. "Whatever information Lange has, we'll pass on to Craig and cable it back to CIAHQ." Stone rose from the bench as the van arrived. "That will be that and off we go. Short and sweet. Unless we run into more trouble."

"I'm getting curious what this fellow Lange has for us."

"So am I."

When they boarded the van, Stone recognized the driver from his last visit to Freetown. They exchanged nods, but he couldn't remember the man's name. Seated, he continued his conversation with Sandra. "It's apparent that there are people, obviously jihadists, who don't want us to meet Mr. Lange. Or maybe someone just doesn't like me."

"You have a tendency to piss people off. Like the terrorists back in France."

From the American compound to the embassy, sections of the route, especially the crossroads, looked familiar. Here and there, homes and buildings lay in ruin, but the people treading along the sides of the road had more confidence in their stride than he'd witnessed in Liberia. Bicyclists accompanied the pedestrians; still, their clothing looked worn and drab. On his last visit, Stone had seen young African children in school uniforms like those worn in England. Not today.

The road winding through the suburbs, wide enough to allow parked cars on either side, narrowed as the van entered the city. Three-story buildings, their facades stained with mold and dirt, lined the streets. Along the curbs, vendors displayed their wares of fruit, breads, and recycled appliances and tools. The driver constantly held down the horn, urging pedestrians to move off the street.

"Ah. There it is," Stone said. "The Cotton Tree."

Ahead, standing in what Freetowners considered the center of town, stood a tree matching in height the nearby eight-story Electricity House, the headquarters for Freetown's spotty electrical supply. It commanded the central square.

"And the significance?" Sandra asked. Her face had regained some color.

"The people here sort of revere it. I was hoping it didn't get chopped down or destroyed during the rebel siege." Stone studied the thick limbs and green leaves extending out umbrella fashion. "I guess superstitions work for the good sometimes."

"How's that?"

"People believe spirits live on the top of the tree. Some claim they see the spirits dancing."

"Have you seen them?"

"Not that I'll admit."

Luke Craig looked in a better mood than he had the night before on the ferry. He sat erect behind the desk in clean khaki slacks and appeared confident in his role as station chief. Peering over his reading glasses, he zeroed in on Stone. Craig informed him he had just reviewed the morning cables from headquarters. "It appears that the executive council takes your visit here seriously. Specifically, Gustav Frederick, who is pretty close to the director, is urging we move swiftly."

"I'd like to interview this Dirk Lange today and get the report out by close of business," Stone said.

Craig looked over to Sandra. "I assume you two will be talking to him."

"Luke, I'm under the weather," Sandra said. "We were told the medical officer is heading off on his road trip today. I'd like to visit him before he departs."

Craig took an exaggerated breath and continued, "The station has very little on what's happening here with your visit. I assume it's important. Care to fill me in?"

Stone related the details of the meeting with Jacob in Monrovia. "Aside from the headquarters briefing back in Washington and what Jacob told me about this fellow Lange, that's all I know." It was time to find out what Craig knew. "So what information does the station have on Lange?"

Craig steepled his hands together. "Headquarters just said to provide support, and, by the way, our personnel resources are a tad thin. We can lend only limited countersurveillance when you conduct your meeting."

"Which gets us to Lange," Stone said.

Sandra jerked forward in obvious pain from a cramp.

"Better get to the doctor before he leaves," Craig urged.

"Sorry, you two. Will be back." Sandra hastened out of the office.

"Occupational hazard in these parts." Craig paused as if he didn't quite know how to handle Stone one-on-one. He started on what sounded like a rundown appearing on a baseball player's stat sheet. "Dirk Lange. Age thirty-two, South African national, white Afrikaner." He moved some papers on his desk. "Let's see, he's been here in Sierra Leone for two years, oh no, more than that now. May have been working somehow with a South African mercenary group. Now works for an export company that handles minerals—"

"Diamonds, I assume."

Craig looked him in the eye. "That's the lucrative commodity hereabouts, yes." He went back to his sheet of paper. "Lange seems to be involved with a humanitarian organization here. Spends a great deal of his free time in the bush finding the victims of the last carnage and bringing them back for rehabilitation." He pushed the sheet away and steepled his hands again.

Stone waited.

"This Lange fellow is typical of your white Africans. Comfortable with his surroundings here on the continent."

Stone nodded.

"Coffee?"

"No thanks," Stone said.

"Lange is rather educated. Engineer. Did postgraduate work at the University of Cape Town in the classics, can you believe?" Craig became evasive. "Went to a religious school in what we call high school. Dominican-run place. Suppose that's where he got his charitable instincts."

That did it. Stone now knew the station had an extensive file on Dirk Lange. A mere cursory trace would have resulted in name, date of birth, and any criminal background. The agency had gone back into his early schooling. Lange was now or had been a person of interest.

"You have an address for him?"

"His office is only a few blocks away. As you probably know from your previous visit here, most businesses are clustered downtown."

"Close to the Cotton Tree." Stone pulled out a three-by-five index card and a pen. "I'll need a business and residence address."

Craig smiled ever so slightly. "Don't know where he lives. Here, give me that card and I'll write down the number and street where he works. I suppose you'll contact him this morning?"

"Yes, but first I'll check on Sandra."

In the embassy's medical unit, Stone found Sandra looking piqued. Asking how she felt, she shook her head. "I'm afraid I'm wasted, damn it. Can't possibly help with the meeting." The driver of the van came to the door. "I'm asking this gentleman to take me back to the apartment."

Stone now remembered the driver's name. Mitchell. Five years before, the man had worked for the RSO, or more accurately Jonathan Worthington, the chief investigator for the embassy's security office. He was a local employee known by the State Department as a foreign service national, or FSN.

"I apologize, Mr. Mitchell. On the bus, your name was on the tip of my tongue, but …"

Mitchell placed his right hand on his heart. "No sir, I should have said something, Mr. Hayden."

"How do I get in touch with my friend Jonathan Worthington?"

Mitchell's face clouded. His eyes filled with tears. Ignoring Stone's question, he looked away and addressed Sandra. "The van is ready, madame."

She rose. "See you later. If I live."

Stone patted her on the back. "I'll be back early afternoon. Can I bring you anything?"

Sandra shook her head and headed for the door. Mitchell closed the door behind them, avoiding eye contact with Stone. The door reopened and Craig stuck his head in, motioning with his index finger for Stone to follow. The countersurveillance team was ready to support Stone for his meet with Dirk Lange.

Two blocks from the central square, Hayden Stone found York Export Ltd. in the shadow of Electricity House. The city roadway in this section of town looked reasonably maintained; however, the sidewalks were cracked and broken. Stone carefully negotiated a deep hole. A twisted ankle was the last thing he needed. The two-story building where he found Dirk Lange's office had recently been painted bright white, which contrasted starkly with the surrounding area of pockmarked structures plastered with faded, tattered posters. A sign hung to the right of the door and in Gothic font stated YORK EXPORT was on the second floor. Stone found the front door locked.

After repeated knocks—the doorbell didn't work—a slight Sierra Leonese woman appeared at the door and asked his business. Stone told her he wanted to speak with Lange, at which she shook her head but opened the door wider and led him toward a stairway. The interior of the building smelled fresh from a new coat of paint, and sections of the wood staircase had been replaced.

He followed her up the stairs where a middle-aged man waited. "Sir. Pity you have missed Mr. Lange," he said. "Presently he travels in the Kono District. He should return from Koidu tomorrow." The temperature inside the building was stifling, and the man dabbed his shiny black face with a handkerchief.

"Made sense," Stone thought. Koidu's was where the diamond fields were located. He continued up the stairs. "May I leave a card for Mr. Lange?" Stone asked with an Irish brogue.

The man nodded and invited Stone into the clean, almost sterile office. The outer space contained four desks at which women worked vintage computers. Their eyes darted up to Stone and returned to their monitors. Three closed two-door safes were positioned in separate corners of the room. Through an open door Stone looked into what looked like Lange's office. An up-to-date desktop computer sat on a credenza behind the desk alongside a satellite phone dock. Maps of Sierra Leone and greater Africa hung throughout the office.

Stone pulled out his Irish passport and looked inside. "Seems I've left my cards behind. May I give you my name and contact number, Mr. ...?"

"I am Amadu. The office manager."

As Amadu searched for a notepad, Stone tried to read the computer screen on the desk next to him. He glimpsed rows of numbers under a heading of what seemed to be a Dutch firm, name not recognized. The office was, as they say in the intelligence trade, clean. Not much could be learned on first sight, but the lack of telltale signs sometimes told more than intended.

Amadu returned with paper and pencil, and Stone said, "My name is Finbarr Costanza." He gave him a telephone number to the cell phone Craig had provided. "I'll drop by again tomorrow afternoon."

"I suggest you call beforehand, sir. If the telephone is

working." Amadu frowned. "May I tell Mr. Lange the nature of your business?"

"I'm a travel writer."

"Really?" The slight lift of Amadu's eyebrow revealed amusement.

"Searching for ideas and possibilities."

Leaving York Export, Stone took the route planned by Craig and his team. They instructed him to walk to the town center and after a few blocks turn east until he came to an eating establishment by the name of Goldie's. The café stood in sight of the once-famous two-story City Hotel that now reportedly served as a base for prostitutes.

Along the way, Stone picked up the countersurveillance. The three Africans and two Americans that Craig had placed on him. Their operational techniques impressed Stone. He had gone three blocks when he heard people singing a hymn. The music came from behind a dilapidated storefront, its front window displaying a taped-on cardboard white cross. He walked in out of curiosity and to puzzle the men following him.

Stone surmised the church was either Catholic or Anglican as the priest wore a white collar and around his neck a clerical stole, a long, narrow piece of purple cloth. At the far end of the dimly lighted room, a gold chalice draped with a white cloth sat in the middle of a table. The congregation consisted of fewer than a dozen people and was, like their minister, black. Heads were bowed and eyes closed in prayer. Feeling like an intruder, Stone turned to leave but saw the stand holding a few lighted votive candles. He walked over and looked for a fresh candle.

"We must hide them," came a low voice from behind. The priest opened a drawer and withdrew a white candle. "Some of our parishioners take them home for nighttime. They have no electricity."

The priest looked ageless, face scarred, his right eye socket sewn shut. An apparent victim of the war.

"Here, Father. For your candle and the parish." Stone emptied his wallet of all but a ten-dollar bill.

Without counting the currency, the priest tilted his head

and returned to his flock, now singing a new hymn. Following a ritual when on a mission, Stone lit the candle for his family and ancestors.

Inside Goldie's café, which matched the hotel across the street for shabbiness, he found Craig leaning against the counter chatting with a wizened woman. He handed Stone a cold Coke bottle that looked twenty years old and had been refilled as many times.

"That was fast," Craig said.

"My client's out of town. Maybe tomorrow I'll see him."

Craig looked disappointed. Was it because Stone wouldn't be leaving as soon as he had hoped?

"Well then," Craig said. "I suppose you'll have time to see the sights. By the way, the team reported you're clean. No one followed you."

"I'm going to look up an old friend," Stone said, debating if he trusted what was in the drink and if indeed it was what the label claimed, or some exotic refill from a backroom vat. "Jonathan Worthington. He worked for the embassy when I was here last."

Stone returned to the embassy. At the entrance, he observed the driver, Mitchell, pulling up to the curb. He approached and inquired about Sandra.

"She was happy to get back to her lodging, Mr. Hayden. Do you wish me to take you back to the compound also?"

"Not quite yet. Let's sit in the van."

Mitchell looked ahead and only responded in short, clipped sentences to Stone's questions about Freetown and the troubles the city had experienced. Stone asked the question that he sensed Mitchell wanted to avoid: Where was Jonathan, and did he no longer work at the embassy.

"This is most painful to talk about, sir." He placed his hands on the wheel.

At this point Stone wondered if Jonathan was alive, a prisoner, or worse. "Please tell me. You know Jonathan and I were friends."

"Three years ago, Jonathan and his family suffered greatly when the rebels, the RUF, entered the city." His eyes watered. "Everyone suffered, but he especially."

Stone rubbed his eyes and looked out at the people in the street. On Christmas Eve 1998, the American ambassador had ordered a post evacuation. The RUF, or Revolutionary United Front, used civilians as shields to launch their attack against the Nigerian troops supporting the Sierra Leone government. The undisciplined Nigerians fell back. The citizenry was brutalized.

"Is he alive?"

After a pause, Mitchell said, "He is at a camp for the rehabilitation of peoples." He tapped the wheel. "I don't believe he would want to see you. Best I give him a message from you."

Stone took a moment to consider whether to respect Mitchell's judgment or push on and insist on seeing his old friend. "I need to see Jonathan. Please take me there today?"

CHAPTER SEVEN

LAKKA BEACH, SIERRA LEONE

Next to the sea, Doctors Without Borders had established a small rehabilitation camp for war victims. Before departing the embassy, Mitchell had traded the van for a four-wheel vehicle. Over an hour they inched their way on roads that hadn't been repaired since Stone last visited Sierra Leone. As they approached the encampment, Stone became apprehensive. What would he find? Mitchell wouldn't say any more about Jonathan than he had back in Freetown.

"Best I find Jonathan and bring him to you, Mr. Hayden." Mitchell parked the SUV next to a large open-sided tent where people lay on cots. He slipped out and disappeared into the campground.

Hayden Stone got out, stretched his legs, and approached the edge of the campsite. Smoke from cooking fires filled the air, and in the distance a rooster crowed. A hush lay across the camp. Men, women, and children limped by on crutches. A boy, speaking kindly, pushed a legless old woman in a wheelbarrow. An occasional doctor appeared among the amputees.

"My friend Mitchell said you insisted on coming to see me." A voice came from behind Stone. With a sense of foreboding, Stone slowly turned.

"Hello, my good friend," Stone's voice broke. Jonathan Worthington, a black man of immense pride and talent, stood before him, both arms missing above the elbow.

They sat on the beach in armchairs that somehow after the war had found their way from a looted home to the seaside. The man who helped Jonathan to light his cigarettes and attended his private needs sat close. Jonathan faced Stone. The two talked about easy things.

"Perhaps you would care to speak privately, Hayden?" Jonathan finally said, and without a word Mitchell and the other man rose and moved a short distance away. "What brings you back to my country?"

"I am to meet and talk with a man in Freetown."

"You are in the same business as you were before?"

"Yes." Stone hesitated. "May I ask what happened?"

Jonathan shook his head and gazed at the sea, which crashed one line of high waves at a time. Typical when the ocean bottom drops off dramatically past the waterline.

"I am no longer in any business." Jonathan's face dropped. "As you can see, I cannot carry my load."

"Where is your family?"

"The embassy can no longer employ me. You know that my father worked for the British embassy during the Second World War. I hoped someday my dear son would work for the Americans, like me. Or perhaps become a doctor like these kind people." He tilted his head in the direction of a woman wearing a doctor's smock.

In a soft voice, Stone asked, "Where is your son?"

Jonathan's eyes went blank, as if he hadn't heard the question. "Do I know the man whom you are meeting?"

"Perhaps. His name is Dirk Lange. A South African."

A smile came to Jonathan's face, something unexpected. Yet Stone knew it wasn't a smile of happiness. "I hope your people are not still angry with Mr. Lange. He is a nice chap. You know."

Stone held a water bottle up for his friend to take a drink. The station in Freetown had issues with Lange. Interesting.

"From your face, it seems you are not fully aware of the circumstances. You will find out."

"May I ask again about your family?"

"A long story." Jonathan now shut his eyes. "They are not here with me."

Sensing Jonathan's reluctance to explain, he decided to

return to the matter of Dirk Lange. "What about Lange? What should I know?"

"Another long story." Jonathan's voice had changed. It lacked the authority Stone remembered.

"I see." Stone might just as well sit there and let this tired old man say what he wanted. He studied Jonathan's face. It hung weary, ravaged. Before him sat a victim of those hophead rebels who had savaged the villagers and townspeople for so many years. All for diamonds.

"Dirk Lange arrived shortly after you departed. He had connections with Executive Outcomes, although he himself was no mercenary." Jonathan looked hard at him. "Already you disapprove of Mr. Lange." He frowned. "Ah, the West's disapproval of the South Africans. During their presence we enjoyed the only peace we had for years. The enlightened Europeans forced them to leave. We had elections, and the RUF went on to ..."

"Executive Outcomes was here as I left. I recall their helicopters flying overhead. I didn't altogether disapprove of them."

"The RUF captured my son and made him into a soldier." Jonathan spoke the words in a whisper. His lifeless eyes met Stone's.

Stone looked away, trying to figure how old Jonathan's son had been at the time. Twelve years old at the most.

"Mr. Lange did administrative work for the mercenaries. When the group regained control of the diamond mines, he went there to work. After a while, when he returned to Freetown, he'd bring back some of the kidnapped." Jonathan touched the pack of cigarettes with the stub of his right arm, asking for a smoke. Stone complied, and after allowing him to take a long drag, Jonathan continued, "I have asked him to look for my son ... and my daughter when he is out there in the bush."

"Why did the station have problems with Lange? Was he working for the bad guys?"

"No. No, a young lady named Marsha worked at the embassy. Those two were very, very close. Your people did not approve. She was sent away."

Holy shit! Lange was poking an agency case officer. "I see why they wouldn't approve." Possible penetration of the station. The COS under the gun from Langley for management laxness. Secrets revealed inadvertently during pillow talk.

"You did not know about all this?" Jonathan asked in the way years ago he would warn Stone that he was about to fall into a trap. "I suppose you can't tell me the details of your being here."

Stone held the lighted cigarette to Jonathan's lips and let him draw until the tip burned bright. The realization that a cloud hung over this interview with Lange came not so much from his brain than from his gut. In the past, when that happened things got melancholy.

"No, Jonathan. I *shouldn't* talk about it." He paused. "People in Washington are concerned about something they wouldn't reveal to me. They sent me to Liberia to speak with an acquaintance from years past, a diamond merchant named Jacob. I believe he's in my line of business, but for another country." Stone held the cigarette for him again. "Jacob sent me here to talk with Lange, saying he had something very important to tell me."

Jonathan closed his eyes. "When I first saw you, my heart leaped. I hoped you had come with news of my son and daughter."

"I'm sorry, my friend. I wish I had."

The old man had grown tired, and Stone was about to wave the attendant over when Jonathan went on.

"You know we lived in the district of Kissy. The RUF took away my son to be a soldier. They took away my daughter to do what they do with young ten-year-old girls. Then the RUF violated my beloved wife, and when they were finished with her, put her and my mother and my sisters into our home locked the doors and set it afire. They made me stand there and watch them burn. Already they had, as they said, dropped my arms with a dull axe—it took many chops."

Stone feared he might say the wrong thing. He placed his

right hand on his heart and offered to obtain prosthetics for him.

Jonathan shook his head. "If you do that, they will send me away from here. And to where? A burned-out home and no family? I will wander the streets and someone will steal my new arms." He waved a stub. "The embassy sends me a stipend. I'm safe here for the time being."

Stone motioned the attendant to come over. "I must go now. If you want anything, let me know through the embassy. I will help."

"It is you who needs help, Hayden. I see Mr. Lange once a week, and he is very distraught. A good man like him should not live in fear."

"Thank you, Jonathan." Stone rose, realizing that with this warning his friend just may have saved his life.

Stone put his cooking skills to work. Sandra Harrington emerged from her bedroom, not because she felt better, but because she wanted company. She agreed to Stone's suggestion that she eat something. He cooked white rice and boiled chicken breasts, which didn't smell appetizing, but he knew she needed bland food.

"So Mr. Lange isn't in town. When's he coming back?"

"Tomorrow." Stone took the chair across the table from her. "Ever hear of a Marsha who worked at the embassy?"

"Sounds vaguely familiar. How were Craig's people with the countersurveillance?"

"Very professional. I guess he's good at being a COS."

Sandra picked at her meal. She asked if he had anything else, and he handed her a slice of white bread.

"Thanks. How about some chocolate?"

"Just what your stomach needs." Stone poured himself a short Irish whiskey. "Don't think you should have this."

"So, this Marsha. Is she an old squeeze of yours?"

"Not mine." Stone told her about his meeting with Jonathan. He provided the details on Marsha and Dirk Lange.

"The CIA Office of Security probably had a heyday

with that."

"Guess that's why Mr. Craig has been such a prick. I don't see how Lange's dalliance with a case officer is going to affect getting the information we need."

"Never know. Christ! Hope Craig doesn't have this place bugged." Sandra pushed her plate away. "How about a taste of that stuff you're drinking."

Stone poured a bit of whiskey into her water glass. As they both drank, he gave her a once-over: unwashed blonde hair, red puffy eyes, sweaty wrinkled robe, and blotchy skin. She wouldn't be well enough to travel for days. No way would he leave her behind.

"What are you looking at?"

"One gorgeous creature."

"You're full of shit. I'm going to bed. Sorry to hear about your friend Jonathan. That upset you a lot, didn't it?"

"Yeah. It hasn't all sunk in yet."

Sandra shuffled to her bedroom. Before closing the door, she called back, "Keep in mind what Jonathan told you about Lange. That South African might have something up his sleeve. Wish I could come with you tomorrow."

Stone finished off his drink and turned out the lights. He decided to retire early. In his room, he opened the hidden compartment in his suitcase, removed his Colt .45, and wiped it down lightly with gun oil.

CHAPTER EIGHT

CAPE TOWN, REPUBLIC OF SOUTH AFRICA
—AUGUST 9, 2002

Dawid van Wartt swirled the glass holding chilled Chenin Blanc from his family's Stellenbosch vineyard. He surveyed his guests who were milling about in the expansive sunken living room that took up one side of the home. His wife's recent redecoration by a well-known designer flown in from Rome provided the occasion for the soirée.

Originally planned for only close friends in Cape Town and the ones who flew down from Johannesburg, the guest list had swelled. Now business associates were included, who gladly joined in to drink his vintage South African wine and nibble on freshly prepared hors-d'oeuvres. A number of the guests had congregated next to the floor-to-ceiling windows to gaze out at the other hillside estates, their white stucco sides dazzling.

The sprawling city below now glowed crimson in the setting sun. White sails dotted Cape Town's Table Bay interspersed with anchored commercial vessels. A few couples walked the terrace that ran outside the windows for a better look, but soon, Van Wartt knew, the winter chill would bring them back inside to stand next to the fireplace.

Van Wartt and his wife, Kayla, watched Abdul Wahab and his wife return from their stroll along the flagstone terrace.

Kayla touched his elbow. "Who are those people?" She slightly raised her perfect nose, wrongly assumed by many of the Cape matrons as being reconstructed.

"Abdul Wahab and his wife, Lady Beatrice Roscommon," he whispered in Afrikaans. "Recent arrivals from London."

"She has a title?" Kayla continued in English with a touch of irony.

"So many of those Brits do." Van Wartt looked for his cigarettes. "Wahab is the one with the royal connections. His number one wife is a Saudi princess." Kayla looked a bit confused, so he explained. "Abdul Wahab has taken advantage of his religion to have two wives simultaneously." "And Lady Beatrice puts up with that?" Kayla cursed under her breath in Afrikaans. "In a way he is rather attractive. Bastard."

Removing a silver case from his inside jacket pocket, Van Wartt removed a cigarette and tapped it on the side. Lady Beatrice reminded him of that famous British actress who had played Cleopatra: long dark hair and ample breasts.

"Please don't smoke. Others will start and the place will reek with tobacco." Kayla brushed back her husband's graying hair, then stiffened. "God. The two are heading our way. They're your friends, dear. You handle them." She moved over to a group of loud Afrikaners from the Orange Free State.

Wahab and Lady Beatrice came up, and Van Wartt immediately guided them to the bar, handing the bartender his empty glass.

"Please, let me have your drinks," Van Wartt said. "I'll freshen them up."

"You do have excellent wines here," Beatrice said, presenting a practiced smile.

Van Wartt agreed and, appearing to gaze into her violet eyes, glanced down her décolleté, admiring the cleavage. Her accent was upper, upper class British, cultivated at that boarding school his people had reported she attended. He had also learned from the same investigators that she had vast funds at her disposal.

"Mr. Van Wartt. Do you think we might have a brief word alone sometime this evening?" Wahab asked, accepting a ginger ale from the bartender.

"Please. Call me Dawid. Now's a good time."

"Splendid," Beatrice said. "I'm off to the powder room."

"The girl here will show you the way," Van Wartt said, motioning to the uniformed servant. As Wahab's wife walked off, he said, "The library's free. We can speak there for a few minutes."

"Excellent," Wahab said. "And do you think someone can bring me a double malt scotch. Neat."

"Of course, Abdul."

They entered the dark-paneled library covered with heads of wild game Van Wartt had taken down over the course of years: an oryx, Cape buffalo, and an eland, among others. He considered this room his private space where he could comfortably make important decisions. Wahab sat in one of the two leather club chairs, Van Wartt in the other. The bartender brought in Wahab's drink and left, closing the door.

"Abdul. Have you and your charming wife found Cape Town up to your expectations?"

"It's a beautiful city to have a villa, if only for part of the year." Wahab adjusted the sharp crease in his trousers. "You have been quite hospitable to us. I wish to thank you."

Van Wartt dismissed the statement with a slight wave of his hand. "Not at all, Abdul. When I learned of your arrival from members of the yacht club, I took the opportunity to seek you out."

Especially when my people told me you had to leave in haste from the Riviera because the French authorities were interested in your terrorist connections.

"I feel that you are interested in entering into some commercial arrangement," Wahab said, sipping the scotch from the half-full tumbler. "You want to explore the business climate in Saudi Arabia?"

"No. More to the point, my friend," he said in Afrikaner-accented English. "I'm interested in some of your contacts in the Middle East. Mainly the disreputable ones."

Wahab leaned back in the chair and placed the glass to his lips without drinking. His cheerfulness had disappeared, and the lines at his eyes accentuated a cold hardness.

Van Wartt smiled. "I'm told we people in South Africa can be blunt at times."

Wahab rose and headed for the closed door. "We must

return to your guests."

"I am so undiplomatic, my dear Abdul. I meant no offense."

Wahab turned back toward Van Wartt. "I'm not easily offended, but I come from a culture where one must be cautious."

"Of course. I understand."

"Really?" Wahab walked back to the still-seated Van Wartt. "You have quite a mix of guests this evening."

"Under the new government we are a multicultural society."

"Is the American ambassador a friend?" Wahab asked. "And I see you have a Jew here also."

Van Wartt rose; now his smile had departed from his broad tan face. "No need to worry. The ambassador is a fool. The Jew's name is Jacob. He is a very useful contact in the diamond trade." He forced a laugh. "We all do business with people who can help us. Why, I've been told that your wife's investments in London are handled by Jews."

"You appear to know a lot about me."

"We both perform due diligence before entering into relationships. Do we not?"

Now Wahab smiled. "We may have common interests after all, Dawid."

"Please sit. Let me explain." Van Wartt waited until Wahab sat. This time his guest ignored his scotch. "You and I face common problems. Here in South Africa, our ... that is, *my* world has changed with the new government. Your world is also experiencing change and threats. I think you have to agree that much of what is happening to us comes from outside forces beyond our control ... it would seem."

"I'm not sure—"

"I'm not happy with what has happened to my world, and I want someone to atone," Van Wartt said.

Wahab looked away, as if to look out the window onto the garden. At last, he said, "Perhaps we should discuss this at a later time. Even though my wife and I have property here, I am still a visitor and must feel my way in your society."

Van Wartt nodded. The man sitting with him was on the run. His father-in-law, a Saudi prince, had blackballed him and would not care to see him return to his country even if he wanted to. The CIA considered him to be involved with the deaths of two of their officers, and everyone knew those people had long memories. Eventually, Wahab would be receptive to his plan. However, he, Van Wartt, had no wish to tarry.

The two left the library and returned to the entertainment area with the other guests, quite a few of whom had found seats on the new couches and chairs imported from Italy. The sun had set and the city lights twinkled in the soft azure dusk. Through the glass doors, the deep ridges of the craggy mammoth, Table Mountain, had darkened.

"Look, Abdul. That brown-haired chap in the Italian suit. The one with the moustache. That's the American ambassador. Standing over there staring out the window at Lord knows what. He is down from Pretoria." He chuckled. "And while the fool is drifting off in some other world, next to him is one of the finest feminine morsels in our city."

"My. Who is that attractive woman?"

"Patience St. John Smythe. An official with the Cape Town city government. Well connected. Especially bright and unattached."

"Quite intriguing. A member of the English tribe to complete your multicultural gathering?"

"My, Abdul. You are learning fast about your new country."

Deep within, US Ambassador Marshall Bunting felt an excitement. He certainly did enjoy taking in the accent of this woman speaking to him. She spoke with that peculiar combination of inflections that comes from speaking British English, Afrikaans, and one or more of the native dialects. He also noted her perfume, light and woodsy. He remembered a similar fragrance one night in Paris a year ago.

However, that strange-looking bird perched on the olive tree branch at the far end of the terrace intrigued him.

"Ambassador," the woman said, touching his sleeve. "We want to thank you for all your help bringing that art exhibit in from the Washington National Gallery."

"You must thank my cultural attaché. He's a wonder."

"I know, but you have been very supportive with the exhibit last month and also with our AIDS conference." She sighed. "Some of the people in my government don't realize what a problem the AIDS virus is."

Bunting turned and studied Ms. St. John Smythe. Age shy of thirty-five, not much younger than he. Hair very black, hanging loose, not too short. She had the ivory complexion of many women from the British Isles. A brush of light freckles across her nose made her face interesting. There was a distant air in her manner, yet she didn't withdraw when he moved close.

"I noticed you watching that bird out there," she said. "You're known as an ornithologist."

"No. I'm just a birder."

"I hear that you have two bird species named after you."

"Yes," Bunting said with a grin. "A swallow and a tern. I'm quite proud of that."

"May I ask? Are you accompanied tonight?"

"No."

"Oh, so you are not ... attached?" Following Bunting's eyes, she began to look around. "Pardon. Didn't mean to be so—"

"Not at all. Hmm. No, I'm not attached, but I am looking for my drink."

Patience hailed the woman carrying a tray of wine glasses, took one, and handed it to Bunting.

"Thank you. And you?"

"Excuse me?"

"Attached?"

"Not seriously."

Both sipped their drinks. She asked him what species of bird sat in the tree.

"That's the problem," he said. "It has all the markings of a golden-breasted bunting. They're not usually found here. They live up north, and in East Africa." He shrugged. "Cape buntings are the birds found here."

"Can't see it all that well. Lost one of my contacts coming

in tonight, but we're talking about birds with your name. They're not named after you, are they?"

He laughed. "No, no." The bird's head swung to the right and to the left with sharp mechanical movements. The eyes looked odd. "Ah well, maybe the fellow's lost."

She moved closer and he enjoyed her presence. "Ms. St. John Smythe, I wonder—"

"That is a mouthful, isn't it? Please, it's Patience."

"Patience. Next week I'm giving a reception here in Cape Town at our mission's residence. It's for a visiting congressional delegation. I have no … that is, would you consider helping me host the event?"

"I'll check my calendar, but I'm sure I'm free." She touched the lapel of his blazer. "Do you like to sail? My family belongs to the yacht club here."

"Yes, I do. Haven't had an opportunity to do any sailing here, though. Your bay looks challenging. Can get a bit rough."

"You must join us sometime. I'm sure you'll have no trouble, coming from San Francisco. I understand the bay there can get tricky."

"Right." *So. She's done her homework. Her arms have the firmness of an athlete. Probably a tennis player. My stay at this posting might prove interesting.*

"There goes your bird." She pointed.

He turned and watched it glide off, but not the way he expected it would. Something about the bird's movements, or lack of certain movements. Something else, the shape of the bird in flight, was peculiar.

It hit him. During his outbriefs in Washington, DC, prior to his posting to South Africa, the Defense Department sent him and two other outgoing ambassadors to an Air Force base in the desert outside of Las Vegas. Their hosts provided them a "show and tell" of the latest military gadgetry. The motivation of the office that ran the military attaché program was to garner favor for their attachés attached to the embassies.

Bunting recalled that it was an enjoyable trip. His friend Valery had accompanied him, and the morning he was to take his classified trip to the airbase, after a very long night partying, he awoke with a throbbing headache and Valery's naked body entwined in his arms. Lying there, he was certain that the night before he had said something to her about wanting to make their relationship a permanent one. He felt ill.

When he finished showering, he found Valery dressed, packed, seated straight in the desk chair, and smoking a cigarette. She asked him to be silent and informed him their relationship was not going in the direction she had envisioned, that he was taking things much too seriously, and that she couldn't possibly handle anything approaching a commitment. She rose, said she was flying to Boston that morning, and said to keep in touch.

Leaving, she blew him a kiss from the door.

He recalled his headache immediately disappearing, and cheerfully ordering a full room service breakfast with a double Bloody Mary.

The briefing at the airbase consisted of PowerPoint presentations on the military's latest and most expensive toys. After a buffet luncheon, he and the other two ambassadors were taken to a vault. There around a large conference table, an affable scientist from one of the Defense research agencies, wearing a Drexel University lacrosse sweatshirt, showed them a number of exotic gadgets.

One particular item had caught Bunting's interest. It was among a collection of drones, unmanned aircraft used for surveillance. Some had five-foot wingspans, some looked like miniature helicopters, and one resembled a saucer. As the scientist brought one after the other out to display, the drones became smaller and smaller. At last, after adjusting his eyeglasses that had slipped down his nose, the man presented his piece de résistance, lifting it and letting it fly about the room.

The bird-shaped drone was the size, shape, and color of the bunting that had just flown from the Van Wartts' olive tree. Identical.

"Ambassador?" Patience placed her hand on his shoulder.

"Oh. I didn't mean to be rude. Just remembered something," he explained. "I think I'm off. Can I give you a lift home?"

"Thanks. I drove."

"I'll call tomorrow."

"Do."

Ambassador Bunting paid his respects to the van Wartts and outside found his driver waiting for him by the embassy's armored BMW sedan. Riding down the winding road toward the sparkling lights of the city, he made a mental note to speak with his CIA base chief at the Cape Town consulate first thing in the morning. Why wasn't he informed of the surveillance, especially since he had announced his daily schedule at the huddle that morning? Unless, of course, it wasn't their drone. Maybe the Russians? Doubtful. Reports were their intel operations were in chaos. Israelis? Possible. Nevertheless, he would get an explanation.

At the same time, he'd get the base chief to do a background trace on Patience St. John Smythe. He did so hope that she wasn't too good to be true.

CHAPTER NINE

FREETOWN, SIERRA LEONE—AUGUST 10, 2002

At nine in the morning, Hayden Stone phoned York Export Ltd. and asked Mr. Amadu, the office manager, to speak with Dirk Lange. Amadu asked the nature of his call, and Stone reminded him of his visit to the office the day before.

"Oh yes. Mr. Costanza, I believe. The travel writer."

"The same."

"I took the liberty of making inquiries for Mr. Lange and could not find your name posted on any of the bibliographies."

"Is Mr. Lange available? If so, put him on."

After a pause and without further comment, Amadu transferred him to his boss. When Lange answered the phone, Stone detected a slight Afrikaner inflection to the otherwise clipped English accent.

"Good Morning, Mr. Lange. The name's Finbarr Costanza. I'm a writer, and a mutual friend suggested I give you a ring."

"And who would that be?"

Stone provided the parole, the password provided by Jacob, to confirm his identity. "A fellow from London said you knew a lot about the forest elephants."

After a silence, Lange asked, "Are you interested in the herds in the Gola Forest North or the Gola East?"

"Both are of interest for my story."

"Let us meet for lunch at the Hill Station Club. The history of the club might be of use for your story," he said, and as an afterthought asked, "What do you look like?"

"White. Dark hair. No facial hair," Stone said. "Oh. I'll be wearing a khaki safari jacket."

"Of course you will."

• • •

Stone drove the small Toyota pickup from the city into the hilly, forested district that overlooked the bay. The meeting with Lange was scheduled for one in the afternoon. As he drove on the narrow lane through the tropical forest, a soft rain fell and the windshield wipers slapped a hypnotic rhythm. Each time the car passed over a rut in the road, the right bumper, the victim of a past collision, clanged against the car's frame.

That morning Sandra had demanded she accompany him on the meet, and at one point became quite adamant, but as they argued, he watched her physically deflate, eyes redden, and finally acquiesce. She trudged to her bedroom.

The station chief was another matter. After making the appointment with Lange, he had touched base with Craig in his embassy office. He showed a strange disinterest in the meet and said countersurveillance was unnecessary. His dislike for Dirk Lange came out rather loud and clear.

"Really can't afford spending resources on someone we know to be a small-time player. The guy's a bum. South Africa's equivalent to Eurotrash. People like him wind up everywhere there's a buck to be made. They're like gypsies."

Stone was relieved to not have Craig involved in his meeting. The man's animosity toward Lange could only make Stone's pitch difficult. He wanted to find out what the man had to offer, report the details back to Washington, and head home. But something nagged at him. Craig's lack of interest in an operation on his turf was hard to fathom. More likely one of Craig's assets worked at the Hill Station Club and would report back to him about the meet.

He turned off the road, drove up a short dirt driveway, and parked in front of a two-story house that served as the clubhouse. Nearby, three weathered colonial-style homes sodden in the rain looked like they hadn't been occupied since the British granted independence to Sierra Leone.

A black man carrying an umbrella came up to the car. A large two-way radio hung on his belt. Behind him the clubhouse sat morose, upstairs windows flung open, the paint faded on the cement block walls topped by a rusty tin roof.

"You are Mr. Costanza? Mr. Lange awaits in the bar."

The guard led Stone up broken concrete stairs to the entrance past scraggly bushes with yellow flowers. "The bar is beyond the ballroom."

The room had not seen a dance in years, yet the wooden floor had maintained a degree of polish. The floorboards didn't squeak underfoot. Scattered around the room were chrome-framed chairs, the type Stone had last seen in an American diner. No tables were visible.

In contrast to the club's exterior, the mahogany-paneled bar was clean and looked cared for. Tall chairs lined the bar, a limited but expensive selection of liquor sat on the glass shelf, and a dated computer cash machine hummed. A local man wearing a striped shirt sat, before him a half glass of Guinness.

At the far end of the bar, under a row of British Navy ship plaques displayed on the wall, in a position where he could see anyone coming in, a sandy-haired man in a yellow tennis shirt sat smoking a cigarette. The eyes gave Stone a long once-over. From a photo Craig had shown him that morning, Stone knew the man to be Dirk Lange.

Stone acknowledged the black man and walked straight for Lange, right hand extended. "Mr. Lange? I'm Finbarr."

Lange's handshake was firm and quickly withdrawn. He motioned for Stone to take a seat next to him. When the bartender approached, Stone ordered a Star beer, then laid a black Moleskine notebook on the table. "Good of you to help me out with my story on the elephants here in Sierra Leone."

"My pleasure. Only hope I can be of assistance." Lange's eyes darted to the man with the Guinness. "They are a distrustful lot, those animals. The ones that manage to survive. In that region there are too many people with AK-47s looking for something to kill."

Stone made a pretense of opening his notebook and scribbling with his pen.

"This is an interesting club," Lange continued. "Has history.

Have you been here before?" Without waiting for Stone to answer, he rose. "Come, I'll show you the billiard room upstairs. You know a famous English writer was a member here during the Second World War."

"So I hear."

"He was also a spy."

Upstairs, a shaded lamp hung over an old, well-maintained billiard table. Not three feet away, a ragged hole in the floor the size of a manhole looked down into the ballroom.

"Termites?" Stone asked.

Lange said, "Probably," and led him to the green painted wall next to the open window. He searched the grounds below. At last, he turned, moved closer, and looked directly into Stone's eyes. "Jonathan spoke to me about you." The words came more as assurance than a statement. "I will come to the point."

He stood close and the nearness made Stone uneasy. The man smelled of a cheap aftershave that airlines placed in travel amenity kits.

"Ronda. A colleague at the aid organization fell in love with an Arab man who lives next to one of the big mosques in town. They slept together and one night began smoking hashish. Three weeks or so ago, she confided in me, being a fellow South African. She is disturbed, troubled." Lange moved away and for a moment listened at the door. Returning, he continued. "She said that while in bed, smoking hashish, the Arab starts bragging about how his people will triumph against Western civilization. That he was helping purchase the means of making a bigger statement than was made with those towers in New York City."

"What kind of statement?"

Lange shrugged. "Ronda came to me about this. Being a sensible woman, she was quite worried."

"Can I talk to her?"

Lange shook his head. "Last week fishermen pulled her body ashore in their nets."

"Did the police rule suicide or foul play?"

"You are joking, Mr. Costanza? The police here are not concerned with the random body that washes ashore. They have a backlog of *explained* deaths to process."

"You believe this Middle Eastern friend had something to do with her death?"

Lange nodded. "I told all this to Jacob, who said he would have someone come and talk with me."

Stone, thinking about his last assignment on the Riviera, asked if Lange thought the Arab had been talking about spreading Ebola or some other disease.

"I doubt it. To me, it sounded like some object they were buying. Something that would prove catastrophic. Ronda told me she thought the Arab inferred one of her own kind, a South African, was selling them this 'thing.'"

"Someone from South Africa?"

"That was her impression."

Stone walked to the window. The still air in the room hung heavy with dust. Down below, the guard stood under the roof of a shed next to the parking lot. He turned back to Lange. "This Arab. What nationality? Lebanese, Syrian? Is he still here? Know where I can find him?"

"Egyptian." Lange motioned that they should return downstairs to the bar. "Saw the bugger two days ago at the open-air beach café on the point. Out Lumley Beach Road."

"Have a name?"

"Nabeel. Nabeel Asuty."

Stone followed Lange to the door. "Mr. Lange. Tomorrow I suggest we go drinking by the bay."

Stone eased the battered truck down the tree-covered lane from the Hill Station Club to the American Embassy. The steady rain washed mud onto the patchy macadam, and at places the runoff poured across the road from the hill above, splattering the windshield with muddy water. The meeting with Lange went well, he thought. The information was a bit sketchy and hearsay, but still Lange gave him a name, Nabeel Asuty, and an address for a place that he frequented—a mosque located downtown.

A cable setting out the results of the meeting had to be sent to Stone's boss, Colonel Gustave Frederick, at CIA headquarters. However, Stone had to follow protocol: Luke Craig had to sign off on the draft before it was sent over the agency's communications network. Craig's reaction would be interesting. Would he blow off the allegation that Nabeel was involved in a grandiose terrorist plot? Did he know this individual and already have him in the agency's crosshairs?

Stone would know by tonight whether he was staying in Freetown to follow up on the case or heading back to Washington. As he drove, he imagined himself opening that café along the Southern California coast. He'd be near his two kids, who attended college nearby. This last thought reminded him that he must email both of them. He remembered his ex-wife lived in Los Angeles, competing for their children's attention. By the time Stone pulled up to the embassy, he decided he wasn't that eager to board a homeward plane.

Craig surprised him. Swiveling side to side in his chair, he read and reread the draft Stone had prepared. He stopped occasionally to make edits with his number two pencil, a practice that Stone knew was instinctual for any boss in the agency who authorized the sending of cables to their headquarters division. Bosses had to make their mark on all outgoing communications. What caught Stone off guard was Craig's interest in the content of the draft. Evidently, Craig had picked up other information that made the account credible. Stone guessed the station's source at the Hill Station Club reported something positive about his meet with Lange.

"The name Nabeel Asuty doesn't ring a bell, but we know about activity at the mosque," Craig admitted. "Most of the hotheads in town gather there to plan their version of *jihad*. As if this country needs any more turmoil."

Since Craig appeared in a cooperative mood, Stone offered, "I suggested to Lange that I'd contact him for a follow-up. What do you think?"

Craig looked off as if in thought. "Why don't you and Sandra stay on for a bit? Contact the source tomorrow and see if this Nabeel can be located. We need a face on this guy." Craig returned to scribbling on the bottom of the draft. "I'm making that suggestion to headquarters."

Stone said he'd get hold of Lange and head for the café on Lumley Beach Road. Craig continued his scribbling. "My people will ramp up coverage of the mosque and try to come up with corroborating evidence," he muttered. Stone knew he was dismissed when Craig lifted the phone and told his assistant to send in one of his case officers for a briefing.

A mixture of cooking aromas greeted Stone as he walked in the second-floor apartment. Sandra Harrington stood at the sink draining pasta in a colander. Her demeanor appeared a lot more chipper than when he left for the embassy that morning.

"We're having spaghetti," she said. "My stomach and head feel a lot better."

The place settings were laid out on the wooden dining table, something cooked in a covered pot, and a short baguette of bread lay on the counter ready to be sliced.

"What, no candles?" Stone asked.

"Not tonight," she said. "But I did get some ground beef and some sort of squash from the commissary here on the compound."

Stone told her she looked a lot better. The color had returned to her face. Her blouse and shorts looked as if they had been washed and ironed that day. Her hair was pulled back in a ponytail and she had put on earrings. His eyes lingered on her legs, tanned and firm.

"So, how did the interview go with Lange?" she asked.

He related the details of the meeting with Lange and Craig's reaction. She turned from browning the ground beef and gave him a look. "Craig knows more than he's letting on."

"I agree." He walked to the counter, cut a slice of Gouda cheese, and put it on two crackers. He handed one to Sandra. "But he wants us to stay and run with it, for how long I don't know."

She studied the cracker. "Imagine getting fresh cheese in this country. The embassy's administrative office must be well run."

"I'm meeting with Lange tomorrow around lunchtime to see if we can get a read on this Nabeel character. Are you ready to go back to work?"

"You bet. And how about you? What happened to the guy who was itching to fly home?" She grinned. "The thrill of the chase got you?"

"Maybe I didn't want to head home as much as lay over in Paris, but to answer your question, something about this case has sparked my interest. Luke Craig knows more than he's willing to let on. That's to be expected." He thought for a moment. "Jacob told me in Monrovia that he's concerned enough that I should contact Dirk Lange, who in turn says this Nabeel character probably had a South African killed to keep her quiet about some big plan to attack the West. Another Twin Towers-type attack. And this guy Dirk Lange turns out to be … interesting." Stone saw his Irish whiskey bottle and two glasses sitting next to the refrigerator. "Shall we? Or is the stomach too sensitive?"

"Water it down for me." She turned off the heat to the frying pan and tossed a few slices of onion in with the beef. "What's your take on Mr. Dirk Lange?"

"Not what I was expecting. You know, the typical tough guy soldier of fortune. Understand, he's no marshmallow, but he has a human side. Seems to be bright and knowledgeable about what's happening in this neck of the woods."

"I believe it, since he's South African. Is he trustworthy?"

"I suppose. After all, a hard-nosed character like Jacob deals with him, and Jonathan and he have a good relationship …"

"Not good enough. What's your gut instinct?"

Stone poured whiskey into the two glasses. It was good to have her cool, no-nonsense thinking back. "For one, he doesn't trust me. I'm sure he thinks I'm agency, and we don't know the whole story of his relationship with that CIA gal."

"I think we know. He was banging our CIA staffer, and the station made it uncomfortable for both of them." She clicked Stone's glass and sipped her whiskey. "Did you get a feeling that he's been trained? That he's a pro?"

"He's trusted to some extent by Jacob, so he floats in

those circles."

Sandra looked hard. "Again, do you trust him?"

"Not yet."

They sat and started eating. She had tossed a light tomato sauce with the pasta, and the whiff of garlic pleasantly added to the taste. Stone saw her appetite had improved.

Laying down her fork, she sat back and looked into space. "So, tomorrow we three go to this outdoor café and look for this Nabeel." Continuing as if going down a list, "The dead South African presumably was murdered by Nabeel because she knew too much about some planned terrorist operation. What happened to her body?" She turned to Stone, who shrugged.

Sandra was right. He should have picked up on that. Lange only said the police hadn't been interested. "The South African Embassy would have made an inquiry," Stone said. "Maybe Craig can find out."

"It's logical to assume that we're dealing with a group of terrorists who have a plan to make a big splash. Like spreading a plague in the US, or poisoning city water supplies. We have to know who we're dealing with, what their backgrounds, educations are."

Stone studied Sandra's face, the sharp outline of her chin and the bright green eyes that, when in thought, appeared to dance with ideas.

"What?" Sandra frowned.

Catching himself, he said, "Nothing. Just thinking about what you said."

"About what?"

"Oh, about ... everything." Stone tried to appear busy twirling the pasta around his fork. "It's good to have you back."

She returned to her meal and after a moment, out of the corner of his eye, Stone caught a quizzical glance.

CHAPTER TEN

FREETOWN, SIERRA LEONE—AUGUST 11, 2002

After fueling up the truck at the embassy maintenance compound, Stone and Sandra picked up Dirk Lange, waiting patiently outside his office building. Lange suggested he take the wheel. "Driving through town from here to Cape Sierra Leone can be tricky for a visitor."

Stone got out of the car and walked around and took the passenger seat. Sandra moved to the middle and introduced herself. After a bit of banter between the two, Lange circled the miniscule square showcasing Freetown's landmark Cotton Tree. He drove southwest on Siaka Stevens Street. Stone noted a change in Lange's demeanor. With smiles and a mellow voice, his attention focused fully on Sandra.

"First time here on the continent?" Lange asked.

"Been to Africa, but never Freetown." Before he could ask another personal question, she said, "And you? How long have you lived here?"

Lange took a moment to answer. "You don't know?" He flashed a boyish grin.

"Just checking to be sure you're the same guy I heard about."

"I've been here off and on for a number of years. First, working for a British-owned security company, now I'm in the mining business." He pointed to the run-down neighborhood of shanties and hollowed-out houses they passed. "You wouldn't think this country is enormously wealthy in minerals, now would you?"

"You also do charity work?" she asked.

"Keeps me busy." He honked at a pedestrian who had stepped in front of the car carrying a live chicken by its feet.

"Have no family except my parents back in Jo'burg. How about you?"

Stone decided to interrupt Lange's questioning of Sandra, which resembled first encounter bar talk. "How far do we have to drive?"

"We go west on the Motor Main Road, cross the bridge to Aberdeen, and then we're almost to the café. Don't expect too much from the kitchen."

"Dirk," Stone said, "I forgot to ask. Do you meet often with Jacob?"

The response came at once and in a flat, deliberate tone. "He didn't tell you?"

Stone looked out the side window. Lange knew what was and was not appropriate when asking about intelligence relationships. Obviously, the man had training. Question: Was he an active member of the South African service or just a runner?

"Jacob only indicated he trusted you," Stone said. "He was also concerned enough about your information to tell me to contact you."

"And you, Mr. Finbarr Costanza, is it? What is your relationship with Jacob?"

Well done, you big prick. "A sporadic one over a long time. Do you expect him to drop by?"

"We both know he pops in and out unexpectedly."

Sandra heaved an exaggerated sigh. "Not to change the subject, but this café we're going to. Is it a local hangout?"

"It is an expat hangout. A very pleasant place," Lange said, his broad smile returned. "It overlooks Man of War Bay, and you can sit and have a cool drink under the palm trees. An escape from reality."

On arriving, Stone had to agree with Lange's assessment. The café sat on the semicircular blue water bay alongside other eating establishments and small resorts that resembled American motels. A far cry from the hovels and trash-laden streets they had passed, this district had a feel of forced relaxation, ever cautious of the possible encroachment of Africa's primitive disorder.

They parked in the café's car lot behind the single-story

metal-roofed building. Lange led them through the main entrance that adjoined the noisy kitchen. Once out on the terrace, he was proved correct—the breeze cooled the soft air and Stone looked out on a scene that could be duplicated at any tropical seaside spot in the world. An invitation to sit and relax and forget where one lived.

Stone and Sandra ordered cool fruit drinks, Lange a beer. The menu resembled one found in an English pub. Again, Lange cautioned them not to expect haute cuisine. They were early, so few tables were occupied.

After the waiter brought the drinks, Sandra leaned toward Lange. "Did the police issue a report on that woman who washed ashore?"

Lange shook his head. "Like I told … Finbarr, the police issue few reports in this town."

"This woman, Ronda, was South African," she pressed. "Did your embassy make an inquiry?"

"Yes, after they examined the body." Lange looked around to make sure no one was near. "They found a small hollow depression in back of the neck, just below where it meets the skull. The spinal cord was cut, they surmise from an ice pick-type weapon."

"They dumped her in the bay," Stone said. "Hope she was dead at the time."

Lange stiffened. "She was quite a decent person."

"I'm sure she was," Sandra said, giving Stone an admonishing look for his insensitive remark.

Across the way a chair fell over, and they saw four bearded men, each wearing black untucked short-sleeved shirts. Lange touched Stone's arm and Sandra, catching the sign, raised her camera concealed in a sunglass case. After a moment, Stone felt assured they had gotten photographs of Nabeel Asuty and his companions, copies of which were now being transmitted by the radio in the case to a satellite overhead. Next, to help the Counterterrorism Center back in Langley do a search on Asuty, they needed a car tag number and, if lucky, Asuty's credit card number.

Their meals came as advertised by Lange. Everyone carefully inspected the food, hoping it wasn't bushmeat. From across the restaurant, Stone was the first to pick up Nabeel's interest in their table.

"It must be me they're looking at," Lange said. "They know I was acquainted with Ronda."

Stone started to say they were giving them all a once-over when Nabeel rose, said something to his associates, and marched toward their table. The man was in his early forties, taller and better built than Stone had pictured. No dandy, he had an arrogant stride.

"Mr. Lange," Nabeel Asuty said in a contrived, unctuous voice. "So unfortunate about our mutual friend Ronda. Boating can be dangerous in these waters."

"Really, Mr. Asuty," Lange said, looking him up and down. "I didn't realize someone who lived in a desert knew anything about boating."

Stone was impressed by Lange's toughness, characteristic of the grit many native-born whites in Africa had.

"One must be careful here in Freetown, Mr. Lange."

Stone gave a purposely false guffaw. "Good God. This man is right out of a very bad grade B movie. Do you practice your routine in front of a mirror before you skip out in public?"

Asuty's face froze, but his right hand twitched. He reached into his shirt pocket for his sunglasses and put them on.

Stone turned to Sandra, who stared at him with a "What the ..." look, then at Lange, who grinned at everyone.

Finally, Nabeel's back straightened, revealing the outline of a gun tucked in his belt. His head bobbled ever so slightly. "Mr. Lange. You should inform your guest that this is not as safe a place as the French Riviera." With that he turned on his heels and returned to his table.

"Why, Hayden?" Sandra asked. "Why did you antagonize the man?"

"I wanted to piss him off. Wanted to have him lose his cool to see if he knew me, or about me. He does." Stone downed his drink. "The only person who got away in the South of France operation was the Saudi, Abdul Wahab, who undoubtedly carries a grudge. I'd wager this Nabeel Asuty works for Wahab."

"Very well done, *Hayden*," Lange laughed. "Good logical reasoning. I bet you were good in your day."

Stone's gray eyes hardened. "The day's not over, pal."

Sandra frowned at Lange. "Where does that put us?" She slowly answered her own question. "That puts us on the track of a terrorist operation with some good leads."

"We still need a license plate and maybe a credit card number," Stone said.

"As for the credit card, I'll get it," Lange offered. "I know the girl at the register. Oh. I'll get Asuty's glass for fingerprints."

"Sounds like a plan," Stone said. *Fingerprints? This guy is a pro.* "I'm headed for the restroom." Stone rose and winked at Sandra. "Wonder if Nabeel knows anything about poisonous snakes in Liberia."

To reach the toilet facilities, Stone had to exit the restaurant's main entrance and walk around the parking lot to a shed attached to the side of the building. He dreaded using public privies in this area of the world and only used them if he had no choice. This one met his expectations. Dark, stiflingly hot, and cramped. The rank odors emitted a unique toxic bouquet.

The door would not completely shut, but he intended to make his visit as quick as possible. Instead of a urinal, Stone discovered at the far end of the room a hole in the floor. He squirmed past a stained water basin and a toilet bowl without a seat, trying not to touch either. Unzipping, he looked up at the ceiling at a collection of cobwebs. From the fresh ones hung spiders of varying colors and sizes.

The door behind him banged open. Stone looked around and saw the silhouettes of two men. "I'm about finished," he called, turning back and pushing to empty his bladder.

As he pulled up his zipper, he realized the two men had entered the room. Spinning around, he recognized them as two of Nabeel's thugs. The first man, carrying a gun, lunged at him. Stone went into defensive stance and kneed him in the gut. He groaned and lurched forward, swinging his automatic pistol at Stone's head.

Stone grabbed his wrist and tried to grasp the barrel of the gun. Slammed against the wall, Stone pushed him away with his leg, but now the second man came from the side and slugged Stone.

Cornered, Stone's only chance was to take away the first man's gun as the muzzle of the automatic came toward Stone's face.

Stone hollered. The second man growled in Arabic, "Shut him up!" Stone spit in the first man's eyes, surprising him. The first man stumbled back over the broken toilet bowl, and as he regained his footing, Stone closed his hand over the barrel and stunned him with a sharp head-butt. The man's nose crunched.

Now Stone had a solid grip on the automatic and was taking it away when the second man slashed at Stone with a knife. Stone ducked, and with his left hand struck the first man's throat with a karate chop, crushing his larynx. Clutching his throat, the man collapsed over the toilet bowl and the gun dropped. The second man now held the knife close to Stone's eye.

The blade inched closer. As it touched the eyelid, a muscular blond-haired arm wrapped tightly around the second man's neck. The hand holding the knife lost strength. The man's face reddened, bubbles formed on his mouth, and his eyes bulged. Stone wrenched the knife from his hand. At the same time Dirk Lange snapped the man's neck.

On the floor, the first man, gasping for air from the broken larynx, picked up his automatic. He aimed it at Stone's groin, but he pushed aside the gun and placed two shots from his Colt into the man's chest. The sound reverberated within the small room as the man flew backward.

Stone and Lange waited, expecting to hear shouts or calls from outside. Only faint music came from the restaurant.

After a moment, Lange went to the door and searched the area. "No one here. I saw these two follow you here to the loo," Lange said. "I heard you shout. Figured you needed help."

"Thanks. You came just in time." Stone bent down at the basin and, using the fetid water from the tap, washed his face.

"What do you suggest we do with the bodies?"

"There's a large rubbish bin outside," Lange said. "We'll dump them there."

Lange's sudden cold demeanor surprised Stone. The fact the man wasn't breathing hard impressed him. Strong mind. Tough body. "Let's empty their pockets first," Stone said.

They found cash, passports, and various shaped keys, which Stone said he'd examine later. It took both of them to drag the bodies one by one from the bathroom to the dumpster. Finished, Stone said, "Let's get out of here." Then stopped. "Where's Sandra?"

"Took the truck and followed Nabeel when he left. She'll ring you on your cell."

"We have to get out of here."

Lange tossed over two wallets taken from the men's pockets and fingered the collection of keys in his hand. "We can use their Mercedes," he said, pushing the release button for the car door. A short beep came from the direction of the parking lot. They headed toward a row of parked Mercedes. Lange pressed the button again, and the horn of a black sedan sounded.

"Hop in. We'll drive somewhere where we can wait for Sandra to call," Stone said. "Do you know someplace by the sea? I'm sweating like a pig."

Under palm trees bent by the ocean breeze, they looked over the Iraqi passports of the dead men and, seeing nothing of immediate interest, searched the car. Stone draped a cloth over the license tag to conceal it from passing traffic. The trunk provided a few surprises: two AK-47s, three Russian-made automatic pistols, and a canvas sack containing what Stone recognized as a C4 plastic explosive.

Lange shook his head. "What on earth were they thinking, carrying this around in their car?"

A truck passed and Stone slammed down the trunk lid. He leaned on the car, and, enjoying the cool breeze, looked up at fat storm clouds forming on the horizon. "Maybe they were on the way to a delivery. That would explain the two cars." He pulled out his cell phone. "I should call Sandra."

Sandra Harrington maintained a discrete distance behind Nabeel Asuty's car as she had been taught at the agency's surveillance school in Virginia. Nabeel traveled through congested neighborhoods similar to the ones she had passed through that morning. It was easy to follow the Honda as it slowed and occasionally halted for pedestrians and animals.

Even with the heat, Sandra kept the windows only partially open. Thieves were expert in reaching in and making fast grabs for purses and jewelry. As she passed the shops and dingy two-story houses, the sounds and smells of West Africa hit her senses—music, much of it Western pop, smoke from the charcoal stoves, shouted sales pitches, wafts from overflowing cesspools, laughter, fragrance from an unseen flower, singing.

Sandra's quarry left the city and started to climb up one of Freetown's many tall hills. Trees and fields replaced buildings as Nabeel's Honda increased speed up the winding road. Traffic was light, but she was able to hide behind a lumbering, smoke-belching dump truck. Still ascending, the air thinned and birdcalls from heavy-leafed trees replaced the noise of the city.

Nabeel's route surprised her. She had expected him to head for one of the downtown mosques, not the countryside. Her cell phone rang. It was Stone. She gave him her location and told him she'd call back when her target had reached his destination. She couldn't talk and at the same time shift gears on the twisting hill.

After a few more turns, she had no one between her and Nabeel's car. She slowed, lost eye contact, but trusted that after a few curves, she'd spy his car again. Around a bend, she spotted his brake lights and watched him turn. For a brief moment she pulled off the side of the road, then proceeded to the turnoff and left the macadam for a red-dirt road. She passed a number of houses surrounded by high cinderblock walls topped with razor wire.

Nabeel's Honda entered a gated compound, the inside hidden by a high wall. She needed a higher elevation. To the right she looked up to where a hill rose. From there she could look down on the compound. Her map showed a road winding up to and beyond the top of the rise.

In less than five minutes she was walking along a ridge, searching for the best vantage point. She chose a place hidden by trees and brush and peered down into the compound. A large housing complex sat surrounded by walls. Seven cars were parked on the grounds where men, apparently guards, walked back and forth smoking cigarettes. The back of the house looked down on Freetown and the bay. A concrete terrace with a lap-sized pool, tables, chairs, and umbrellas provided a vantage point for the owner.

Sandra found a tree stump, checked for bugs and snakes, settled herself, and looked over the scene. The rich, green hilly landscape overlooked the city below. It was quiet except for an occasional rooster crow and a dog bark. She called Stone.

"Are you okay? Where are you?"

She told him. "Are you two still at the café?"

"No. We had a problem with two of our target's friends. I'll explain later. Be careful. They play dirty. How long do you intend on staying at your location?"

She studied the woods around her and scanned the compound again. She felt a shiver as if someone was watching her. "Not long."

Placing the phone in her pocket, she tried to interpret Stone's statement about having a problem. From the last mission they were on, she knew how he solved problems. Very decisively. *He did attract trouble.*

She thought about Stone and Lange. What was Lange's part in all this? She had noticed tension between the two men on the way to the café and again at lunch. Was she the cause? Two men posturing before a woman? She smiled while lowering the binoculars. Dirk Lange was a charmer. No wonder that CIA gal fell for him. The strong jaw. That deep, confident voice.

Had she detected a note of disapproval on Stone's part

when she joked around with Lange? What was that about? Was he jealous?

Sandra caught movement below and raised her binoculars, scoping the complex. Men filed out the back door onto the terrace. They sauntered around the pool; a few moved to the edge of the terrace, taking in the view of the city. No women, just men talking in small groups with many hand gestures. Most had beards and a few wore *thobes*, ankle-length robes. As she scanned the group, she spied Nabeel. He had donned one of the ivory-colored billowy *thobes* and glided from one group to another. Again, the flying hand gestures.

While panning, she stopped on a man's face. A face she knew, but didn't belong in this scene. Whether in denial or just confused, the person's identity didn't register at first. Then she realized who the man was, standing by the pool, in sunglasses, in deep conversation with Nabeel Asuty.

Her former partner, Farley Durrell.

CHAPTER ELEVEN

CAPE TOWN—AUGUST 12, 2002

At the morning "country team meeting," Ambassador Marshall Bunting sat to the right of Whitmore, his consul general for Cape Town. Bunting allowed Whitmore the position of honor at the table. Rightly so, for it was his post, and the fussy little man had earned one of State's posh assignments through years of dedicated service in many of the hellholes of the world.

The staff assembled around the table inside "the bubble," a Plexiglas compartment designed in the 1960s as an anti-eavesdropping device. American security professionals had questioned its effectiveness from the beginning, but it did provide some protection from sound and voice emanation. The contraption was useless against a technical attack, a method the South African intelligence service, one of the best in the world, certainly used. The nation's science capablitiies were first-rate, having performed the world's first heart transplant and having tested a nuclear weapon over the southern sea near Antarctica. American counterintelligence knew South Africa's intelligence organization would be no less accomplished. In addition it wasn't a particularly friendly one.

A few moments into the meeting, one of the junior counselors brought up a personnel problem, setting out the sexual proclivities of a young staffer. The CIA Base Chief M. R. D. Houston, in his early thirties with a short haircut that emphasized his jug ears, squirmed in his seat. An enemy agent overhearing this conversation could use the information as blackmail to target the unfortunate American being discussed. The information would be leverage to turn the young staffer into a spy for the South Africans and the United States.

Bunting spoke up. "Perhaps this matter should be discussed one-on-one, don't you think, Consul General?"

Flustered, Whitmore agreed and moved on to another topic. The meeting continued for a half hour. As they adjourned, Bunting asked Houston to remain behind. When the room had cleared, he pushed a three-by-five card across the table with the writing:

WHERE CAN WE TALK IN PRIVATE?

Houston nodded. "Let's go for a ride."

They drove in Houston's car, a battered green Land Rover Defender, through crowded Cape Town toward the bay. After fifteen minutes Houston found a parking space near the lighthouse off Beach Road. The two got out and strolled along the waterfront. Bunting took in the deep blue ocean, rough with white caps, and off to his left, Table Mountain. The air sparkled.

"That's called Three Anchor Bay." Houston pointed down the coast. "I guess they named it so because it takes three anchors to hold your ship in place." He surveyed the area, and apparently comfortable with their surroundings, finally said, "I believe this is a place where we can safely talk, Mr. Ambassador."

Bunting wasted no time getting to the point. "Mr. Houston. I attended a soirée the other evening at the residence of one Dawid van Wartt."

"Yes, sir," Houston murmured.

"I observed out the window, perched in a tree, a drone in the shape of a bird. Remarkably realistic, I might add." Bunting stopped to let what he said settle in and continued. "One of yours, Mr. Houston?"

He stammered and shook his head. "It wasn't my operation." Houston looked directly into Bunting's eyes. "I only know about it because the team flew in from Washington and hit me for hotel accommodations. They arrived two weeks ago. I'm not in the loop."

"I trust your boss, the station chief in Pretoria, is aware of what's happening on his turf."

Houston nodded.

"For two weeks this operation has been going on?"

No answer at first, then a nod.

"The target is ..." Bunting pretended to hesitate before asking, "Me?"

"Good God, no. Not you, sir!" he blurted. "That Arab fellow. What's his name? Wahab something."

Bunting tried to remember the people he had met at the party. The name Wahab didn't ring a bell. "What does he look like?"

"About our height, a little less than six feet. Fortyish. Well groomed and dressed. Trimmed black beard."

M. R. D. Houston knew enough about the operation that he was certain of the target's description. Bunting let the young man fidget. Finally, he asked, "This Wahab is important if you're spending all these resources on him."

"Yes, sir."

"Why is he so important?"

"Well, sir ..." Houston took a deep breath. "You'll get this from the station chief, so ..."

"I'll act surprised when I talk with your boss. Please, go on."

"A couple of months ago, Wahab was involved in the death of two case officers on the French Riviera."

"I see," Bunting said. He started walking back to the Land Rover. "I return to Pretoria tomorrow afternoon. Tell your boss I want to meet with him on this matter."

"Yes, Mr. Ambassador."

As they climbed into the vehicle, Bunting looked at his watch. It was close to noon. He wondered if his colleague, Colonel Gustave Frederick, had arrived in his spacious seventh-floor office at Langley. A call to him was in order. Did he have a hand in this operation?

Ambassador Bunting chose a table within the enclosed patio area set off from the main dining room. Dusk was in the process of bringing its shadows and warm colors onto the waterfront of Cape Town's Victoria and Alfred complex. He readjusted his silverware setting, placed the blue linen napkin on his lap, and sipped his ice water. He would wait to order his cocktail until Patience arrived.

She fluttered in, looked around, saw him, and hurried to his table. She reminded him of one of those English schoolgirls: bright, fresh, earnest. Her motions at times were birdlike. Is this what had attracted him?

"Sorry I'm a bit late. Last minute details at the office. Traffic."

He rose and pushed in her chair. "No problem. Care for a drink?"

"A wine. Riesling, please."

He ordered a South African vintage for her, and for himself, a negroni cocktail. She wore a charcoal pinstriped business suit. Skirt cut to the knee. She had a curl to her hair, and her eyes were deep blue.

"So," she said. "How are the arrangements for the reception coming along?"

She had agreed to help him host a dinner at the official ambassador's residence the following week. The US Embassy had two ambassador's residences: the main one in Pretoria, the other in Cape Town.

"Coming on quite well. We'll have about seventy guests, and the household staff is getting things organized. I'll be back from Pretoria the day before the event."

"Anything special I should do for you?"

"Not really. I passed your name and telephone number on to my secretary, and of course I'll be in touch with you during the week. I really appreciate your help."

For the first time since arriving, she appeared to relax. As the drinks came, the Italian ambassador ambled by with his wife, acknowledging Bunting with a wink. *Nothing like being seen in public with a beautiful woman.*

As the maître d' led the Italians to their table, he turned back to Patience. "I'm glad we met at the Van Wartts' party. It was a rather interesting affair, don't you think?"

She nodded, and as if pondering the question, asked, "How so?"

"I don't know. Quite a varied group in attendance. Do you know that fellow Abdul Wahab?"

"Oh, that dreadful man married to Lady Beatrice. He has two wives. Can you imagine?"

"How does Lady Beatrice handle that?"

Patience shrugged. She remained close to him, and he caught whiffs of her perfume. The same scent she had worn at the Van Wartts' party. For a brief second, he imagined how it would be to unbutton her blouse and, quickly, unsnap her bra and massage what had to be luscious breasts. The skin matching her ivory complexion.

"This Abdul Wahab," he continued. "He and Dawid van Wartt are close friends?"

She placed her elbow on the table and rested her chin in her hand. Controlled now, looking as if she was waiting for his next question, her eyes became vivid blue.

"You're probably thinking I'm trying to pump you … for information."

Gradually the warmth returned to her face. She picked up on the double entendre, straightened, and said, "Shall I order for both of us?"

They had the same seafood main course. The linefish catch of the day, something foreign to Bunting, was well prepared, moist and with a unique meaty texture. In the distance, the setting sun spotlighted Table Mountain, and the city lights started to flicker. While debating dessert, Patience again leaned toward him, motioning that he should do likewise.

"You're going to tell me a secret, aren't you," he said, his hand touching hers.

"Wahab is being watched by the government."

"I see."

"He arrived recently and has been using all his contacts in an effort to remain in Cape Town. There are important people here who sympathize with his political views. Van Wartt is a risk taker when it comes to business, and somehow he and Wahab have something cooking."

"That's very interesting."

"I'll skip dessert and have a cappuccino," she said.

"Me too." He was still whispering. "I know you sail, but perchance do you play tennis?"

"I'm very good at sports."

CHAPTER TWELVE

CAPE TOWN—AUGUST 12, 2002

Abdul Wahab, shielded from the wind in the protected veranda, glared out over the choppy sea. The winter August wind brought the temperature down below sixty degrees Fahrenheit. He turned up the collar of his Harris Tweed jacket and leaned back in the white wicker chair. Next to him, on the table, rested his leather-bound copy of the Koran and a dog-eared copy of Chaucer's *Canterbury Tales* in Middle English.

The butler, Dingane, a handsome man with streaks of gray in his close-cropped hair, laid down a Limoges tea service next to him. A chocolate-coated biscotto lay next to the cup and saucer. Without asking, he poured his employer a cup of Ceylon tea. Wahab enjoyed the English custom of afternoon tea, although he preferred having it, like now, during late morning.

The home, built into a steep mountain slope, overlooked the expansive shoreline of Bantry Bay lined with white beach houses. A relaxing view, yet somehow he found it boring. His wife Beatrice had purchased the home a while back, while married to that American tycoon from Silicon Valley. Absentmindedly, he stroked his neatly trimmed moustache and goatee. He had to admit, Cape Town was pleasant, but it lacked the panache of the French Riviera.

Thinking about the Riviera made him uncomfortable. Only a few months ago, he had to flee Villefranche before the French authorities arrested him for importing narcotics. His father-in-law, a Saudi prince, had for all practical purposes disowned him. Of course he, Wahab, for that matter, had all but abandoned the prince's daughter to a mental asylum near Jeddah. There was the matter of his connections with the terrorist groups—the brothers no longer viewed him as reliable. And of course the CIA. Had they connected the death of their two people on the Riviera to him?

All these problems because of one man: Hayden Stone. Now that same man had come to Africa, and Wahab's first attempt to even the score had failed. Whoever talked him into that snake stunt in Monrovia? That weasel, Nabeel Asuty. Then he sends four fools to Monrovia to kill him. Idiot.

Behind him the glass door slid open and his wife, Lady Beatrice, marched out. She wore a beige twill suit over a pink blouse. A matching scarf covered her hair.

"Dear Abdul. Don't tell me you are sitting here moping."

"Just having tea, my dear. And a cigarette." He pulled out his silver cigarette case.

"Don't light up now. That awful Egyptian is in the reception area waiting to speak with you." She went to the railing and looked back and forth across the landscape. Turning back to him, he said, "Really, you shouldn't invite that type to our home. For God's sake, join a club in town to entertain people like that."

"A good idea," he said, starting to rise. "Where are you off to?"

"The museum. I'm meeting with women from the National Gallery."

Next to the marble pedestal displaying a bust of Apollo, Nabeel Asuty sat in a gray cushioned accent chair, legs crossed, dangling his right shoe, a knockoff Gucci. Dingane hovered about the reception area, keeping an eye on him. Wahab approached and extended a cordial greeting. Nabeel rose and presented a saccharine smile. Wahab thought the man's obsequiousness complimented his coarse facial features.

"Nabeel, my friend, let me show you to the garage."

A dark shadow crossed Nabeel's eyes. Wahab knew him to be touchy on matters of courtesy. Could it be his humble origins? Quickly, he followed up by saying, "I have purchased a new toy I want to show off." He whispered, "Much more private out there."

The saccharine smile returned.

Wahab led him along the driveway to the detached garage that overlooked a fifty-foot drop to another home.

"You live well, Abdul Wahab."

In Arabic, he responded, "God is good." They entered the garage, and he pointed to a green Jaguar XK-150 roadster. "A beauty, no?"

Nabeel agreed, walked up to the car, and sat on the front bumper. "May I smoke?"

"I'd rather you not." Wahab tensed to the man's impudence. "And if you don't mind, do not sit on the car." Nabeel rose and walked to the closed garage door and stared out at the ocean below. "What news do you bring?" Wahab asked.

Nabeel made a display of changing his attitude to one of cordiality. "My friend, our brothers in Sierra Leone are an undisciplined lot. They talk jihad, but are more interested in dealing in diamonds and gold."

"And there are other problems, yes?"

"Yes. This American, Hayden Stone, is a nuisance. Have you ever met him?"

"I have seen him … and met him." *In Afghanistan and on the Riviera.*

"In Freetown, I met him in a café and learned that he is arrogant. I sent two of our people to handle him." Nabeel glowered.

Wahab shook his head slowly. "They are now enjoying Paradise. No?"

Nabeel looked down at his feet.

"And in Monrovia, the snake made a mistake and bit the wrong man. Then you send four of your men to kill him and that ends badly. And Mr. Stone lives on. He appears too much for you."

Wahab watched Nabeel stiffen as he walked up to his Jaguar, took out his handkerchief, and wiped down the front bumper where Nabeel had sat. "I have a complicated task before me. This task, if accomplished, will far surpass Osama bin Laden's

9/11 glorious victory. Our world will cheer our work, and they will write poems that will be recited for centuries." Wahab laughed to himself. If he continued on this vein, the rich, poetic Arabic language he was speaking would soon take him off in irrelevant directions.

He cleared his throat and brought himself back to business. "I need assistance from competent people to carry out this mission."

"You need not worry about me, Wahab." Nabeel smirked.

"I do when you murder your lovers. The ones you tell too much in the heat of passion. While smoking hashish. Especially when those lovers are Afrikaners."

Nabeel froze. His body appeared to shrink within his suit. The eyes pleaded.

"Yes, I know what goes on in Freetown," Wahab said in a low tone. "Now go back there. Await orders, and come up with a sound plan to kill Hayden Stone. Rather, come up with a number of plans. Contact me before you do anything."

CIA HEADQUARTERS, LANGLEY, VIRGINIA

Elizabeth Kerr knocked on the door twice, and then stepped from the quiet corridor into a noisy room filled with people in motion. Twenty-four hours before, top officials on the seventh floor at CIA headquarters had given their imprimatur to form this ad hoc working group to address the problem in Namibia. The group's team leader, John Matterhorn, an older man with thinning brown hair and wire-rimmed eyeglasses, came up to her.

"Good to see you, Elizabeth. Come with me. We'll find a corner and talk a bit."

She knew John and his wife, who was also a CIA case officer. Kerr's family and his were old friends. He had recommended Elizabeth to an acquaintance for employment at NIMA, the National Imagery and Mapping Agency located in the suburbs of Northern Virginia. Another case of Washington beltway networking in the intelligence community.

"I got the word to report here this morning," she said, looking around at the controlled turmoil. Some of the staff chattered happily as they lugged computers and pushed file cabinets around the room. Others slowly arranged desks and chairs, pausing at times to assess their fellow workers. Elizabeth surmised the happy ones were glad to be assigned to the group; the others looked as if they wished they were back at their old jobs.

"Bit hectic for now," John said. "But in a day or so, things will be running smoothly. Always does." Pushing two chairs together, he motioned for her to sit. "You're responsible for all this." He waved his hand. "Good work on finding that nuclear thermal source. The director is very, very interested in this project."

"John. One problem. I can't be here all the time. My organization insists that we keep monitoring the target from our location. Anything we pick up will be transmitted or carried here."

He pushed his glasses back on his nose. She knew what he was thinking. Her people would not allow CIA to have control of their equipment or their sources and methods. Agencies in Washington, DC, didn't survive lending their techniques to other agencies, even for a short term. Rarely were they returned.

"I understand. In that case you'll be travelling back and forth a lot. I want you to know the success of this program rests a great deal on your shoulders. Any new developments out there in the Kalahari?"

Elizabeth opened her briefcase. "Here are some photos you'll find interesting. They were taken about two weeks ago, ten o'clock in the morning Namibia time." John studied the overhead photographs taken of a boxcar sitting on a railroad siding in the desert. Two figures stood nearby next to an ATV. He flipped through the pictures quickly, stopping to closely examine one in particular.

"Is this their helicopter?" Without waiting for an answer, he asked, "French make?"

"It's an older Aerospatiale SA 330. Called a Puma." She

pointed. "See, they stowed the ATV in it."

"How many people, all together?"

"We saw four men standing around the helicopter. Two drove in an ATV to the site but didn't stay at the boxcar for long. They took some readings with what we think was a Geiger counter and hurried off."

John pointed to a spot some distance from the boxcar. "Who are these two figures over there?"

She paged through the photographs John held and pulled one out. "Here's a closer shot. Two young men or boys were watching from behind a bush. Appeared to be hiding. Afterward, they walked toward the nearby town of Bruin Karas."

"Which direction did the helicopter take?"

"North toward Angola. That's when … we lost our window." Kerr hesitated. "The satellite had to be switched to a target in Iraq."

"You're kidding! Who the hell ordered that?"

"A request from *you people*. The CIA."

"I see. Any idea who the four were?"

"All four were male," Kerr said. "Caucasian or light skinned. Dressed European fashion. That's all."

John sat back, silent. Elizabeth thought she saw his mind working. This would be the first time she had seen him engaged professionally. In the past they had been together only socially for dinners or at the Tuckahoe Tennis Club.

He picked up the stack of photos and snapped through the sheets while he talked. "This is some form of nuclear device. Large, not suitcase size, which we all worry about." He paused at one photo showing the two men at the boxcar. "South Africa had a nuclear weapons program a while back when they controlled Namibia." He restacked the photographs on the desk. "Lord knows how many of these things are floating around the world."

"I'll get a cable out to the chief of station in Luanda. Don't know how good our Angolan sources are, but we'll try to come up with their identities. Did you get any markings or numbers on the that helicopter?"

She handed him a sheet of paper.

"Good. We'll get this out right away." He looked around the room. "That is once we get the computers up and running. Namibia is another story. That's a one-case officer post, and she's back stateside for surgery. The COS in Embassy Pretoria is covering that post, which may work to our benefit."

The noise level increased in the room as people jostled one another, avoiding bumping into the incoming office furniture. John suggested they go to the ground-floor cafeteria between the new and old office buildings and have a cup of coffee.

Seated in the glass-enclosed dining area, Elizabeth Kerr let her coffee cool and looked around. Even though it was between normal breakfast and lunch hours, the spacious area was busy, attesting to the fact that the CIA operated around the clock and on irregular shifts. Outside the windows, she saw the lawn sculpture in the open courtyard. The artist had placed a lengthy coded message on the four copper plates. The artwork had been the subject of numerous articles in magazines and the *Washington Post*. "Anyone break that cipher out there?" She pointed.

John shook his head. "Break the Kryptos? Not that I know," he said without looking, his mind apparently on something else.

She felt her cup and decided it cool enough to sip. John took his time to say something he seemed hesitant to say.

Finally, he said, "Afghanistan is sucking up a lot of our resources. We're having success there, but not for long, I'm afraid." He looked at her. "The White House wants to go into Iraq. We've begun redirecting our resources."

Kerr laughed. "Let the good times roll."

John didn't smile. "With all the focus on the Middle East, there's a question: How can we address other issues when they come up. Like this bomb, for instance." He set his coffee aside. "We need to take possession of this weapon or neutralize it. Quickly. Before some terrorist group gets hold of it."

"Send in a SEAL team plus a HAZMAT team from the Department of Energy for protection against any radiation."

John shook his head again. "Not so simple. It'll take time to put teams on the ground and organize an extraction process. We need time. That's why they sent Gus to South Africa." He apparently saw her quizzical look. "Colonel Gustave Frederick from the director's executive staff. He's headed there to work with the COS in Cape Town."

"Those men who came in on the helicopter," Elizabeth asked. "Think they're members of a terrorist group?"

"Hard to tell. Don't think terrorist groups have the kind of network to use helicopters ..." He stopped. "But their cousins managed to hijack four commercial airliners; still, I think the word has somehow gotten out about this thing sitting in the desert, there for the taking."

"The French? It was a French helicopter."

John shrugged.

"The Iraqis, Iranians, Libyans? Any one of the crazies out there."

"Either someone who wants to use it against somebody," John said, "or someone who wants to prevent it being used against them. Doesn't matter. We must get it first." He shook his head. "And the thing is leaking radiation, for God's sake!"

They drank their coffees for a while. Elizabeth asked, "What kind of resource does this colonel of yours have down there in South Africa?"

"The COS is Charles Fleming. Base chief is M. R. D. Houston. Gus also has Sandra Harrington. All top-notch people. They better be, and they better move quickly." All at once, John straightened in his chair and grinned.

"What?"

"Colonel Frederick also has an ace in the hole. A fellow by the name of Hayden Stone."

CHAPTER THIRTEEN

FREETOWN, SIERRA LEONE—AUGUST 13, 2002

Hayden Stone sat back and watched Luke Craig's eyes darted back and forth from his computer screen to Stone. The afternoon before, after Stone and Dirk Lange had killed two of Nabeel Asuty's henchmen, Stone had returned to the embassy and reported the incident. As he related the details, Craig's bronzed face turned dour and the scar over his right eyebrow became prominent. All he did was nod and scribble notes. Finally, he ordered Stone to prepare a detailed report while he notified CIA headquarters.

Five minutes later Craig read the response from headquarters that appeared on his computer. "They want to know why you didn't think it was a routine robbery." He looked up. "They're right, you know. Crime is rampant here in Sierra Leone."

"You're shitting me. Right? I explained what happened at the café. Nabeel and I had words. Afterward, his henchmen came after me in the restroom. They weren't interested in my wallet." Stone felt himself becoming impatient, so took a deep breath. "Nabeel is connected somehow to Abdul Wahab, who carries a grudge against me because of what happened in France." Stone's head ached. He never had migraines, didn't know how they felt, but this one had to be as bad. "Abdul Wahab is responsible for the deaths of two CIA case officers."

"Yes. I know." Craig returned to the computer.

"There's the matter of the guns and explosives in the trunk of their car." Stone waited and got no response. "What's wrong? Do they want to know if you authorized my actions?"

Stone knew the routine: Monday morning quarterbacking by the people up the chain of command in the CIA's Africa

Division. Would there be repercussions with the Sierra Leone government? What if the incident became fodder for the press? Craig was caught in the middle. Was Craig thinking of a way to direct the flack in his direction?

Craig's face hardened, yet his voice stayed calm. "Look, Stone. You're not a staffer. You may think you know how we work in the agency, but you don't." The computer beeped with an incoming message and he looked back at his screen. "Shit!" He shoved his face closer to the monitor while saying, "I don't have time to discuss this." His head shot around. "You're just a damn cowboy. The word is everywhere you go there's gunplay. Get yourself reassigned to a teaching post at the Farm. They're gearing up for Iraq. They need your type. Or better still, go back to Afghanistan."

Stone's head throbbed. He was about to tell this bastard to take a flying leap when a knock on the door interrupted him.

"That's Sandra." He waved Stone off. "I'll talk with you later. Don't do anything unless you check with me."

As Stone passed Sandra coming through the door, she avoided eye contact. She looked concerned.

A few minutes later, at the front door he met Sandra rushing down the stairway. Obviously distraught, she said she didn't want to talk and dashed down the hallway. The meeting with Craig hadn't gone well.

Outside, Stone spied Mitchell, the embassy driver, and walked up to him. "Do you mind taking me to the housing compound?" he asked. "I'm calling it a day."

With nervous jerks, Mitchell steered the van back and forth through the crowded streets of Freetown, eyes intent on the rearview mirror rather than on the road ahead. Approaching an outdoor bazaar crowded with people in gaily colored clothes, he swerved to the right into a narrow alley. Hawkers leaped from in front of the vehicle. He shot a glance at Stone. "I'm taking a circuitous route, sir. One suggested many times by the RSO for security purposes."

"Fine. But slow down before you hit somebody." Stone waited for him to ease up on the throttle. "What are you looking for in the mirror?"

Mitchell gave a high-pitched laugh. "Just traffic, sir. Just traffic."

Now Stone found himself looking in the mirror. He realized that Mitchell was on edge, and no doubt the reason he was frightened was the word had gotten out that Stone was a marked man. Mitchell had no intention of being caught in crossfire. Stone understood—it wasn't Mitchell's fight.

At the compound gate, Stone hopped out and waved good-bye to a visibly relieved Mitchell, who sped away. After Stone passed the guard shack, he decided not to go to his apartment but headed for the clubhouse. An airy glass-sided structure that served for informal gatherings by the residents, it faced the swimming pool where parents reclined in deck chairs, watching their children splash in the pool. Palm trees shaded the lawn and pink bougainvillea bloomed along the walls of the buildings.

Inside the clubhouse the air was chilled a few degrees lower than outside. Still, the air conditioning hadn't eliminated the touch and smell of dampness. Stone found himself alone in the lounge.

The vending machine buzzed a tone that signaled it was on its last legs. Stone inserted coins for a soda and took a chair with a view of the pool. After allowing his thoughts to gather, he took stock of his situation. Obviously, his mission to Sierra Leone was over. Operationally, he was a liability for the agency. He was on the local jihadist hit list. By now the local authorities had gotten word that he was involved in the deaths of two men. He had accomplished identifying Nabeel Asuty and the terrorist's apparent connection with Abdul Wahab. As for the nature of his plans—the local CIA office had to follow up on that.

The soda helped relieve Stone's headache. His eye caught sight of a lizard sitting on a low rock wall outside the window. Slender, with a thin tail, at times its greenish-gray body sparked with a touch of fluorescence in the sunlight. Every few seconds the lizard did a push-up, and then it darted a glance from side to side. A little African comedy.

Stone wondered how his friend Colonel Frederick would receive Craig's situation report. Would he think Stone had let him down? Had he let him down? And what of Dirk Lange's wisecrack at the café about him being over the hill? A guard who opened the door interrupted his musings. He said a gentleman at the gate wanted to speak with him.

Dirk Lange stood at the guardhouse, and although he appeared poised, perspiration stained his blue dress shirt. "Got a minute, old boy?" His demeanor sought a positive response.

When Stone led him into the clubhouse, Lange looked around and whispered, "Can we speak privately here?"

"For the time being, while we're alone. Let me get you something to drink." At the machine, Stone waited for the can to clang down the chute, then offered it to Lange. "Let's sit."

Lange looked nervously around the room. Not without a bit of sarcasm, he said, "You chaps have it made here, don't you."

"A pleasant place after a day in the salt mines." Stone waited for him to get to the point. It didn't take long.

"I'm settling my accounts here in Freetown and leaving tonight by boat for Conakry. My sources tell me that you and I are on the local jihadist kill list. Seems our boy Nabeel doesn't have much of a sense of humor." He took a swig of his drink and looked over at the wall. "What are your plans, Hayden?"

"It appears I've also lost some of my charm with the locals."

"Who shot that?" Lange pointed to the large wild boar head mounted on the wall. "Looks like that specimen came from the Atlas Mountains."

"Beats me. Nice tusks though."

"Don't want to end up like that bugger." Lange crushed the can in his hand. "Just dropped by to say good-bye and, oh, a little tidbit for you. Our mutual friend Jacob advised you should be aware that Nabeel is in business with an influential South African in Cape Town." He started to rise from the couch. "Don't know this man's name, but Jacob indicated he's up to no good. Has to do with something big aimed at the US or Europe."

"When did Jacob tell you this?"

"Last night." Lange started for the door.

"Let me walk you out." Stone followed him out to the gate. "Funny, Jacob didn't contact me."

Lange turned and shook hands with Stone. "He didn't want to stay in town. Asked that I pass you the message."

"What's your final destination, Dirk? South Africa?"

"Eventually. Perhaps, we'll meet there."

"Are you seeing Jonathan before you leave?"

"No." Lange frowned. "I've made provisions for him with the doctors out at the camp. Nabeel's people may follow me, so I don't want them to know Jonathan's a friend of mine. I suggest you not go out and see him either."

Stone nodded and saw Sandra push through the turnstile at the guard gate. Lange's face brightened for the first time. Seeing them, Sandra stopped. She did not look happy. Lange approached and told her he was leaving Freetown and hoped to see her again someday. She gave him a quick hug and they exchanged more pleasantries. He went out the gate and disappeared.

Sandra said, "We're heading back home." She took his arm and led him to the apartment. "I know it's early, but I need a drink."

In the apartment Sandra slumped on the couch with the whiskey Stone had handed her. She avoided eye contact. Obviously, her day had been as bad as his. Her meeting with the station chief had not gone well. She would tell him about it when she wanted.

Her voice was raspy. "You're not joining me in a drink?"

He shook his head.

She did a double take. "Something wrong?"

"Headaches," Stone said. "Hope I don't get those weird dreams again."

"You didn't have problems after the Marseilles shoot-out." She thought a moment. "Unless you were keeping it a secret. I recall specifically asking you about that."

"I know. Maybe it's the anti-malaria medicine I'm taking. Maybe I'm just tired." He leaned forward, elbows on knees. "What's this about heading back home?"

She sipped her drink, studied the glass, and placed it on the coffee table. "We've got to start packing. We've been yanked from the job. Our plane leaves tonight for Paris."

Stone started to ask for the details, but she interrupted. "Bad scene with Mr. Craig. Let's take a walk around the grounds and have a chat."

Walking the compound's pathway under the shade of the palm and banana trees proved pleasant even in the early afternoon heat. A breeze coming in from the sea a half-mile away helped. Sandra walked with her head down, as if intent on not stumbling on imaginary debris scattered on the path, unlikely as the grounds were kept in immaculate condition.

On hearing about their orders to leave, Stone had become resigned to events he considered out of his control. The game was over for him—let someone else pick up the sword.

"I didn't give you the whole story yesterday," she said in a low voice. She related the details of her surveillance of Nabeel Asuty the day before—that she followed him to a walled compound in the hills overlooking Freetown. "What I didn't tell you was I saw Farley in the compound talking with Nabeel."

"Farley who?"

"Farley Durrell. The guy who double-crossed me."

"The guy at the airport. Holy shit."

Sandra stopped walking and wrapped her arms tight against her chest. She took deep breaths. "I had to tell Craig. Afterward, we composed a status report to Langley. Their response this morning was for you and me to leave immediately. That's why they're sending a special plane to take us to Paris."

Stone attempted to craft his words. "I guess it's good that you saw Farley. Now the agency knows he's in contact with those people."

"Ready for the whole story?" Her eyes teared. "Farley is CIA. He's under non-official cover, a NOC, and not supposed to have any contact with people like me. He was deep cover. I wasn't allowed to fraternize with him."

"So? That was a year ago."

"Someone from Nabeel Asuty's organization may have noticed that altercation at the airport. The point is I wasn't supposed to know about him being inside this terrorist organization. They think I've jeopardized the mission."

Stone knew what that meant. A big career hit. Good-bye, interesting foreign assignments. Hello, dead-end job at some warehouse in Fairfax County, Virginia. He tried to think of a positive spin on their situation, but muttered instead, "Looks like we stepped in deep kimchi."

Trying to laugh, she cried instead. He took her in his arms and she relaxed for a moment, pressing her body to him. She stiffened and pushed away. Now she looked him in the eye for the first time that day. "Time to pack. Craig picks us up at seven tonight."

The bright moon broke a path on the rough surface of the bay as the embassy's boat cast off from Freetown. Luke Craig had organized a quick extraction for Stone and Sandra, which included taking them from the city to the landing across the bay where they would meet the armored SUVs. From there they would drive to the airport and board the agency's jet.

Stone and Sandra stood by the helm, holding on to grips as the Boston Whaler skimmed across the water. Just enough light allowed them to make out the silhouettes of anchored ships on the starboard side, many derelict.

"Nice boat," Sandra said to the helmsman, a young man with a crew cut and eyeglasses.

"Most of the American posts in this neck of woods have this model boat," he shouted over the noise of the twin outboard engines. "We have two boats. Part of the emergency evacuation plan. We have enough fuel to make it to Guinea. Another West African *rectum mundi.*"

Twenty minutes later, the boat eased alongside a dilapidated wharf, and the young man helped them with off their luggage. Craig waited on the pier with two other men, whom Stone had never met. Both carried submachine guns.

"We're behind schedule," Craig barked, waving them on to the SUVs.

Conversation was limited as they raced to the airport. Craig was eager to send them off as soon as possible. Still, he ran a well-organized program, and they could thank his efficiency in getting them out safely.

The farewells alongside the executive jet were brief and formal. As soon as the two were seated, the engines started, and in a matter of minutes they were in the air, the city lights of Freetown below. The plane banked in a northerly direction, the moon shining in the windows, and they began to ascend.

The plane held ten passengers in two rows of single seats on either side of the aircraft. Stone sat in front with Sandra across the aisle. In the rear of the plane sat two long-haired men in dirty clothes who didn't acknowledge Stone's greeting when he boarded and didn't speak the rest of the trip. Deep cover operatives, Stone assumed, going from one hellhole to another. Sandra had closed her eyes before takeoff, and they remained shut for an hour.

As the plane flew over nighttime Africa, Stone looked down at the moonlit vastness. Here and there he saw soft glows from single points of light. Oil lamps from villages somewhere in the backcountry of Mali or Guinea, their owners far removed from Stone's universe. He imagined someone looking up at the blinking aircraft lights and wondering who flew above their world.

Stone had a strong attraction for Africa, but at the same time knew he could never understand it, nor be at home. Always he anticipated going, always he was happy to leave. Now it appeared he was leaving for the last time. Another tasking from Langley appeared unlikely, and even though his future now was in California near his two children, he would miss the action and the excitement. His headache returned.

"I forgot to tell you, Hayden." Sandra reached across the aisle. "You're supposed to lay over in Paris." She handed him a white index card. "This is your hotel."

Stone switched on the overhead light and studied the address, immediately recognizing it. One block off the Boulevard Saint-Germain, the small hotel was on a quiet street and very chic. A favorite haunt of his friend, Colonel Gustave Frederick.

CHAPTER FOURTEEN

PARIS, FRANCE—AUGUST 14, 2002

Like so many things Parisian, the hotel had lost none of its charm over the course of time. It had been three years since Stone's last visit to the hotel. The four-story, mansard-roofed structure sat on the Left Bank, hidden off the busy Boulevard St. Germain. A guest entered through a courtyard, wisteria climbing the gray stone walls. Sections of the building dated from the seventeenth century. Inside, the salon was still decorated in dark, richly upholstered furniture and damask wallpaper in rose patterns, and a blend of antique prints and modern art was displayed on the walls. Here, Stone always felt he was entering a world that had existed between the two great world wars. A comfortable one.

A stylish, impeccably attired woman greeted him. Her hair perfectly coiffed, she wore a single strand of pearls. She spoke to him first in French, and frowned when Stone answered in kind, and switched to English. His French didn't go well in Paris.

"Mr. Stone, we have been awaiting your arrival." She took his passport, had him sign the register, ordered the bellman to take his bags, and led Stone to his room, again set out with ornate furnishings. The US Government expense allowances would never come close to covering the cost of these accommodations. Good thing he was on a CIA operational expense account.

Stone took his time unpacking, pausing occasionally to peer out the window and reacquaint himself with the surroundings. The empty courtyard and neighboring gardens added to the feeling of tranquility. Late afternoon shadows darkened the walls and building facades. He would dine at a restaurant he knew of a short distance from the hotel. Perhaps he'd have the paillard of veal along with the house white wine. Nothing fancy. He'd be dining alone, which in Paris he always considered a waste of setting. Too bad Sandra wasn't there to dine with him. Still, he intended to make the best of his stay—not knowing when he'd return.

The next morning Stone made his way down to the hotel's cellar lounge and helped himself to the continental breakfast. While he read the *Herald Tribune*, the concierge approached and handed him a sealed envelope. Stone's full name appeared in type on the front. Opening it, he found the following message, handwritten in blue ink and undated:

> *Bonjour, Hayden,*
> *Await further instructions.*
> *Relax,*
> *F*

His friend and mentor, Colonel Gustave Frederick, had authored the instructions. Was Frederick giving him a short vacation?

"Who delivered this?"

"A woman from your embassy. Just before you came down for breakfast."

"Blonde? Green eyes?"

The concierge tilted his head. Obviously, Sandra Harington was in contact with Frederick. The two were probably putting their heads together to salvage her career. Meanwhile, he, Stone, was set adrift for a time in Paris. Not a bad place to plan one's future.

Tossing the newspaper aside, Stone phoned the US Embassy and asked for Roland Deville. The secretary told him that Deville and his family had taken vacation in a little town outside Nice. Stone sighed and flipped his cell phone shut. *I wonder if Deville and his wife will visit Contessa Lucinda Avoscani?*

Deville was the FBI's legal attaché assigned to Paris. FBI colleagues for over twenty years, Roland was someone whom he could confide in. It had been only a few months since the two of them participated in the assault on Lucinda's palace in Villefranche. That misguided adventure to capture Osama bin Laden's lieutenant had resulted in disaster. The team found the lieutenant already dead, but wrecked Lucinda's palace in the process. Lucinda held Stone responsible.

Lucinda. Maybe he'd phone her. On the other hand, why not fly down to Nice and see her? He saw the bright sky through the window. Perhaps, a morning walk around Paris would clear his mind.

Turning left out of the hotel entrance, he walked toward St. Germain. He passed the corner restaurant where he had dinner the previous night. Now it was empty, the tables outside bare. He thought of the dessert he had, frangipane tartlet with plums.

At the Boulevard St. Germain, he again turned left and headed toward the Pont de la Concorde, one of the bridges crossing the Seine. Midway across the bridge, he stopped and watched the tour boats passing below.

Stone took in the moist, mineral smell of the river. Farther down the Seine, he spotted rows of *bouquinistes*. Their owners were opening their green stall boxes and extending the short awnings, where for over a century proprietors hawked their used books and prints. Being August, with many Parisians taking *vacances*, walking the city was a delight. Stone decided to stroll along the open-air market and see if he could find a treasure to take home.

He visited the stalls one by one. Most of the books were in French. The few ragged English titles were uninteresting or already in his personal library back in Virginia. Still, he welcomed the distraction of exchanging greetings with the proprietors and ducking his head under the makeshift awnings to inspect their wares.

Half an hour passed and he reached the end of the line. He paused to look at Notre Dame over on the Île de la Cité, and continued browsing until he spotted an interesting faded poster displayed in a wire rack stand. The edges were only slightly frayed. Removing it, the script advertised in English the Trans World Airline. The message was: Fly TWA on a Lockheed

Constellation to Paris and visit the Eiffel Tower.

"Ever fly in one of those?" A familiar voice came from over his shoulder as a hand reached across and seized the poster. "It took forever to cross the Atlantic. But those were the days when people dressed up to fly on a plane, were served their meals on china, played cards to pass the time, and the flight attendants were oh-so-gorgeous."

The plummy New England accent belonged to Stone's pal and boss, Colonel Gustave Frederick. His thick graying hair was combed back from his face. He pulled a pair of reading glasses from his shirt pocket and placed them on his long nose.

"*Bonjour, mon ami*," Stone said. "I was wondering when I'd see you—"

"Both of us are being followed. I suspect you knew that." He continued to inspect the poster as if he intended to purchase it.

Stone shrugged. Fact of the matter, he didn't care. He had assumed he'd be under surveillance by the French authorities. He'd be disappointed if he weren't. He took back the poster.

"See if you can shake the agents tailing you," Frederick said. "I know you old FBI types can do it. We'll meet at the Luxembourg Gardens. In two hours. Enter from the north side, from Rue de Vaugirard. Wander around. You'll find me sitting on a park bench." At that, Frederick meandered back up the row of stalls, stopping occasionally to pick up and replace a book.

Stone purchased the poster. He knew his son would like it.

At the entrance to the Luxembourg gardens, Stone believed he had successfully dry-cleaned himself. At his hotel, he had dropped off the travel poster at the front desk, slipped out the back door, walked two blocks, found a cabstand, and told the driver to head for the Petit St. Benoit restaurant. Halfway there he instructed him to pull over. After paying the fare, he walked one block, went into the first café he found, took a table where he could survey the street, studied the scene, searching for surveillants, then satisfied on detecting none, finished his caffè Americano and headed in the general direction of the Luxembourg Gardens. He alternated walking busy and empty streets, stopping to check his surroundings.

From past experience, he knew the French were expert in conducting surveillance, so he avoided being obvious in his countersurveillance. If they detected him acting suspiciously, the French security people would gear up for a full-court press.

As Stone entered the park, he felt the quiet, and as he continued walking, the sounds of the city faded, replaced by his footsteps crunching on the raked gray pebbles. Chestnut trees, alternately mature and young, formed a canopy, and the clean air filtering through the leaves felt cool on his face. Ahead some hundred feet, Frederick strolled with his hands clasped behind him, casually looking side to side. Stone watched him nod to a woman pushing a pram, and after she passed, Frederick took a seat on one end of a bench and crossed his legs.

Stone pulled out his Paris tour book and pretended to study it, all the while checking the movements of the passersby. Frederick would expect him to do this. Over the years, the two of them had formed a close but proper friendship. Even though they had fought the Taliban side by side in Afghanistan—and had saved each other's lives—Frederick kept a certain distance in their relationship.

Making eye contact, Stone sat down next to him. "I believe I'm clean."

"Same here, but one can never be sure with French intelligence." Frederick took a deep breath and gestured at the surroundings. "They do know how to do it with panache, don't they? Ah, the French. This park is a downright treasure."

"Best I tell you what happened in Monrovia and Freetown while we're alone." Without waiting for a response, Stone related the details of the attempt on his life in Freetown and his meeting with the Mossad agent, Jacob, in Monrovia. He summed up his impressions on Jacob. "We're not high on Jacob's list of favorite people. But if he thought it important enough to contact us, I think he believes the threat is serious."

"Agreed. What about this South African, Dirk Lange?"

"I got the feeling he's a member of the South African Secret Service."

"Makes sense," Frederick said. "SASS has ties with the Israeli Mossad, and both services are concerned with al Qaeda activities in Africa."

They sat quiet for a while. The closest person was the woman with the pram who had passed by earlier. Now she sat about fifty yards away, tending to the blanket-wrapped bundle in her arms.

Stone asked the question that had gnawed at him since arriving in Paris. "When do I head home?"

Frederick didn't answer at once, apparently preoccupied in thought. "What were Station Freetown's thoughts on all this?"

"I got the impression they were annoyed by Sandra's and my presence."

"That's to be expected, but what did they think of this Nabeel? Did they have any intel on him?"

"Craig, the COS, said no, but I think they did. He wasn't surprised when I reminded him we found guns and C-4 explosive in the terrorists' car trunk. I emphasized the connection between Nabeel and our nemesis from the Riviera, Abdul Wahab."

"And?"

"Even after I reminded him Abdul Wahab was responsible for the deaths of two CIA officers, he still pretended to not care. Craig's quite the asshole."

Frederick laughed. "You have a way with words."

"Now, what about me?" Stone asked. "What do I do?"

"Huh? Oh yes. I thought about that." He smiled. "You have a reputation in the agency as a person who comes in the room and breaks up all the furniture. Take the demise of those four jihadists in Monrovia and the two thugs in Freetown as examples. By the way, one of those bastards in Freetown murdered a pregnant CIA spouse in Jordan six months ago. After he had raped her."

Stone gritted his teeth. "Payback time."

"Yes. Well done."

"The South African guy took care of one thug. The other

one was mine."

Frederick nodded. "Yes, which is important, but back to you. In only a few days, you have managed to get on the radar of all the important players: the CIA stations in West Africa, the South African intelligence service, the Israelis, al Qaeda, and we can assume Abdul Wahab."

"So? What do I do?" Stone became encouraged.

"You're flying to South Africa. I'll give you the details at dinner tonight. By the way, do you have any ideas for a good restaurant?"

"Yeah, sure. But about my assignment?"

"We have a couple of taskings going on down there in Cape Town. All against this target, this threat. We're not clear what it is yet. I assumed you knew that you've been let in on only a piece of this operation."

"SOP. I'm given a piece of the operation and expected to move on after it's completed."

"However, somehow you always make yourself indispensible. I take that back. No one's indispensible in this line of work."

"I wasn't ready to head home and take up gardening."

Frederick leaned toward him. "You'll go down to Cape Town, hang around, and see who knocks on your door. It won't take long for people to start showing up. The first may be that fellow Dirk Lange."

"What about these other *projects* going on down there?"

"Best you not know about them now." Frederick looked around. "I think we've stayed here long enough." He gave a hand signal to the woman with the pram, who got up and leisurely pushed the carriage away. "We'll split up. We're at the same hotel. Let's meet at seven in the lounge."

"How about six. I'd like a drink earlier than seven. Can we get Sandra Harrington to join us? By the way, how's she doing?"

"I'm heading back to the embassy now to work on her problem." Frederick's tone made it known that Stone shouldn't have asked that question about Sandra. Evidently, the situation was tougher for him to handle than he had expected. Frederick rose, casually taking in the surroundings. He leaned toward Stone. "Do you know anything about nuclear weaponry?"

"They make a big noise."

With a dismissive glare, Frederick marched off across the grounds in the direction of a roofed bandstand where musicians assembled.

The sun overhead worked its way through the leaves, bringing the August afternoon heat. Over at the bandstand the musicians had begun a classical piece Stone didn't recognize. Frederick had disappeared into the gathering spectators.

He got up and stretched, his attention caught again by the extensive lawns and shimmering flowerbeds beyond the trees. As he strolled, his mind searched for names of places and contacts he knew in South Africa. The operation was more important than he had imagined. Abdul Wahab, his adversary from France, was involved, and Frederick had him back in business.

A passing young Parisienne in a tight tank top surprised him with *the look*. Stone hadn't realized he'd been walking along with a smile on his face.

CHAPTER FIFTEEN

CAPE TOWN—AUGUST 15, 2002

Marshall Bunting lay face down on his bed, searching with his hand for a cool spot on the sheet. There wasn't. Through the night he and Patience had worked over the entire king-sized bed. She lay on her back now, breathing gently, peaceful, her head turned away. The sheet had slipped off one breast. Bunting found the nipple enticing, soft and plump. His hand came up to caress it with his fingertips but stopped. He didn't want to wake her just yet.

He carefully rolled on his back and shut his eyes. Too bad he had early meetings at the consulate. He'd like to spend the rest of the morning here in bed. He enjoyed this period after lovemaking, lying around, letting his imagination wander. At the same time, he learned a lot about his partner as the two lay naked. As if baring their bodies made it easier to bare their souls.

What would Patience's reactions be to their lovemaking? Good God! His old flame, Valery, used to issue what amounted to formal critiques.

His eyes wouldn't stay closed. They drifted over to the beguiling nipple. He felt a warm surge and an insisting twitch. Oh hell, he thought and turned to let his finger touch its satiny surface. Its texture changed.

A small sound came from her throat. "That's nice." She smiled but her eyes stayed closed. His fingers worked the nipple to a hard point, and then strayed down. Her legs opened. She sighed, and flipped over, and in one motion straddled him.

It was pretty quick. She clutched and dug in her nails when she came, but she wasn't a screamer. She collapsed on him, then slipped off and turned on her back with a soft laugh.

He smiled. He hadn't been laid like this since when? Ever? Patience gazed at the ceiling, around the room, finally coming to rest on his face. "Hello there." She slid out of bed and made a beeline for the bathroom. "Don't go away. Be right back."

He admired her body as she scampered out the door. Long legs, great ass, and other dimensions he'd always been partial to. A few moments later, she hurried back, jumped into the bed, and pulled the sheets up halfway. With chin resting on her raised hand, she announced, "I think everything unfolded quite well last night. Are you satisfied as well?"

Bunting broke up in laughter and slid close to her and ran his hands through her black hair. He gave her a soft kiss on the lips. "Now, my dear, are we speaking about the great dinner reception we put on for those visiting Washington congressmen?"

She ran her finger from his forehead down the length of his nose. She drew back and looked up. "Mind you, I don't do this sort of thing as a matter of course."

"Hosting a splendid dinner, or having wild sex with me?"

She didn't answer, just gazed at him with her sparkling blue eyes. A moment passed and her expression changed. "What time is it?"

"About seven."

"Bloody hell! I've got to get home and get myself ready for the council meeting downtown." She jumped out of bed and began looking for her clothes.

"Take a shower here and I'll get us some breakfast."

Bunting found his robe and relaxed in the chaise, listening to messages on his cell phone. The butler brought breakfast on a large silver tray—scrambled eggs, rolls, juice, and rich coffee. Patience called from the shower asking for shampoo, and the man barely suppressed a smile as he set the tray down on the table. He poured Bunting a cup of coffee and discreetly left the room.

Last night's tryst had come as a complete surprise. Of course, he had made his normal seductive moves, more out of fun engaging in the chase than expecting a conquest. He had learned years ago not to expect to always grab the victory torch. Fact of the matter, it was when the object of a quest suddenly agreed, or better still, surprised the hell out of him by unexpectedly dropping her drawers, he became lightheaded—in that confused way that men experience as they hurry to slide their zipper down.

He thought back at the previous night's events. The last guest had departed the mansion and his household staff had started the cleanup to be finished the next day. He had taken Patience in his arms and kissed her, thanking her for helping him out with the reception. They moved from inside the mansion to the outside portico and had brandies. She drained her glass, looked up at the Southern Cross in the clear sky, said that she was too tired to drive home, and said it was time to go to bed. Just like that!

In bed, she showed no sign of being tired. She clutched, nibbled, scratched, and wouldn't let go of him whether they were on the bed or after they had fallen to the floor. Somehow, during their journey around the bedroom, they found themselves on the French embroidered loveseat. By this time, after two serious coital encounters, Bunting was hoping for time to refill, but she was impatient for more. Taking him in her hand, she repeatedly squeezed as she blew and licked his ear. Her persistent efforts along with his breathing in her body scents of sandalwood and musk proved fruitful, and they had one last spasm of love.

He was smiling to himself as Patience burst from the bathroom, claiming she had time for only coffee. Eyeing the breakfast spread, she announced she'd have some eggs. After talking about the traffic she would encounter going into the city, Bunting asked matter-of-factly if she heard anything new about Dawid van Wartt or Abdul Wahab.

"For some reason, you appear obsessed by those men."

Bunting paused; perhaps he was revealing more information than he could possibly obtain from her. "Maybe I just don't understand the South African social milieu. Van Wartt dealing with this man Abdul Wahab doesn't make sense. I only inquire because Van Wartt had sent me that invitation to attend his function two weeks ago."

"In your capacity as ambassador, you must receive many strange invitations."

"Yes, but enough of that. Let's talk about you. I want to know everything about you."

She looked at her watch. "Perhaps later? I must be going."

"Will I see you tonight?"

The question appeared to catch her off guard. Carefully placing her cup on the delicate china saucer, she said, "Yes, but ..."

"I'll pick you up and we'll have dinner at a quiet place."

"That will be splendid."

She rose, found her purse, and as they left the bedroom, Bunting caught her arm and drew her to him. "You realize five minutes after you leave I'll begin missing you." He kissed her gently.

From the front door, he waved good-bye and returned to his bedroom to get ready for his day. Draining the last of the coffee into his cup, he found he had a few moments to spare. He pulled back the draperies, threw open the French doors, and gazed at his garden below. The early morning had brought a sky turning from purple to pale blue, dotted with rose-tinted clouds. The air coming in had a fresh earth smell from the fields in the near distance. A mating pair of hoopoes fluttered in the olive tree. The peculiar-looking birds were residents in the garden.

The reception the night before had gone well. No mishaps with the visiting congressional delegation. He had to admit Patience contributed greatly to the success. She looked stunning in her black dress, just the right amount of cleavage, and seemed to have a sixth sense in choosing which staffer she should spend time with and which congressman's arm she should touch. Quite the hostess.

His thoughts drifted to the two memos, one from the regional security officer and the other from the CIA station chief. The reports covered Patience St. John Smythe's background. Born in England, she moved with her family to South Africa when she was twelve. After attending Catholic secondary school, she attended the University of Cape Town, where she received a law degree. She went to work with the city government. Her position became tenuous when the new government came into being, requiring a proper ethnic mix for official positions. Her contacts and talent for multi-cultural politics so far had kept her in place.

Bunting turned and headed for the shower. As the warm water flowed over his head, he wondered. Was she a spy? If so, for whom did she work? The South Africans or the British? Or both?

Dingane stood outside the kitchen door listening to his wife chatter about how he spoiled their son, how their son was disrespectful to Lady Beatrice, the woman who had most graciously provided the funds for their son to attend university, and how he, Dingane, showed little initiative to gain the respect of Abu Wahab. The lady's husband.

"Soon. I know this to be true. The madame will tell us to leave the estate," Dingane's wife cried, coming out the door carrying a large pot of steaming vegetables. "You know this to be true." She placed the pot on a warped wooden table and sat heavily onto a bench, wiping her face with a bandana.

Shaking his head slowly, he walked over to the wall, picked up an old pair of snippers, and began trimming dead leaves and flowers off the plants growing in a line of boxes. The air from the ocean below had a touch of iciness, which the sun blazing down over his shoulder fought. Now and then he heard a wave crash.

"You need not fret yourself, woman. All this will move along."

"What? What will move along? You, who are so passive?" She heaved an exaggerated sigh, and her ample bosom rose and fell while her black eyes teared.

"Madame knows how to handle her new husband."

Dingane's wife jumped up from the bench. "Hush!"

"Be still, woman. The lady is in the city."

"This house has ears," she whispered. "Many troubled

spirits here." She waved her hand across the mansion, to the sea, and back toward the rocky ridge above. With that, two shaggy baboons began to yell to each other high up on an outcrop.

Dingane knew it was useless to try and calm her now. She was correct. Trouble brewed in this house ever since Lady Beatrice married that Arab, and for what reason he could never fathom. Wahab was a decent enough chap. He treated Dingane and his wife well, but it was the company he kept. That weasel-looking man who visited Wahab the other day. The man Wahab had shown his prized car to and this same man, Nabeel was his name, treated Wahab disrespectfully. A day later he saw Nabeel and a stranger come out of the garage when Wahab was not at home. On investigating, Dingane found the car vandalized. He gave Abdul Wahab full details.

"Do you still listen?" she asked in a nervous voice. "Leave those flowers and talk to me."

He placed the tool on the wall and walked over to his wife. "We will perform our duties. I know you worry." She started to say something, but he interrupted. "All will be well."

She settled back on the bench and stared ahead. Dingane thought of the Afrikaner who came to visit Wahab. The man called Van Wartt. One of the *Broederbonders*, the zealots who constituted the hard-line believers in apartheid. This one would always have hate in his eyes when he looked at a black man, a *kaffir*.

Whenever Dingane met with his secret service control, the agent always began his debriefs with questions about Van Wartt's visits. The secret service was very interested in this Afrikaner. Dingane smiled. How things had changed with the new government; black men were now investigating the former white rulers.

From over the ocean came the familiar sound of a passenger plane coming in on time from Europe. It was making its approach to the airport north of the city. Dingane watched the huge plane bank and head in a northerly direction. The size of a Boeing 747 amazed him, and he wondered why with the plane moving so slowly it did not drop out of the sky.

A chill ran through Dingane's body, followed by a feeling of dread. Years before, he had felt the same sensation hours before the ANC guerrillas had marched into his village. They were there to accuse the elders of collaborating with the Apartheid government. Seven were executed and their huts put to the torch.

"What is wrong, my husband?" The wife looked up, fear in her eyes.

"Someone comes, bringing trouble. Maybe death."

Hayden Stone wiped his face with the warmed towel and handed it back to the flight attendant, who also took his breakfast tray. He returned his seat to the upright position as ordered and gazed out the plane window to the scene below. The white buildings of Cape Town shone in the morning sun, bright, clean, and orderly, contrasted against the ragged mountain standing above it. The sea appeared choppy, wave lines hard along the shore. Only good sailors could handle those currents; those who couldn't met the sharks waiting beneath the surface.

This was the Africa he enjoyed, a place where one could find excitement and challenge. A forced sophistication awaited the visitor who toured the city or went out to the wine country, yet danger was always near whether down a dark alley or out in the bush. Stone had an eerie feeling, as if somehow he was returning to his prehistoric origins. After a few moments, he sat back and the sensation left. He was going to work.

PRETORIA, REPUBLIC OF SOUTH AFRICA

In the US Embassy, M. R. D. Houston sat across the walnut desk from the newly appointed station chief Charles Fleming, a serious middle-aged African-American who sported French-designer glasses. The scuttlebutt from headquarters had Fleming marked as a comer in the CIA, yet he was someone who had an evenhanded perspective of personnel management and agency operations. Fleming was a diplomat when it came to dealing with both subordinates and the many agencies that constituted the embassy team.

Houston decided to feel out his new boss by bringing up the ambassador's irritation with the station, specifically the CIA base in Cape Town. "Ambassador Bunting is pissed that he wasn't in the loop about the drones."

"Was he posturing or genuinely annoyed?"

"He read the riot act to your hastily departed predecessor."

The two men were in the embassy's enclosed station. The embassy, a solidly built, highly secure structure, was in the style of an "Inman building" built by the US in response to the debacle in Moscow. There the new embassy had to be torn down and rebuilt after it was discovered to have enough KGB listening devices to make the embassy a virtual broadcasting station, capable of transmitting secrets to Soviet intelligence.

"I know. Colonel Frederick from the director's office briefed me about Ambassador Bunting. Seems Frederick and Bunting worked together in the past. Sounded almost like Bunting was one of us. Who knows? With his connections, the ambassador may someday be the Director of Central Intelligence." Fleming adjusted a family picture on his desk. "I have a meeting with him this afternoon." He rose, walked around his desk, and took the armchair closest to Houston. "What happened to the bird, you know, the drone?"

"Damndest thing," Houston said. "It was on its way back to the control post when a damn hawk attacked it. Swooped down in flight and struck it hard. The drone ended up in someone's swimming pool."

"Did we get it back?"

"Yeah, but not without a little, err, incident."

Fleming waited for Houston to continue.

"We sent a new officer over the fence to get it." Houston waved his hands around. "Well, to make a long story short, our guy goes in the pool, he dives down to the bottom to retrieve the bird, and when he surfaces, he's looking into the barrel of a shotgun held by the irate homeowner." Houston ran his hands through his hair. "Luckily, we had another officer standing by with her wits about her. She runs up to the fence and asks the man holding the gun if her model airplane was broken. She sweet talks the owner of the house, who grabs the bird from our guy climbing out of the pool. Our gal is, shall we say, attractive, and she establishes a rapport with the guy, we get the bird back, and all ends happily."

Fleming sighed and appeared to be in thought, which made Houston nervous—had he explained too much about the disaster that could have happened?

"Do we have another bird ... drone, that is?"

"Should have one operational tomorrow."

"So, our technical coverage of Van Wartt in Cape Town is presently down." Without waiting for a response, Fleming continued, "We'll have to rely on human sources. How are we down in the Cape for assets?"

"Thin."

"The station is getting a new operative. He should be arriving in Cape Town as we speak." Fleming sighed. "Hayden Stone is his name."

"Do you know anything about him? Is he good? Controllable?"

"Yes and yes to the first two questions." Fleming went back to his desk. "As to the third question, Mr. Stone has a tendency to wander on his own. He's former FBI." Fleming did an eye roll. "Wait. I take that back. Three months ago he worked for me in the South of France. More apt, he was assigned to me when I was in Paris. Mr. Stone is hard to control to say the least, but his instincts are spot on, if you know what I mean. You must have heard about the shoot-out in Villefranche and then the termination of that terrorist in Montpelier? Stone was instrumental in both actions."

"We can always use good people," Houston said. "But back to Van Wartt. We still have a wiretap and random physical surveillance on him. He's been in contact with Abdul Wahab. Something fishy going on there."

Fleming sat with his hands lifted to his chin as if in prayer. "The agency has unfinished business with Mr. Abdul Wahab.

Are we on Wahab? Is he being covered?"

"At the time, indirectly. The other service, actually two other services have coverage of Wahab. The locals, and we only get from them what they think will keep us happy, and the other service."

"And the other service is who?"

"The Canadians."

"You're shitting me. I'll be damned." Fleming smiled. "God, at last someone we can trust." Fleming crossed his legs and examined the crease in his trousers. "What's your read on the relationship between Van Wartt and Abdul Wahab?"

Houston let a moment pass, then answered carefully, "Their connection might be commercial, in some way." He knew Fleming wouldn't be satisfied with this response.

"I was stationed in Paris when Abdul Wahab operated down on the Riviera. His people murdered two of our officers. Killed, we believe on his orders."

"Are there plans to take him out?"

"Nope, and if you want to discuss it, we have to go into the bubble."

They both remained silent for a few moments. "Now what about our ambassador and his love ... that is, his extra-curricular activities," Fleming asked.

Houston squirmed in his seat. "Again, boss, we should discuss that in a secure environment, like the bubble. The situation you'll find quite interesting."

CHAPTER SIXTEEN

CAPE TOWN—AUGUST 16, 2002

Outside Hayden Stone's hotel window, the morning sunlight washed over boats tied up at the Victoria Wharf. In the distance Table Mountain loomed over the tops of high-rise buildings floating above a soft haze. He had slept well, comfortable in the fact that the agency still valued his services. The potential danger he faced made his mind as sharp and clear as this bright winter morning by the sea. He still had to find out the full story behind the mission. It had to be good.

When he arrived at the hotel the night before, he refused the first room offered and asked for one on the second floor. If somehow he had appeared on the SASS intelligence watch list, they would have a bugged room waiting for him. This change of room would complicate matters for them, but again the entire hotel might be pre-wired.

His stomach growled and he debated whether to have breakfast at the restaurant downstairs or find a place along the wharf. He decided on the latter. He placed some intricate traps in his room, including the obligatory single hair over the lock of his suitcase, which any respectable intelligence service would find and replace after they had gone through his belongings. He turned on the TV, put the DO NOT DISTURB sign on his door handle, and departed. Outside he walked along the quay toward the shops and small eateries.

Already tourists and visitors began to filter into the area. Stone wore European-style shoes, trousers, and a long-sleeved shirt to blend in with his fellow strollers. He put on his Italian sunglasses and changed his gait by placing his hands behind his back and assuming a leisurely shuffle. Just another tourist taking in the sights.

Stone's orders were to be available for any approach. He reasoned that the most likely would come from Jacob or Dirk Lange, but he had to be alert for an encounter with henchmen of Nabeel Asuty or Abdul Wahab. Operational protocol called for the local CIA base to place countersurveillance while he wandered about. Stone hoped his faith was not misplaced.

It took less than an hour for Stone to cover the whole Victoria Wharf waterfront. As he meandered, he made phone calls on the non-attributable cell phone provided to him on arrival at the airport. He had also received a pistol, not a Colt .45, but a .40 caliber Sig Sauer P226. Unfortunately, he had little luck in reaching his old contacts. One had moved to Australia, another was in prison, and a third had died mysteriously. He remembered one other, a woman named St. John Smythe. He'd try her later.

Still hungry, he decided on a small storefront eatery where he took a seat looking out on the people passing by. The coffee was weak, but the egg concoction wrapped in phyllo dough was satisfying enough. In the back of the restaurant a jazz piece by Dave Brubeck played on a dusty tape machine. After an hour sitting at the table and drinking a second cup of bad coffee, he started to become an object of interest for the two bored Portuguese waiters. Settling his bill, he was heading back to his hotel when he spotted him.

A hundred yards away, Jacob, wearing expensive leisure clothes, rose from a café table under a blue-striped umbrella. The Mossad officer threw coins on the table and, tapping a rolled-up newspaper in his right hand three distinct times, indicated it was safe to make contact. He turned away from Stone and headed toward the far end of the waterfront complex. Stone followed at a discreet distance.

As they passed by various shops and exhibits, Stone's antennas worked overtime. A number of times he saw what he believed were police or intelligence agents—and they probably were, he reasoned. The local authorities were keen on keeping this tourist attraction as free as possible from crime, and they'd be on the lookout for anyone suspicious. He believed he wasn't their target. He also hoped Jacob, walking in front of him, hadn't attracted attention.

At the far end of the waterfront, Jacob stopped on the pier, leaned on the railing, and appeared to study the watercraft passing by. From the left a brisk breeze blew in off the Atlantic, and Stone zipped up his jacket. Few strollers had ventured this far from the center of business activity. Stone came up and leaned on the railing a few feet away.

"I believe we're clean," Stone said.

Jacob looked over. "I'd like better assurances than that, my friend."

"Hey. I did the best I could." Stone waited. "After all, your people probably trained the local service."

Stone recognized the annoyed look on Jacob's craggy face. The man had extensive sources in all tribes of the South African community: black, white, mixed races, and Asians. His intelligence organization had tight liaisons with the predecessors of the SASS. However, Jacob appeared uneasy with the domestic intelligence organization, the National Intelligence Service, the South African equivalent of the FBI. The NIS would be very interested in both Stone's and Jacob's activities inside South Africa.

Stone spoke without looking at him. "I met Mr. Lange in Freetown. We had a very interesting time together."

"He told me."

Both men faced toward the water and talked into the wind.

Stone said, "I understand an old opponent of mine is in town. Abdul Wahab. We had an encounter in France."

"Yes. I know."

Jacob's complexion looked more sallow than it had in Monrovia when they last met. Perhaps it was the chill in the air. Stone knew that Jacob would tell him what he wanted, when he wanted. He had to be patient.

Jacob took a deep breath, turned, and looked around at the people on the pier. Satisfied, he faced back into the wind.

"Our Afrikaner, Dirk Lange, was impressed with you.

Thank you for not embarrassing me.'"

Stone felt like saying he should shove his backhanded compliments, but again noted Jacob's unhealthy pallor. A doctor's visit was in order. However, Stone exercised caution. The only time Jacob showed any warmth to him was years ago at the memorial service for Jacob's daughter in New York City. In the synagogue he had approached Stone and told him if Stone was to wear a yarmulke, for Christ's sake wear it properly. Then gently he patted Stone's shoulder twice. That was it.

Stone let a moment pass. "You look like shit."

Finally a reaction. He shook his head and released an ever-so-thin smile that vanished as quickly as it came. "I'm concerned." He coughed and spat over the railing. "Something is in the works and it may be too big for us to handle."

"I see." Stone waited a moment. Jacob had good sources in this country. "What can you tell me?"

"I'll be brief. We can't stay here long." Jacob spoke quickly as if reciting from a numbered list. "Mr. Lange can be trusted just so far. He has his own issues. His intelligence service is going through a bit of turmoil. Lange may be looking for new employment."

A pause. "The changeover from apartheid is bringing party people into the secret service. They are not professionals, just apparatchiks. That is good for us." Another pause. "Nabeel Asuty is coming in from Freetown to meet with Abdul Wahab. Both men are trouble. Neither has a particular liking for you." After one more coughing spell, Jacob continued, "Wahab and Dawid van Wartt have established some form of arrangement. This looks to be our major problem."

"Who's this Dawid van Wartt?"

"We've been here too long. Let's walk back into the crowd."

They walked in tandem back to the throng of shoppers and stopped at a storefront tourist shop. Behind dark wood African carvings, a little brightly colored desk flag stood upright in a penholder. It was the old regime's flag. Jacob handed it to Stone after paying the proprietor in rands.

"Van Wartt is a hard-line Boer. Wealthy. Connected with

the intelligence service. High-ranking army officer for a while." Jacob took the flag back from Stone. "He despises the West, especially your country."

"So?"

"He's selling something to the jihadists, something they are very anxious to get their hands on."

"Sounds like an arms deal."

"One would think, except for one thing, or two things for that matter. The first is Van Wartt isn't concerned about the price they'll pay."

Stone looked around at the people milling about. "So whatever it is, he wants them to have it. A biological, chemical, or nuclear weapon."

Jacob tensed and moved away, their meeting over. Stone would have to wait to know the second thing about Van Wartt's dealings with Wahab and the jihadists. He walked to the entrance of the wharf complex and stopped at the parking lot. As he turned to go back to his hotel, a beat-up Land Rover pulled next to him and the driver, a young man with a set of jug ears, called out the parole, the recognition phrase to identify him as CIA. The young man instructed him to be at the Mount Nelson Hotel promptly at eight that night. The Land Rover sped away and Stone continued on to his hotel.

From the pilothouse of his yacht, Dawid van Wartt watched Bull Rhyton lumber down the wooden pier. A big rock of a man with a "bull neck" and arms that bowed out from his muscular body, he approached the yacht's gangplank and was stopped by the guard. Van Wartt called down and the guard allowed Rhyton to board.

He led his visitor to the lounge and closed all the doors. Gusts blowing in from Table Bay rattled the hatches and slightly rolled the vintage thirty-meter craft. Rhyton settled himself into an armchair and rubbed his right knee.

"Drink?" Van Wartt asked in Afrikaans. "Perhaps for that knee."

"Too early." Rhyton's red face inspected the inside of the cabin. "Nice."

"She's an old craft, but sturdy." He pointed. "You should have that Communist shrapnel removed. I know a good doctor."

He shook his head. "Agh." Bull's favorite negative expression.

Van Wartt sat across from him and inwardly smiled. At fifty years of age, Bull still resembled an overgrown Boer teenager. His eyes spoke more than his tongue. Twenty-four years ago this man had been his sergeant when, as a new lieutenant, Van Wartt's airborne unit was called up for the 1978 border raid into Angola. Their unit dropped into a rebel base, killed many Cubans and guerillas, and since, every year on May 4th, celebrated Cassinga Day. Last May, Van Wartt had asked his former sergeant if he would help him with his plan. The man had readily agreed … at first.

"Well, my friend." Van Wartt said. "How are things up north in the desert?"

"Warmer than here." The burly man had just driven three days from Bruin Karas, a hamlet sitting across the border in Namibia, South Africa's former territory of South West Africa. He hadn't changed his soiled bush clothes.

Van Wartt wished that it wasn't so early in the morning. A little drink would loosen Rhyton up. He must take his time with the man. A few lazy questions before zeroing in on the subject. "How are our friends up in Bruin Karas?"

"Do you have coffee?" Rhyton asked.

"Come. We'll go to the galley."

As Rhyton drank his coffee from a heavy mug, the two stared out the portholes at Cape Town. The hot coffee loosened his tongue. "Bruin Karas remains the same for the most part."

Van Wartt knew that Bruin Karas had not changed. It would be difficult to call it a town. It was more of a settlement, with two stores, a petrol station, and an eating establishment that also served as a bar. Like all farming or ranch communities, it served as a central place for supplies, relaxation, and gossip. Relatives of Bull Rhyton lived there, and Van Wartt had met them on the occasions when he had visited and inspected the boxcar, sitting off on an unused siding, appearing for all practical purposes abandoned.

Strange. His friend had just hinted that things were *not* all the same in Bruin Karas.

Seated again in the salon, Van Wartt knew the time had come to get to business. "What is wrong up there?"

"Our friends say it started three, maybe four months ago. When the temperatures were still high." Rhyton leaned forward. "Around the *trein*, the boxcar, some young fellows found dead animals."

Van Wartt raised his hands as if to say, "So?"

"The same boys, one is a nephew, developed rashes, like burns. Their parents want the boxcar moved."

Van Wartt tapped the arm of his chair with his fingers. "Did you go out to the siding and look at it? Was it broken into?"

"The lock on the door was broken. The boxcar still stands out at the end of the spur. Nothing around for miles. I saw no dead animals around it." Rhyton paused, thinking. " Screws were off one of the plates on the bomb. I touched the sides for heat. Nothing." At this, he inspected his hands.

"This is not good. Must be a leak. A very bad time for this to happen." Van Wartt thought a moment. "I wonder how much time those children went there. They were probably curious and tried to get inside it."

"I don't like any of this anymore. We shouldn't have this thing. The bomb belongs to the government."

Van Wartt jumped up. "Good God, man! We don't have the old government. This is not our government." He looked up at the ceiling light. "Return *it* to the *kaffirs*?"

"We should get it out of there."

Van Wartt took his seat again. He did his best to look composed. Rhyton mustn't think this worried him. He spoke in a low voice, "I will push our plan along with this man, Abdul Wahab. I'm sure someone in his group is an expert in these matters. They want to take delivery soon."

"How will Wahab take possession? Where will he take it?"

"He's not specific. I didn't tell him where the device is located," Van Wartt said with a wave of the hand. Truth to be told, he had no idea if Wahab had the means to move it from the middle of the Namibian Desert to wherever he intended.

"I don't like this whole matter anymore."

"What do you say?" Van Wartt yelled. "This is payback to those who have taken away our world. Our way of life!" His fists clenched and he watched Rhyton intently study his face. He breathed hard. "Your people and mine have been here for hundreds of years. The same, no, longer than the Americans have been in their country. *Fok hulle!*"

"I don't believe it is God's will that we kill innocents." Rhyton stood. "These are evil people we are dealing with." Now, he spoke softly, "Dawie, my friend, are we sure we are in control of this? I think not. Those devils may turn this thing against us."

CHAPTER SEVENTEEN

CAPE TOWN—AUGUST 16, 2002

Following the waiter wearing a short white jacket, Abdul Wahab passed the bar toward the far end of the room. At a window table sat Dawid van Wartt, who had a view of the bay and at the same time could watch the patrons entering the grill. He noted that Van Wartt's right leg twitched. No doubt, Wahab thought, this was his usual table here at the Bay Yacht Club.

Wahab had intended to be late for their luncheon appointment, just to keep the South African off balance, but as he drove to the club, he wondered if that was wise inasmuch as he wanted Van Wartt to sponsor him for club membership. No matter. Today they had important business to conduct, and the matter of his joining this pretentious establishment could come later.

"Sorry for making you wait, Dawid," Wahab said. "Traffic and my driving."

Van Wartt rose. "Ah no, Abdul. I lost track of time looking out at the bay. See. The wind has died and the white caps have disappeared. Just a lovely view."

Wahab took a seat, told the waiter he wanted some sparkling water, and while looking out at the moored yachts, asked, "One of those is yours?"

"Yes."

"Which one?"

"The big one." Van Wartt leaned forward. "Abdul. We have urgent business to conduct. Before this place begins to fill up, let's settle a few matters."

Wahab took offense at Van Wartt's rudeness. Afrikaner or not, he expected to be treated with deference, and why do all these Boers wear the same absurd mustache? "Please, begin," he said.

"The packet we have talked about is ready for pickup." Van Wartt spoke softly. "Because of circumstances, the timing of the delivery has become critical. First, have we reached an agreement on price? Second, are your people prepared to take possession?"

Wahab watched him sit back and play with his napkin. His eyes focused on the embroidered anchor emblem on Van Wartt's blazer. No doubt he would have one of those when he became a member of the club. He detected some sense of urgency on Van Wartt's part. Why? Did the man suddenly need the money?

He said in a low voice matching Van Wartt's, "About the price of the merchandise. We talked about ten million dollars—"

"Euros. Ten million euros," Van Wartt corrected.

This interested Wahab. The man across from him was concerned about the amount of money. Euros were worth more than dollars. He might have some fun. "Dawid. My people tell me that such a sum is not available at this time. They are thinking half that amount. Perhaps at a later time something more would be added."

For the moment this was true. Since his misadventure on the Riviera, al Qaeda considered him a risk and had placed middlemen between them. He was forced to work with the weasel Nabeel Asuty, who only had his Egyptian contacts, but they knew how to bargain. Not like his Saudi brothers flush with their dollar stockpiles.

Van Wartt's cold eyes fixed on him and appeared to move off to empty space beyond Wahab. At last, he said, without looking directly at him, "Five million will do. Can you take delivery within a week?"

"A week?"

"Yes. This is the bank number where you forward the funds." Van Wartt wrote on the cocktail napkin. "I'll arrange transportation for your pickup of the device. You will need five … no, six men. I suppose one of them will be versed in nuclear technology. We'll provide the necessary test instruments and equipment."

"I'll let you know by tomorrow morning." Wahab coughed. "Where will my men go?"

"There's an airfield up north. Driving distance from here. They'll be flown to the site, and when they take possession we'll take them to some reasonable destination of your choice." Van Wartt made to rise from his seat. "You do have a place to take it? Don't you?"

"We'll have one."

"I'll expect your call. Meanwhile, I have an appointment." Van Wartt got out of his chair and turned to the waiter who had hastened to his side. "Mr. Wahab will stay and have lunch. Put it on my tab." Leaning down, he said, "Abdul. Time is of the essence. Oh, the crab salad is especially good."

In time, the waiter brought the crab salad. Wahab found himself picking through lettuce for the crab morsels. He swallowed the chunks but didn't enjoy the succulent meat. For what it was worth, he could have been eating the bland African corn porridge, *putu*, as his mind raced from one perceived obstacle to another. Van Wartt had surprised him with the deadline. It would be difficult to keep.

Wahab laid down his fork. Perhaps it was, as they say, a blessing in disguise. Nabeel was on his way here to Cape Town, and when he arrived he would be told to get six men together. Meantime, to cover his bets he would get in touch with his al Qaeda contact in South Africa. This development would be of interest to them. All this could work.

As for Dawid van Wartt, Wahab must be careful. This man had a bad reputation. Men like him were doubly dangerous if they were under pressure, which he seemed to be.

Noisy gulls outside the window attracted his attention. The wind had picked up again, bringing in a gray cloudbank. Wahab dropped his fork. Nabeel had called and told him he was hurrying here from Freetown.

In addition, Hayden Stone had arrived in Cape Town. This time Wahab would make sure that the man who had caused him so much trouble in the past would be eliminated.

• • •

At a little before eight that evening, Hayden Stone approached the front desk of the Mount Nelson Hotel and as the man in the Land Rover had instructed that afternoon, inquired if "Finbarr Costanza" had any messages. After searching through the message folder, the desk clerk handed Stone an envelope.

He waited to open it until he found a quiet place and took the hallway off the main lounge. When he entered a side room he discovered a wedding party in progress. He stopped in the middle of the room next to a round table holding an arrangement of white flowers that towered over his head. The Mount Nelson oozed chic and always seemed a bit over the top, but their martinis were the coldest in town. The barman stored the vodka in a small freezer. He read the message, smiled graciously to the bride and groom, and headed for the bar.

The message inside the envelope had come as a pleasant surprise. MEET ME IN THE PLANET BAR. It was signed "Harrington" in Sandra's elegant script. He carefully folded the message and slipped it into his inside jacket pocket, smiling. Colonel Frederick had somehow managed to get Sandra off the agency's bad girl list. *Wonder what her old boyfriend Farley Durrell is up to? Would he accompany Nabeel Asuty here to Cape Town?*

In the bar he moved toward two empty seats next to the fireplace and saw a blonde seated with her back to him. She stood, retrieved her evening bag from the cocktail table, turned, and walked by him, giving him a slight bump. He caught a whiff of Sandra's perfume as she passed. In a navy blue pantsuit, she obviously had been watching for him in the wall-to-wall mirror behind the bar.

Acting as if he couldn't decide whether to stay, he turned and followed her. With a determined stride, she went out a side door, took a path through the lighted gardens, and approached a black sedan waiting in the darkened parking lot. The back door opened and she slipped in. A few seconds later he was sitting next to her in the backseat. Discreetly, she reached over and squeezed his hand and held on for a moment. In the front seat one of the two men said, "We're on our way," to a hidden microphone, and the car sped from the hotel grounds and drove south on the M3. Stone knew the road as the Simon van der Stel Freeway or known locally as the Blue Route. They were headed toward the coastal town of Fish Hoek.

The city lights faded behind them. They rode in silence as the CIA officers in the front seat constantly checked each passing car. When the lights of a car shone in the face of the driver—an African-American in Rastafarian attire and dreadlocks—Stone caught his eyes studying him. Evidently, Stone's reputation had been broadcasted on the agency pipeline. *The cowboy was in town*.

The driver tilted his head back and asked Sandra, "Is our guest staying overnight?" Rasta man had a distinct Philadelphia Main Line accent. Probably a Bucknell or Penn graduate.

"Yes. We have a lot to talk about."

Therefore, Stone would be staying in a safe house tonight. He hoped the accommodations weren't too bad, what with the budget crunch. Who else would be there besides these three in the car? The base chief, no doubt.

Sandra touched his hand again. "Someone will make sure your room back in the hotel looks like it's been used." She kept her hand on his. "Like I said, we have a lot to discuss."

The safe house was a five-room villa facing south overlooking False Bay. A soft breeze brought in the smell of sea foam. The furnishings were basic, but clean. Rasta man, whose name was Owen, had prepared two platters of *bobojtie*, the Cape Malay dish of lamb, nuts, raisins, and chutney, with a baked egg topping. Its rich aroma filled the dining room as they waited for the arrival of the CIA base chief. The chief of station would also be there, Sandra told him. He had flown in from the embassy in Pretoria for the meeting.

An hour passed and M. R. D. Houston came in with the COS, who to Stone's surprise and relief, turned out to be Charles Fleming, wearing as usual a bespoke gray suit.

"You left Paris for South Africa?" Stone asked, exchanging

warm handshakes. Fleming had been assigned to the Paris station. It had only been months before in the South of France when he, Colonel Gustave Frederick, and Fleming had been involved in a counterterrorist operation.

"My family hasn't gotten here yet, but, yes, it's a good move and a very good slot." Fleming looked over the remnants of the meal on the table. "Looks like you're all finished eating. Let's get to work."

He ushered Stone, Sandra, and Houston into a bedroom at the end of the hallway. Again, sparsely furnished, with only a long table and eight metal fold-up chairs. Cold water bottles stood upright in the center of the table on an old serving plate.

"I just visited Paris," Stone said. "Didn't have time to look you up."

"I knew you were in town. Colonel Frederick told me." Fleming glanced over to Sandra. "He was busy with a lot of things."

Sandra coughed. "Yeah. He can work miracles sometimes. That's why I'm still here."

"And that's why I'm still here." Stone tapped the table. "Now, I suppose you want to know what Jacob had to say." Stone related the details of his morning meeting, including what appeared to be Jacob's ill health. "He's concerned with Abdul Wahab as he should be, but he's got this South African, Van Wartt, under his claw. Believes he's the real problem."

Fleming rubbed his hands together, looked over again at Sandra, and said to her, "Might as well get right down to it."

She nodded and sipped water from a bottle. She'd lost weight and had circles under her eyes.

Fleming started. "Hayden, this is all supersensitive, but things are moving so fast that ... I can't tell you everything. You know, compartmentalization."

"You mean I won't hand over the whole story before the jihadists chop my head off." Stone pulled out a cigar and asked if anyone objected. Houston, his arms bulging from his dark blue polo shirt, surprised him by also pulling out a cigar. Sandra said she didn't mind if she could have a drag or two.

"If we all have burnished our macho credentials, can we move on?" Fleming said, his handsome black face creased in a frown. "Stone, let me give you a little history in the South African nuclear weapons program."

"The what?" Stone handed Sandra his cigar and reached over to the sideboard and got two ashtrays. After taking a long puff, she handed it back.

What Fleming related didn't surprise him. Years ago Stone had heard South Africa had a nuclear bomb, but it was never really much interest to him. He wondered what this had to do with the operation.

"Back in the late sixties, early seventies, the white government here had a viable nuclear weapons program. You have to remember the country was ostracized for the most part by the world for its apartheid policy. Trade embargoes, the whole package of sanctions by the world to force them to change and become more democratic. One of the results was that South Africa decided to become self-sufficient economically and militarily. Ironically, because of that they're now the most viable economy on the continent.

"And back then one of the ways to stay in power was to build the bomb," Stone said.

"Yes. They had legitimate worries. Angola had become independent from Portugal, and a communist insurgency arose with Cuban support. In fact, the Cubans had quite a military presence and they had their eyes on the South West Africa territory that South Africa controlled. A nuke or two would be quite a deterrent against the spread of communism."

"South Africa developed the bomb themselves?"

"They had help. Their chief partner was Israel."

Stone leaned forward and tapped his cigar in the ashtray. "I see a story developing here."

"I'll spare you the complete info dump just to say the two countries had a lot in common. Both felt like outcasts, both had this God's Covenant thing going, and both needed a solid military stance. South Africa needed the experience—they had the expertise in nuclear development but not weaponry. Israel needed a place to test their device."

Stone had lost interest in his cigar and let it lay in the ashtray. Houston did the same.

Sandra put her elbows on the table. "My understanding is the apartheid government destroyed their bombs just before relinquishing control."

"Ah. Now here we come to the interesting part. A little numbers game. One report says that they developed eight nuclear bombs based on the gun-type principle—that is, creating an explosion by shooting one piece of subcritical material into another." Fleming paused. "Follow me, Stone?"

"No." Stone frowned. "Let's skip the technical stuff."

"No matter. It's the old-fashioned method of making a bomb. The first US bombs were made on that principle."

"So they were bulky?"

"Yeah. About two feet by five and weighing close to a ton. That's going to be of interest to you later."

"So the eight bombs were dismantled after South Africa signed some treaty," Sandra said.

"Well, no. We know there were supposed to be eight bombs, because the Israelis were providing eight Jericho missiles for them. The South Africans were afraid that the Cuban antiaircraft batteries would bring down their Canberra or Buccaneer bombers, so they had asked for Israeli long-range missiles. Now here comes the numbers game. In nineteen eighty-seven we had a report that eight bombs had been produced. Then in nineteen ninety-four, six fully completed bombs and one partial were dismantled."

"But it's believed they tested one near Antarctica," Sandra added.

"Back in September nineteen seventy-nine."

Stone sat back. "Okay. There are your eight bombs."

Charles Fleming slid an eight-by-eleven photograph across the table to Stone and Sandra. "Take a look and count the bombs. This picture was taken up there at the Vastrap facility up in the Kalahari Desert around ten years ago."

Stone looked at the photo showing fat bullet-shaped,

brass-colored bombs, two to a rack, except in the back row. A single ninth, fully completed bomb sat on a cradle. "Looks like someone lost count."

"We think we located the unaccounted-for bomb. Also, we're certain someone wants to hand it over to Abdul Wahab."

Stone let the last statement sink in. Abdul Wahab, a man in league with al Qaeda, in possession of an atomic bomb. "Shit! There's no telling what Wahab wants to do with an atomic bomb. No wonder Jacob looked worried when I saw him this morning."

"What exactly did he tell you?"

"He said that Nabeel Asuty is heading here from Freetown. Some big shot here in Cape Town, Dawid van Wartt, wants to sell them something. This guy is well connected. When I asked if it was an arms deal he was talking about, Jacob said he didn't know. He did emphasize that this Van Wartt is big trouble."

"We know Dawid van Wartt is vocal in his hatred of the Western countries and especially America. We believe he's the one who wants to sell Wahab the bomb."

Stone looked around the table. "Thank God it's not a suitcase nuclear weapon. You know where this thing is?"

"Another agency that does a lot of satellite recon advised they've picked up a possible nuclear glow in Namibia."

Sandra huffed. "They must pick up hot spots every day."

"Namibia is located north of South Africa in the Kalahari Desert." Fleming took back the photograph. "We had a report that Mr. Van Wartt had a meeting this morning with an old army colleague who had just driven down from the area where the hot spot was seen."

"I'll get a hold of Jacob again and question him about this," Stone said. "I also have to find Dirk Lange, who I'm certain is with the South African Security Service, but Sandra and I have built a working relationship with him."

"Don't ask Jacob any direct questions about the bomb." Fleming tensed. "He was bouncing around this country during the seventies. He knows more about this than he's letting on."

"Maybe that's why he's so worried."

"Can you trust those two—Jacob and this SASS guy

Lange?" Fleming asked.

"As much as they trust me," Stone said. "Are we checking out that area up there in Namibia? Why not drop in one of those DOE response teams or maybe a SEAL team?"

"We're working on options. You and Sandra may come into play on that angle."

A little after midnight, Sandra knocked gently on Stone's door. She whispered to meet her in the kitchen. He put his clothes back on and quietly went down the hallway. She sat on a stool sipping a glass of wine.

"Want some?" she asked and motioned for him to sit. "I didn't want to go into your room. These people have big ears and big mouths, if you know what I mean."

Stone knew that as gossip went, the sexual kind was the juiciest. It wouldn't be the first time men and women on a mission got involved in a little side action.

"Frederick put his neck out and saved my ass from going to a bureaucratic Siberia," she said. "There were two catches. One, I work with you on this mission, which is turning out to be bigger than I thought."

"Bigger than I expected," Stone said. "We're not letting Wahab get ahold of this nuclear device. What's the second catch?"

"It has to do with that prick Farley Durrell." She leaned closer. "Farley's position with Nabeel Asuty and his gang is not going well. Some of them are suspicious of him. Evidently, he's not as valuable to them as he was. You know what that means with those shits." She took a deep breath. "You know how much I hate Farley, still ... Anyway, Frederick told me one of our jobs might be to extract him from their clutches."

"Nothing I like better than a good shoot-up."

"Hayden! Be careful what you say around here! That's why they call you a damn cowboy."

"Tomorrow I head back to my hotel. Hope Dirk Lange contacts us. We're going to need him."

She poured more wine. "I'll check in at the same hotel.

That'll double the odds of Dirk finding us."

"There's one more source for me to contact," Stone said. "Few people know this town better than Patience."

"And how well do you *know* her, Hayden?"

"Well enough, toots," he said. "Don't stay up too late. You need your beauty sleep."

CHAPTER EIGHTEEN

CAPE TOWN—AUGUST 17, 2002

Hayden Stone phoned his old acquaintance Patience St. John Smythe. After four rings, she answered. He identified himself and following a pause, she asked where he was. She always held conversations on the phone to the minimum. Stone attributed this quirk to the fact that she had been raised in a country that made it a practice to listen to their citizens' telephone conversations. However, when he had gotten to know her, he found she was smart and kept a tight schedule, only allowing herself to slide into niceties when her calendar permitted.

"Hayden. My, we haven't talked in ages."

"Let's get together."

Silence, then, "Do you have transportation?"

When he said he didn't, she told him she'd pick him up in a dark blue Honda in an hour at the corner of Wale and Adderley Streets. In front of the St. George's Cathedral. End of conversation. Still the professional. Even if the conversation had been overheard, the secret service would have a difficult time setting up surveillance in one hour in the middle of downtown business traffic.

Stone holstered his new Sig Sauer, left his hotel room, and took the stairs up to Sandra's floor. She waved him in and went back to unpacking her suitcase, laying the clothes on the couch. He told her about the phone call. She showed interest in the details.

"The woman seems pretty savvy. Who does she work for?"

"I've always thought the Brits, but I'd noticed in the past a lot of inconsistencies in her stories."

"What information does the station or Charles Fleming have

141

on her?" Sandra asked. "And how long have you known her?"

Stone looked at his watch. "Look. I have to go. Only have a little more than half an hour before I meet her."

When he reached for the doorknob, she said, "Fleming doesn't know about this? You're playing the lone ranger. This isn't how we do things. You know that."

"I'm meeting someone that in the FBI parlance is a hip pocket source." He detected no reaction from Sandra, so continued, "Basically there's nothing about her recorded on paper or in a file. I just collect information from her and attribute it to another source."

"Sounds fishy and not according to the rules. You're not in the bureau anymore, and if you keep up this shit, you're not going to be with the CIA either."

Stone had learned the hard way he shouldn't argue with a person giving him good advice. As he was about to fall back on old habits and say something dumb, Sandra saved him.

"What's your relationship with this *Patience*?"

"I hope we're still good friends, but the last time we were together ..."

Sandra sighed and held up her hand. She reminded him of one of his grammar school teachers having lost patience with him. The "patience" crack made him smile.

"Don't smile, smart-ass. Give me that gun." Taking it, she asked, "Are you familiar with this?"

He told her no, that for some reason they hadn't given him the Colt .45 that he'd asked for. "At least it's a forty caliber S&W," he said. "It looks like a pistol, not some high-tech toy." She took the gun and gave him a thorough rundown on the Sig Sauer. Had she been a firearms instructor at one time?

A taxicab dropped him off at the House of Parliament, and then on foot he took Government Avenue through the extensive gardens to the cathedral. He took in the crisp morning air and walked briskly, glad that he had his leather jacket. He mused about his first meeting with Patience. Two years ago, in June or July, he had visited Salzburg, Austria. The weather was invigorating. Tourists strolled the streets from one music performance to another, and the river Salzach ran fast and cold from the melting snows in the Alps.

As he had sat in an ornate music room waiting for an afternoon string quintet to begin, she slipped in the seat next to him. Rows of empty chairs surrounded the two of them, so it was evident that she wanted to meet him. The encounter was pleasant; the quintet's set was dreadful.

Their relationship had been semi-intense, platonic. She said she couldn't help falling in love with a married man, but she didn't have to bed him. Her words.

Stone made sure that he came to the street corner at the precise time Patience had given. A dark blue sedan approached the curb and the headlights flashed. He went up to the passenger door, looked in, and climbed inside. Patience leaned over halfway to give him a perfunctory kiss on the cheek and sped off. He had forgotten she had a heavy foot on the accelerator. He'd let her get her bearings before making conversation, but a minute later she started in.

"You haven't changed much." She glanced over, then up to the rearview mirror. "Put on a little weight around the middle."

"You, my dear, on the other hand, simply glow."

She did. Her features had softened. She was on the way to becoming one of those women other women secretly hated—one who improved with age. He expected her to be in a business suit, but instead she wore taupe twill slacks and a cashmere sweater over a turtleneck. Gold flats matched an expensive watch, bracelet on left wrist, and rings on both hands. Causal chic. However, her perfume signaled business office, not boudoir.

"Are you here on holiday?" She looked over. "Of course not. Spying on my country?"

"No. As a matter of fact, I'm working with elements from your local government."

Stone, at times like this, got a kick out of semantics. He and Dirk Lange did have something of a working relationship. Also, he had to clarify which country he was referring to. She held a British passport as well as a South African one.

"I almost left you hanging there on the corner. You deserve to be stood up."

"We didn't part on the best of terms, did we?" Stone knew diplomacy was in order. "The whole thing bothered me. A lot."

"Let's get this over with, so we can move on."

She looked for agreement on his part, so he nodded.

"You are insensitive and in the realm of personal relationships, wholly unreliable." Once again, she glanced in the rearview mirror. "Now let's get to whatever you called me about. Shall we?"

Stone felt relieved they had gotten past that hurdle. The car headed out of the city. He needed a safe place where he could question her about Van Wartt. If he was lucky, she might even know something about Abdul Wahab. He suggested lunch.

"We are going to a cheetah sanctuary about forty-five minutes from here. It is located on a wine estate. They have a restaurant."

"Is it a game park?" Stone enjoyed safaris, but this was not the time to go touring.

"It's part of the Cheetah Outreach Programme. I'm going to let you pet a real live cheetah. Sometimes they bite."

They drove through the famed Stellenbosch wine country. Except for the backdrop of jagged mountains, one would believe they had been transported to Napa Valley in California. Hilly, with neat divisions of vineyards interspersed with tidy homes favoring Cape Dutch architecture. This was not the raw Africa of legend. Patience was true to her word, and they arrived at the sanctuary in forty-five minutes.

A regal, lean animal, stretching six feet from head to tip of tail, the young cheetah reclined on top of a three-foot high metal cage. The face with big amber eyes resembled any placid household cat. No sign of an efficient killer, the fastest mammal on earth. So calm and friendly now, but when, like so many of

Stone's quarry in the past, would they turn on you?

Under an open wooden pergola within a high-fenced compound, other cheetahs that had been taken in by the sanctuary for rehabilitation lounged and made soft guttural sounds. A staff person in khaki shorts and long-sleeved shirt stood close to Patience and Stone as she stroked the animal's back. The cat acted as if it was normal to be in close contact with two-legged animals.

Stone had seen a change in Patience the minute they entered the gate. She showed affection for the animal, and the cat displayed easiness with her. Africans, he knew, had a strong attachment to the animals of their continent. Moving closer to Stone, she took his hand.

"Just stroke its back like this," she said softly. "I think it's a female."

"It is, miss," the uniformed attendant said. "She has been here for close to one year now."

The vision of a full-grown cheetah taking down a gazelle flashed in Stone's mind. "What do you feed her?" Stone asked, running his hand along the soft, tawny, black-spotted fur.

Patience moved close and whispered, "American bastards." She returned her attention to the cat.

Inside a rustic wooden building, not unlike one would find in the American West, the sanctuary's restaurant served basic South African fare along with wines from the vineyard located on the property. Stone ordered a Cape-style smoor with spinach and jus. She had a salad. They sat outdoors, where the sunlight brought out the sheen in Patience's hair. Her almost mauve eyes studied Stone and he knew she wanted to talk business.

"Before we start on your inquiries ... that is why we're here, correct?" she said. "You want some sort of information from me, unless you are in Cape Town to resume our relationship, and if you are, you're too late."

"That's getting to the point," Stone said. "Yes. I hope you can help me, but first, what's this 'too late'?"

"I met a man who is, well, special." Patience looked off. "However, in the beginning stages, you know? Now, what do you want to know? Wait, what are you doing here? The FBI has no jurisdiction here."

The last time they'd been together, he was in the FBI, working cases in New York City. The two had attended a diplomatic function on the East Side. Her "people"—Stone assumed British MI6, though he could never confirm it—and the FBI were interested in a particular Russian intelligence officer. They had orchestrated a pitch to the Russian to defect, with no success.

"I retired early from the FBI and now I'm sort of doing freelance work."

"For the right side, I assume." Her eyebrows had lifted just enough to show she had shifted to professional mode. Well, almost. "Are you and your wife still separated? It's been a while now since the two of you have gone your own ways."

"Along with my retirement, we made the separation official."

She tapped the table with her fingers. "Too late for us." She said it with finality. "Now, what is it you want?"

As he began, her eyes darkened. "I'm interested in a South African by the name of Dawid van Wartt. We have reason to believe he is in league with Middle East terrorists who want to target the US. Do you know anything about him?"

"Seems all you Yanks are interested in is dear Dawie." She glared. "Stone. You realize you are asking me to give you information on a fellow South African. There are legal issues here."

"You're a lawyer. That shouldn't bother you, but to reassure you, I'm working with a South African intelligence officer on this."

"He knows about me?" She looked alarmed.

"No one is aware I'm talking with you. This is between you and me." He decided to chance it. "You might know him."

Before he could give her Dirk Lange's name, she slumped back in the chair and looked skyward. "There goes a Wahlberg's eagle. Beautiful birds, aren't they?" She reached for her glasses.

When had she started wearing them?

The graceful bird soared then dropped fast behind a tall tree. Mealtime for him.

She saw that Stone picked at his meal. "If that dish is too spicy, you could tame it with a beer."

Stone indicated his water was fine.

"I remember from New York you'd never drink while on duty like the other agents we worked with. Bureau regulations, you would say. Are you on duty now?"

"Just trying to keep my wits about me."

"You're a bit of a stuffed shirt. Won't change with the times. At least you don't double knot your shoe laces." She hesitated, then almost whispered, "I don't bed married men, like you were back then, but you could have done me the favor of trying harder."

A family passed by their table; having finished lunch, they headed for the cheetah enclosure. The parents wore short shorts and heavy sweaters favored by Africans . The father had the distinctive Boer moustache. The boy and girl went barefoot like many of the white farmer children in South Africa.

He caught Patience watching him. "Tough lot, aren't they?"

"I like them."

"They don't like you, Yank," she said. "They blame your kind for the end of apartheid and their way of life."

They watched the family head for the entrance to the sanctuary.

Patience changed her tone of voice and spoke softly. "Hayden, you must realize you caught me by surprise. I had no idea you were onto Van Wartt. All this is becoming awkward for me. Let me explain." She moved her chair next to him and whispered, "The love of my life is your ambassador to South Africa. He is also interested in Van Wartt. My people are interested in Van Wartt. One person in the local secret service who I know is interested in him is ... Dirk Lange."

Stone attempted a nonchalant smile. She knew Dirk. Small world. However, he let sink in the fact that her lover was none other than Marshall Bunting, the American ambassador.

147

"Dirk Lange is a sweet man. Also, very *reliable*." She looked him over. "However, dear Dawie on the other hand is a bloody rockspider. You know, not quite what we call a hairyback Afrikaner, but still one of those thickheaded Boers." She put her glasses away. "No. I'm not generalizing. I have many Afrikaners for friends, but most are quite impossible. And," she said with emphasis, "it's not an English–Boer thing." She smiled. "Perhaps it is."

"How well do you know him?"

"Attended some mutual functions. Met his wife at the Museum of Art a few times. She's as bad as he is." She clicked her tongue twice. "Met him numerous times at the yacht club. Oh, Hayden, do you still sail? No matter. Back to sweet Dawie. He occasionally has hit on me without success, and that sums up the personal contacts. Now for what you Americans say, the nitty-gritty."

"I wish I'd brought my notepad."

"None of this is to be written down. Understand?"

"You know how I operate."

"Checking." She placed her hands over her mouth. "He's a member of the *Broederbonders*. That's a secret society of apartheid zealots. Under the old regime any senior member of government had to be a member. They also controlled the police, education, broadcasting, and the censor board, everything important.

"Van Wartt's money and power comes from an engineering firm, some mining, and real estate investments. He holds a general's commission, but that's inactive." She paused to sip her soda. "This is interesting. His status with those *Broederbonders* is shaky. Reports are his fellow loonies consider him too extreme. Some are beginning to maintain a distance, not completely, mind you. After all, that crowd isn't on everyone's dance card and their social circle is thinning."

"Extreme in what way?"

"Rants in public, especially when he's in his cups—about settling the score with those who caused the downfall of apartheid. He tried to enlist others in some wild schemes, like computer hack attacks against Wall Street. That didn't go over big with that crowd, most of whom have their money parked there. Lately, he's tamed down." She waited a moment. "One incident that I'm certain has hardened him. Just as the new government took over, a massacre occurred up north. During Sunday service, in one of those Dutch Reformed churches in the farm area, a group of blacks, rebel types, entered and machine-gunned everyone. No one survived."

"So Van Wartt's religious?"

"I'm not certain. All I know is his parents and sisters were in the congregation."

"Damn," he said. "An incident like that would make anyone seek retribution." He thought a moment. "Were the killers brought to justice?"

"Of course not. Reconciliation for past crimes and all that nonsense the new government is pushing. You must realize that for Van Wartt this is home. There's a strong connection with his ancestors, blood, and history." She met his eyes. "Not unlike your feelings for the United States."

Stone mulled over what she said about Van Wartt. The thought occurred: How much of an attachment did Patience have with this country after living here since she was twelve years old? "I heard he has something going with a Saudi named Abdul Wahab. That he wants to sell Wahab something very big and dangerous."

"Yes." She gave him an admiring glance to say he was on the top of his game. "My people picked up on Abdul Wahab when he fled France a few months ago. One of his two wives is Lady Beatrice. Quite an extraordinary woman, even though her taste in men is questionable." Pause. "Wahab is knee-deep in the terrorist trade." She stopped, her eyes left him, returned, and narrowed. "You visited the Riviera recently, didn't you?"

It was Stone's turn to churn the information he'd learned. Patience was not just a South African lawyer who happened to work occasionally for MI6. She was a full-blown case officer. Granted, she might not have known why he had come to Cape Town, but she knew a lot about Abdul Wahab and Van Wartt's activities. Were MI6 and the CIA exchanging information?

Finally, he said, "Yes. I did."

"You're here to kill Wahab for murdering those CIA officers in the South of France, aren't you? You work for the CIA. You were involved in that big shoot-out in Villefranche."

"Get this straight. I'm not an assassin. You know me better than that."

"I don't know you at all." She seemed to fret. "Well, not all, all."

Stone grinned. She was quite dramatic at times. "Patience, dear." This time he moved closer. "What I do, I do in the service of my country. Always have. I'm a minor player. Just a contractor on a job to obtain information to prevent another 9/11 in the US, London, Paris, or Israel."

"Were you truthful about no one else knowing about us?"

"Neither the station here nor the man I work for at Langley knows about you and me."

She put her face close to his. "How about that blonde I saw you scoot out with last night at the Mount Nelson Hotel?"

"Your eagle is back. Finished lunch, I suppose."

"Surprised?" She smiled. "I was in the bar with a friend. You didn't see me. Maybe you are slipping. I notice a gray hair here and there." She leaned against him and with that mischievous look he recalled from the past, whispered, "You have another surprise flying into town."

CHAPTER NINETEEN

After Hayden Stone left the hotel to meet with his contact, Sandra Harrington took a stroll along the waterfront. It was time that she establish contact with Dirk Lange. Walking through the Victoria Wharf complex might provide an opportunity for a casual encounter. A bright sun warmed her face even though the air chilled her legs. Aside from cries of sea birds flying overhead, quiet settled on the area. The seaside smelled of fresh fish that drifted up from open tanks in trawlers tied along the quay.

Noisy tourists boarded a double-deck sightseeing boat at the end of the pier. The sign at the gate announced two-hour tours of the bay, and Sandra considered spending her afternoon on one of the boats. Then she remembered the meeting the night before with CIA station chief Fleming. When he had told them about the nuclear weapon that could end up in the hands of Abdul Wahab's terrorists, even Hayden Stone's *sangfroid* had slipped a little. Was considering a little sightseeing at this time a way to shove such a horror out of her mind?

She loosened her scarf, shook her hair, and leisurely continued along the dockside, inspecting the various boats, curious at the many configurations and conditions of the craft moored along the way. Just as she was about to take a break from her trolling for Dirk Lange and find someplace to get a cappuccino, that *feeling* came. In the back of the head, down the neck, and along her spine came the sensation, not a chill nor shiver, but something almost akin to a touch of a warm finger. She was being watched.

Don't alter your pace nor movements. Just walk a minute, stop, adjust your scarf, and gaze out at the boats. She cursed herself for leaving her sunglasses in the hotel room. *Squint. Now look around for the person or persons who are following you*. She stopped and went through her routine. Then reversed course, heading back toward the end of the pier. No sign of Lange. She strolled, placing one foot in front of another as if she was walking a line. One would suppose her in deep thought.

Still no sign of him. Suddenly came a shiver. What if it wasn't Lange who was watching her? Nabeel Asuty and his cohorts were in Cape Town. Nabeel saw her in the café in Freetown, where Stone and Lange had killed two of his men. Her pace quickened and she headed for the hotel.

Instead of waiting for the elevator, she raced up the stairs and hurried to her room. The hotel maid stood at the door, pulling her cart out of Sandra's room, about to start cleaning the one next door. Sandra tipped her, looked up and down the hallway, closed the door behind her, and leaned back on the wall. Sweat dripped down her back. Why had she lost her composure? Don't worry. The instructor at the Farm, the CIA training facility, had advised her class years ago that it happened now and then. Rarely did it happen to her.

Light knock on the door. She tensed. She reached for her Glock and carefully slid back the cover to the door's peephole. Dirk Lange's handsome face appeared through the smudged circular glass. She quickly let him in.

"Did you just check in? I see that you haven't fully unpacked," Lange asked.

She eyed his black turtleneck shirt under a brown leather jacket. With his sandy blond hair and close-cropped beard, it all came together. Quite attractive.

"Don't know how long I'll be here. Besides, I get tired packing and unpacking." She pointed to one of the armchairs for him to sit. "I thought I sensed you following me." She sat on the edge of the bed. "How long have you been in town?"

"Two days. Did you see our friends from Freetown?"

"Nabeel Asuty?"

"Nabeel and some of his *chinas*," Lange said.

"His what?"

"A South African term for one's buddies."

"Should I have seen Asuty?"

Lange stood and stepped to the window. Keeping to the side, he carefully tilted one of the blinds. "I spotted them just after I got a glimpse of you. You were wandering around Victoria Wharf for me to make contact. Yes?"

She mumbled a yes, went over to the other side of the window, and looked down from the second floor onto the walkway bordering the moored boats. Her instincts had proved right. Lange had spotted her and had waited to make contact. Whether Nabeel was looking for her or not, more importantly, he was in the area.

"Where did you see them last?" she asked.

"Two blocks from here." He pulled out a phone. "Pardon, while I make a call to my partner." He talked with a fellow operative and flipped the phone closed. "Nabeel and his boys will pass by in a jiff."

Down below, only a few people sauntered by, most holding something to eat or drink. Directly across from the window, not twenty yards away, two bearded men stood in the stern of a motorboat that needed a fresh coat of paint. They were watching the passersby intently.

"There they are," Lange said. "Uh. Oh. What's that all about?" He took his phone from his pocket and spoke to his contact.

Sandra saw five men coming from the left, appearing to head for the boat where the two bearded men waited. One of the five men was Farley Durrell. Something was wrong—Asuty held Farley's right arm, a large thuggish-looking man with a prominent bald spot grasped the other. He was being taken for a reluctant boat ride.

She heard Lange's phone click shut. "That fellow down there is in a bit of a bind. Doesn't look Middle Eastern."

"He's Polish-American. One of ours. He's in deep shit."

Now Lange yanked the blinds apart. "I have only one chap to assist. Don't know if the three of us have the time. Could call the Harbor Police "

"Forget it. Help me open the window." She pulled out her

gun. "Just a few inches."

"What?"

"No time. He must have blown his cover. He's a dead man if we don't do something now." She watched the group below prepare to board. One of the two waiting men went forward in the boat and started the engines. White diesel smoke rose from the stern.

"We can't start a firefight with all these tourists here!" Lange clutched her arm. She pulled free.

"Only one shot is necessary," Sandra said, amazed at what she was about to do. "I'm shooting Farley."

"Good God! You people will take out one of your own?"

Sandra knelt, rested the Glock on the windowsill to steady her aim, judged the distance, held her breath, and fired. She watched the bullet tear a chunk of cloth from Farley Durrell's right pant leg. "Not kill him. Just shoot him in the leg."

"Good shot! Can't believe my bloody eyes."

Down along the walkway, people scattered at the sound of the shot. Asuty's men drew their weapons and looked in all directions except up at them. Farley Durrell had fallen, but rose and hobbled away from the group. Two of Asuty's men jumped into the boat. Police whistles sounded from both directions. A siren wailed.

"We best be out of here," Lange urged. "Good thing you didn't unpack." He hurried over to the couch and threw her clothes into the open suitcase. "I'll check the bath for any of your belongings."

Sandra watched Farley, who had distanced himself from Asuty's thugs, stumble into the arms of a large redheaded policewoman, who held him upright. She grimaced. "Typical Farley."

"Where to, *maat*?" Lange called.

"Stone's room. Downstairs at the other end of the hotel." Sandra shut the window and closed her suitcase. Where was Stone when she needed him? With some old squeeze?

• • • •

At the seaside villa of Abdul Wahab, the butler, Dingane, observed the girl dust Lady Beatrice's grand piano with haphazard flips of her wrist. She stared off to some distant place. Dreaming into the eyes of her new boyfriend, Dingane surmised.

He startled her, speaking in Fanagalo, the half Zulu, half pidgin English spoken in the mines where her parents lived. "If the mistress of the house, Lady Beatrice, catches you slacking, lazy girl, it's the end. Hand me that." He took the feather duster from her and demonstrated how she should use it. He thrust it back. "Now do it correctly."

The girl returned to her task, now chastened. Dingane continued on his rounds of the villa, assuring that the staff was not shirking its duties. His wife remained in bed this morning. She said her stomach had cramps, blaming the *tokoloshe*, ground-hugging night gremlins. "He visited last night when I slept, I'm sure," she moaned. "Build me a bed of bricks to stay off the floor to keep him away."

He berated her for bringing up old myths, reminding her they were Christians. However, this afternoon he would arrange to get bricks from his cousin, who worked at the villa down the road. Building a traditional brick bed was preferable to her going to that old hag witch doctor.

He paused in the foyer, inspected the floor for dirt and the two Greek marble busts for dust. None. He stopped and sighed. His family had become a strain. Lady Beatrice had arranged a scholarship for their son, but the boy was more interested in playing his *igopogo*, the oil can guitar contraption favored by the South African bands. The young men in this new South Africa had many temptations. He was the only child who lived after his beloved wife's six pregnancies, and Dingane knew they spoiled him. He must watch his son, or he would become a *tsotsis*, a young gangster roaming the streets.

Noise from outside interrupted his thoughts. From behind the carved oak door, he heard a car stop in front of the house and two doors open and slam shut. A hard knock on the door immediately followed. Must be rude visitors for madame's husband. He looked in the TV monitor covering the outside entrance and saw that despicable man, Nabeel Asuty, with another ugly Middle Easterner. Both men looked around nervously as if they were fleeing from someone or thing. Dingane took his time opening the door.

"I want to speak with Abdul Wahab," Nabeel said, not looking at Dingane. "I must see him."

Dingane arched his back, as he had seen the British butlers do in old films, and said, using his best English diction, "I shall see if the master is receiving guests." As he turned to go to the sitting room, he noted with humor the man's face contort with anger.

He found Abdul Wahab and Lady Beatrice sitting on the opposite sides of the room, both reading portions of *The Star*, the Cape Town daily newspaper. Beatrice lifted her eyes and asked who was at the door. When told, she shouted at Wahab. "Damn it to hell, Abdul. I told you to keep those swarthy buggers out of my home." Wahab rushed from the room.

She called after Dingane. "Keep an eye on them."

He nodded and went back to the foyer where Wahab was leading an agitated Nabeel to the library. The other man, who had a prominent bald spot, remained standing. Dingane motioned for him to sit. The man scowled and sat roughly into a chair. Dingane couldn't help thinking how inappropriate it was that the delicate French armchair should host the backsides of such a crude person. Intending to keep a watch on him, Dingane busied himself sorting the morning mail on the table.

"*Ureed ma'*," the man shouted in Arabic.

Dingane feigned ignorance, but knew the man had asked for water.

The order came again as if *he*, Dingane, was the inferior, only there to do this man's bidding. Again, Dingane acted as if he didn't understand, and the man rose, making a cupping motion with his hands. At this, Dingane's wife appeared.

"My dear. How do you feel?" he asked in Zulu.

She made various faces that said she felt better, but not much better, and glowering at the visitor, asked in Zulu, "What is this pig doing here?"

"Fouling the place," Dingane said. "He has ordered water."

"Shall I get it while you wait here with him?"

"Yes. Take your time. Make it warm and dirty it."

Dingane leaned on the opposite wall and motioned to the man that his water would come. The man looked away, not bothering to conceal the pistol in his belt. Perspiration ran down his neck.

Dingane heard the faint voices of Wahab and Nabeel coming from the library. Obviously, something was amiss, as Lady Beatrice was wont to say. That husband of hers was trouble. Much trouble. He remembered the time Lady Beatrice and he had that short conversation out in the gardens.

"You Zulus don't have problems with multiple wives, do you?" she had asked.

Somehow, he had always thought it odd that she had mentioned the fact that Wahab had another wife in Saudi Arabia. However, from the time he had told her that his blood was royal Zulu, the two of them had formed an understanding.

He had answered her, "Not with Zulus, no, mum, but one must remember it was allowed in the holy book, the Old Testament."

She had thrown her head back and laughed. "But Dingane, my good man, that helps me not. I'm all New Testament."

From down the hallway the pantry door creaked, then closed. Without seeing, he knew Lady Beatrice had switched on the recorder hidden behind the side panel. Later on today, she would retrieve a little black object from the machine, which no doubt held the conversation of her husband and that vile man, Nabeel Asuty.

Before dinnertime, Dingane could expect to be paid a visit from his friend in the South African Secret Service wanting to know about the visit of these two Arabs. Two days ago his friend said he would bring another person from the SASS who was interested in questioning him about both Wahab and Lady Beatrice. Dingane had no trouble providing information on Wahab; however, they need not know about Lady Beatrice's suspicions of her husband and things like her electronic device.

The SASS people would be happy enough when he handed them the water glass with the fingerprint impressions of this bald-headed thug.

Abdul Wahab allowed Nabeel to rant. Both remained standing in the middle of the book-lined library. Nabeel's dark face glistened with sweat, which in Wahab's mind made him appear even more unctuous. They spoke in Arabic.

"We were infiltrated! They placed this man within our group. This, this Englishman."

"Who is *they*?" Wahab demanded. "And who is this man?"

"The British MI6. I'm certain." Nabeel paced and wiped his face with a dirty handkerchief. "He is English. A convert to our faith, he insisted."

"Who allowed this Englishman into the group? Why was he allowed in? Why was I not informed?"

The number of questions appeared to slow Nabeel's fuming. He ceased pacing. "Our group decided he was of value. He had contacts with airlines and shipping companies. He was very devout."

Wahab eased into his chair at the desk and studied the man standing before him. In a way, it was a pleasure to watch him squirm. Truth of the matter, he neither knew nor cared about Nabeel's group of thugs. They were all uneducated, except for their reading the Koran, and had one-track minds—jihad and the destruction of Western civilization. He asked again, "Why was I not informed about bringing in a Westerner?"

Nabeel shrugged. "It seemed of little consequence at the time."

"Let me go over this again. You discovered this man was a spy. You neglected to say how you found out, but that matters little right now. You planned to take him in a boat to the middle of the bay and kill him. What happened at the wharf?"

"Someone shot him."

"Your people shot him on the pier? Why?"

"No. Most strange. None of my people fired. Someone else

did. The police came and arrested two of my men because they found they were carrying guns. Mohammed, sitting outside, and I escaped and came here."

"You came directly here, you idiot!"

"No. We took a roundabout route. One other member of our group escaped. Don't know his whereabouts." Nabeel folded his arms across his chest. He didn't like being called an idiot. "The Englishman was taken away by the police."

Wahab leaned forward and rested his arms on the desk. His beautiful plan for a major terrorist blow was unraveling. Van Wartt demanded that he take possession of the nuclear device within the next few days. Now they were minus two men and didn't have sufficient manpower to transport the nuclear weapon.

"When we take possession of the bomb, we need at least six people to transport it to ... Where have you planned to take it?" Wahab asked, realizing that he had mistakenly placed a great deal of the plan in the hands of this fool.

Nabeel regained his composure. "Where is the bomb now?"

"Up north in the desert. How and to where will we move it?"

"We were thinking to Douala, Cameroon."

"Who are we?"

"The Englishman had contacts with a shipping company. Now, that plan is—"

"How did you discover he was a spy?"

"By chance. He wanted a woman and we all went to a whorehouse he knew. We caught him passing a piece of paper, a message of some kind, to one of the prostitutes. A fight broke out between the Englishman and two of our men. We were thrown out by the pimps."

"Where were you at the time?"

Nabeel looked down at the floor. "In one of the rooms. Busy."

That poor woman, thought Wahab. Having to share a bed with this slime. He gathered himself. "My good friend. Things have gone astray, but we shall prevail. The greatest strike against the infidel is in our grasp. Go. Stay alert and await my call."

Nabeel blinked, turned, and hesitated with his hand on the

doorknob. "One more thing. That man Hayden Stone is in Cape Town. I will find him and kill him."

"I told you before, Stone is mine." Wahab rose. "I'll show you out."

After he watched Nabeel and his man drive off, Wahab asked Dingane to bring him a cup of fresh coffee. Back in the library, he eased the door shut, hoping his wife would not interrupt him with a tirade on Nabeel's visit. He needed time and quiet to think. The plan to explode the nuclear device off the shores of Los Angeles, San Francisco, or Tel Aviv needed immediate fixing. After an hour the realization came that his control of events was tenuous. Perhaps, control had never been in his hands.

Wahab thought back to the events on the Riviera and how all his plans, organization, and contacts had been lost. The support and trust of his benefactor, the prince, father of his first wife, had vanished. Saudi Arabia barred him from his homeland. Al Qaeda and other terrorist groups mistrusted him. The French intelligence service made him flee his beloved South of France. The CIA wanted retribution for his hand in the deaths of two of their operatives, and they had sent Hayden Stone to settle the score. As for Stone, the man had constantly hounded him from Afghanistan, to the Riviera, to here in Africa.

Perhaps Stone was not the jinn he had believed, haunting and hounding him. The fault might lie within. He picked up his worn copy of the *Canterbury Tales* from the table, opened it, and saw the Middle English text. He thought of his Oxford don in the worn cardigan sweater and his days as a student in England. A young Arab in a strange, fascinating world that he had reluctantly grown to love.

Wahab laid the book on the desk, keeping his hand on the leather binding. He heard his English wife's voice from beyond the closed door. He closed his eyes and wondered, who was he, really?

CHAPTER TWENTY

CAPE TOWN—AUGUST 18, 2002

As Dawid van Wartt maneuvered the curves of Kloof Road, he pressed down on the accelerator, enjoying the power of his new Bentley coupe. The way the car held to the road impressed him. At least something was going well today.

The first thing that morning, he had received an urgent telephone call from the manager of his real estate firm. A sizable group of trade unionists were demonstrating in front of his main commercial building downtown. The reason given by the strikers to the press was "inadequate wages" for their maintenance people. What had really happened was Van Wartt's corporation had been late and parsimonious with the requisite *omkoop*, the bribes to the union leaders. A second phone call determined that certain politicians had offered to help in easing tensions—that meant more bribes. Such was the cost of doing business in South Africa.

The visit later that morning from his friend from Namibia, Bull Rhyton, concerned him most. A little before noon, Bull had phoned and said he was outside the gate of Van Wartt's villa and had to speak to him. Van Wartt met the burly, unshaven man and led him to the garden. They sat in the warm sun on a concrete garden bench. In the cooled winter ground, a few flowers gave off weak fragrances while a brown and black bird fluttered in the bladdernut tree directly above them. Stretching below, the houses and buildings of Cape Town sparkled. Farther out, ships crisscrossed a calm bay.

Quick pleasantries were exchanged and at last Bull got to

the point of his visit. His voice carried an edge. In Afrikaans, he addressed Van Wartt using his nickname. "Dawie, this morning my nephew phoned me. He said two weeks ago he saw two men by the boxcar. They broke inside."

"Two weeks ago? You just came from Bruin Karas. You hear this now?"

"He knew he was to stay away from the boxcar. His mother found out and made him call me."

"Did these two men who broke inside take anything out?"

"No. Corneliu said when they came out of the boxcar, they acted concerned. One had an instrument in his hand. I suppose it was a Geiger counter."

Van Wartt frowned. "Then what?"

"They left on an ATV. Headed west, Corneliu said. Out of sight. However, going back home, my nephew saw a helicopter fly."

"The two men weren't locals?" Van Wartt guessed the answer.

Bull shook his head. "Do you know who they were?"

An unexpected turn of events. Van Wartt searched for the right words. He knew that however he explained it, Bull would be unhappy, disappointed. "I neglected to tell you. I formulated a backup plan. I reasoned we must get rid of the bomb quickly, one way or another."

Bull Rhyton ground his boots in the gravel beneath the bench. His eyes didn't blink. Finally, he said, "*Ja*?"

"I offered the bomb to the Libyans."

Bull cursed and spat. He used Van Wartt's formal name. "Dawid. The Libyans and our new ruling party, the ANC, have been in league for years. They supplied the explosives and guns that killed our people. Why did you deal with *them*?"

"It was only a backup plan. In the event these jihadists wouldn't take the bomb." Van Wartt lifted his hands. "How they found the boxcar, I don't know. What they intend to do, I don't know."

Bull turned his face away. When he looked back at Van Wartt, he said coldly, "You assume it is the Libyans. Maybe someone else knows about it. My nephew said they looked European."

"*Ja.* They may not be Libyans." Van Wartt folded his arms. *Then who for God's sake are they?*

Van Wartt stood, started pacing, stopped, and whispered, "We have to move quickly. I'll contact Abdul Wahab and tell him he has to take possession of the nuclear device within two days." He sat down. "Can we move it somewhere else?"

"The damn thing is leaking radiation! Who will move it? Not me. Not my kin." He slapped his leg. "This is all bad. We've gotten ourselves in too deep with these evil people. I don't like it anymore."

"Think what these hypocrites in America and the West have done to us."

"Dawid, we have been through much, hey? We have fought together up in Angola. Truly I believe this plan has gotten out of control. We must give the bomb back to the government." He waited for a response from Van Wartt and, getting none, rose. "I'll let myself out."

Van Wartt watched the big man push past the guard, open the gate, and leave. Bull should have been told about the Libyans, but he had known what his reaction would be. He would have objected just like he had now.

He lingered on the bench and lit a cigarette. The words of his father came to him: In Africa, the strong eat, the weak are eaten. He crushed the cigarette under his shoe and looked again at the beautiful city below. The damn Americans and Europeans were responsible for the embargo of his country during apartheid. Making his people pariahs to the world. His Afrikaner people became hated and made scapegoats for the West's own failings. Forcing them to relinquish control of their government, of their country. America deserved the Twin Towers attack. Many of his friends had cheered when they watched the burning towers on TV. See how it feels, you sons of bitches, his friends had shouted.

Two minutes after Van Wartt hastened back inside his villa, the brown and black bird tipped forward, lifted from the branch with a flurry of its wings, and sailed down the mountain.

• •

The meeting with Bull Rhyton had disturbed Van Wartt, but as the Bentley neared the Camps Bay residential area, he rehearsed what he would say to Wahab. The man had been dragging his feet. Was it the money? He had assumed these terrorists had an inexhaustible supply of funds. Perhaps Wahab didn't have the network he claimed to have. Today he must get a timetable from that man.

More and more the need for revenge against the Americans and Europeans took a backseat for the need to dispose of this nuclear device as soon as possible. Bull's uneasiness, no, hostility to the plan, disturbed him.

Van Wartt found Abdul Wahab not in the fish and chips restaurant as agreed, but across the road. Here the ocean edged Victoria Road. The sea floor dropped dramatically, and at certain times of the year Southern Right whales came up, almost within touching distance, exhaling water from their blowholes. Wahab stood with the other onlookers gaping at two immense mammals surfacing in the black water.

Van Wartt stepped up next to him. "Fascinating animals, no?"

Wahab continued to look ahead. He appeared disturbed.

"Abdul. Shall we walk along the shore?"

"I decided to forgo a meal of fish and chips," Wahab said. "If you don't mind?"

"I agree. We do have important business to discuss, and this is a perfect place for it."

"Why are there no waves along here?" Wahab asked. "There is surf where I live."

"Deep water. No waves," Van Wartt said impatiently. "Will you be ready in two days to travel north and pick up the … package?"

Wahab stopped, looked around. "We are experiencing a delay. It's a matter of getting enough people. We had a setback.

I need more men for my team."

Van Wartt thought a moment. "Damn! Those Arabs who were involved in the shooting at Victoria Wharf were your men." Getting no answer from Wahab, he said, "Dammit to hell!"

"A minor setback. As we speak my headman is obtaining additional men." Wahab looked directly at Van Wartt. "Not to worry. The plan goes forward." He looked away as if he knew he failed to be convincing.

"You have two days from now. Call me tomorrow at this number. I would be most appreciative having an update tomorrow."

Wahab pronounced, now more evenly, "I shall, if I can. If not … *maleesh*." He shrugged and walked away.

Van Wartt cursed and hurried to the Bentley. He had to contact the Libyan chargé in Pretoria and set up an emergency meeting to determine if it was the Libyans who Bull's nephew had seen two weeks ago up in the Kalahari.

CHAPTER TWENTY-ONE

CAPE TOWN—AUGUST 18, 2002

Hayden Stone watched Sandra fidget and fret while driving the rental car. They had just left the city and were heading for a conference called by the ambassador. The meeting was to be held at the official ambassador's residence, a distance from center city in a treed suburb. The ambassador promised a *braai* afterward. Since COS Fleming didn't want them staying at Victoria Wharf after the shooting incident, the two would then head for the safe house.

Fleming had phoned and advised that Ambassador Bunting wanted the meeting at three o'clock in order to hash out issues that had come to his attention. One issue on the agenda was Sandra's putting a bullet in Farley Durrell's leg. True, she had saved Farley from being murdered by Nabeel Asuty and his thugs and should be commended by her superiors for quick thinking, if not flair for improvising, but both knew their bureaucracy would view the action outside the norm. As very "sticky." Administrative criticism could be expected.

Shifting her weight and hitting the wheel with both hands, Sandra let out a long groan. "This mission sucks! Nothing has gone right. I want to go back to Paris."

"Pull over. I'll drive," Stone said, and surprisingly she pulled off onto a dirt shoulder. Stone hoped he'd have the good sense to remain silent and allow her to talk, tell him her concerns.

The surrounding neighborhood consisted of elegant homes placed on expansive lots. Traffic had been almost nonexistent since leaving the city, but as they exited and walked around the car to change positions, a black SUV approached from the other direction, slowed, and stopped opposite them.

The moment the SUV's windows lowered, Stone, standing in the open, yelled, "Take cover!"

His Sig Sauer was out at the same time gun barrels emerged from the front and rear windows of the SUV. Bullets whizzed by Stone's head and slammed into the car. The windshield shattered behind him.

Stone ducked behind the open driver's door, using it as a shield. He returned fire.

Crouching in front of the grille, Sandra began shooting with a controlled two-shot sequence. By now the front window of the rental was gone. The attackers' rounds penetrated the car door Stone used for cover. Gun empty, he needed the other magazine inside the pocket of his coat, which was lying on the car seat.

He dove headlong into the car and squirmed over to the passenger side. Finding the spare magazine in his coat, he scrambled out the other side.

Sandra had shifted position from the front of the car to the trunk area and was in the midst of reloading. The SUV crept along the road, maintaining rapid fire. Reloaded, Stone bent down next to Sandra and steadied his pistol with both hands. He aimed and fired at the SUV's tailgate window. The window fell apart, revealing a bearded man in sunglasses.

Stone lined his sights and eased off two rounds. The man's sunglasses flew from his face, and his gun dropped out of the vehicle. The driver accelerated, peeling rubber from the SUV's rear tires.

The two watched the vehicle disappear. Out of breath, they leaned on the car's trunk. She said, "Good thing they left. I'm out of ammo."

Examining his Sig Sauer, Stone said, "Not a bad weapon. Fairly accurate. I nailed one of them."

"By my count, there were two more. One looked like Nabeel Asuty."

They straightened and looked around. No movement came from the nearby homes. Either they were accustomed to gunfire in their neighborhood, or were wise enough to stay indoors when shootings occurred.

"I'll phone for help," Sandra said. "This car isn't going anywhere. A bullet must have hit a hose in the engine compartment. Hear the hissing?"

In less than ten minutes, a car arrived from the ambassador's residence. Owen, dreadlocks flopping, who the two had met at the safe house the previous night, jumped out. After assuring neither required medical attention, he inspected the rental car. "The rental company won't like this, but then carjackings aren't unusual here." He ordered them into his car. "We have to get out of here in case they return."

They retrieved their luggage from the trunk while Owen checked the inside of the car for any belongings. Before getting into the car, Stone ran over and with his handkerchief picked up the pistol that had dropped out of the SUV. He came back and asked, "Shouldn't we gather up our brass?"

Owen looked puzzled.

"The brass. The expended cartridges lying on the ground." After Stone had said it, the absurdity of the question hit him. "Guess we shouldn't be worried about the crime scene." Handing the pistol to him, Stone said, "Here's one of their guns. We may get a make on a fingerprint."

They drove away at a normal speed. Owen asked Stone, sitting in the backseat, to check behind them for any suspicious cars, and he began a dry-cleaning run along the back roads to the ambassador's home.

Sandra spoke up. "I'll bet Nabeel Asuty's pissed."

"Stupid move on his part," Stone said. "Makes me wonder why he did it, and if they are the terrorists who want the bomb, why are they still here in Cape Town?"

CHAPTER TWENTY-TWO

CAPE TOWN—AUGUST 18, 2002

Hayden Stone watched people file into the high-ceilinged room used by the ambassador as an informal meeting area. French provincial chairs had been arranged in a circle. Two of the room's walls, painted a rich yellow, darkened as the afternoon shadows advanced. Colonel Gustave Frederick stood next to him, waiting for the stragglers before he began his briefing.

"I guess that little fracas out on the road got your juices flowing," Frederick said.

"It got my attention," Stone said, coming down from the adrenaline rush caused by the gunfight. His stomach growled and he felt edgy. A drink would help.

"Glad headquarters is on the ball, sending you here to smooth this operation."

The COS, Charles Fleming, entered the room and introduced Colonel Frederick to the assembled group, which included the base chief, Houston, and the four agency people, whom Stone had met at the safe house. Then Fleming said, "The ambassador wants to talk with us—oh, here he is."

Ambassador Bunting rushed in and told Frederick that he wanted to speak alone with him and Stone and Sandra. The four gathered by the fireplace, and Bunting came to the point.

"These shootings have put the embassy in a delicate position." He raised his hand, knowing Frederick would protest. "I know your actions were reactive, well for the most part, but the South Africans are sensitive about firearms. Certain unfriendly factions would have a heyday with these two shootings."

"So far we haven't been identified or connected with the incidents," Stone said.

"So far."

Frederick said, "I plan to send these two to Namibia tomorrow. That should allay your concerns."

"Wait 'till the ambassador up in Namibia hears."

Stone said, "We hope to have this problem solved before anyone knows we're there."

"Considering the serious nature of this mission, it better be quick," Bunting said. As he left he told Frederick, "I'll let you conduct your meeting."

To the group Colonel Frederick went over the situation and the obstacles they faced. CIA Headquarters considered the nuclear device up in Namibia a top priority and had sent him to oversee the operation.

"Are we going north to Namibia to seize that thing?" Houston asked.

Colonel Frederick held up his hand. "Before we get into specifics, let me tell you what Langley cabled to us an hour ago. As you are aware, we have a fix on the nuclear device, which is located in the southern region of Namibia on the fringe of the Kalahari Desert.

"Two weeks ago our satellite tracked two, rather, four men, identities unknown, scoping out the boxcar that has the nuclear device inside. They flew in by helicopter and two of them searched the boxcar, entered it, and took some readings. They took off and flew north toward Angola."

Stone said, "Two weeks ago? That's quite a time delay. Do we know where in Angola?"

"No," Fleming interjected. "For some reason they lost coverage. Maybe technical."

"Our people in Angola are attempting to identify the helicopter. They have make, model, and markings. It had a peculiar livery and logo, probably bogus."

"What is the station in Windhoek doing?" Stone said.

"The COS in Windhoek is stateside in the hospital." Colonel Frederick pointed to Fleming. "Since you're the backup

COS for Namibia, that will smooth administrative issues." He looked at Stone and Sandra. "We have to step lightly, especially after that ambush today. The ambassador expects to take heat from the South African officials. Apparently they feel they have enough problems with the homeboys shooting each other. They don't need to import sideshows."

The snickers from the three men from the safe house disturbed Stone. He expected more from them, no matter how unseasoned they appeared. Across from him Sandra stiffened when Colonel Frederick turned in her direction.

Frederick regarded his notes. "Sandra. Very quick thinking on your part, by the way. You saved a fellow case officer's life. Well done."

Sandra relaxed and shot Stone a look of relief. Both now knew where Colonel Frederick stood regarding Sandra shooting Farley Durrell. He was definitely in her corner.

"Back to those four men up there in the desert," Stone said. "Any indication they were Abdul Wahab's people? Or Van Wartt's group?"

"Houston, did you research that?" Colonel Frederick asked.

"We've tracked Wahab and Van Wartt in town. No linkage between the unknowns and either man." Houston paused. "But here's something. Our bird, that is drone, picked up a meeting yesterday between Van Wartt and a fellow from Namibia. The two were sitting outside Van Wartt's residence. Believe the fellow's name is Rhyton. We're checking him out. Anyway, both seemed on edge. When Rhyton left, Van Wartt drove to a gas station and called the Libyan consulate. Later he met a man at the Bo-Kaap Museum."

"What's that?" Sandra asked.

"It features Cape Muslim culture."

"This guy. Did you ident him?" Stone asked.

"Looked North African, but nobody we know from the Libyan consulate."

Stone looked at Colonel Frederick. "Could be an intelligence officer from Libya."

There were a few nods among the group.

Stone continued, "Now about the bomb. We've got to take possession before Wahab's people get there."

"That's one of our hang-ups," Colonel Frederick said. "We don't have the aircraft or ships in the vicinity to take something like this on. The navy is sending an amphibious ship with marines and helicopters, but won't be in position to launch a team for at least forty-eight hours."

"We could neutralize the opposition." Stone's suggestion met silence.

Finally, Colonel Frederick said in a quiet voice, "Van Wartt is a South African national, and we can't touch him on his home turf. As for Abdul Wahab." He looked at Fleming, who squirmed in his seat. "Let's forget about Wahab for the time being. The people he's dealing with are the major targets. What's that man's name who is working for Wahab?"

Stone caught Sandra's eye. She'd picked up on the same undertone. *Why was Abdul Wahab off limits all of a sudden?*

Fleming spoke up. "Nabeel Asuty. The one who today tried to kill our colleagues here. Asuty's the guy who's gathering men to take possession of the bomb."

Colonel Frederick said, "Stone, I want you and Sandra to fly to Namibia. Secure that boxcar. Leave here early tomorrow."

Stone nodded and turned to Sandra, who seemed to be thinking the same thing he was. How in hell would they to travel to the Kalahari Desert, find the boxcar, and secure it for two days?

"We'll provide logistical support from the station," Fleming offered. "We have a plane available."

Houston said, "You'll need a little more than water bottles and field rations. You need some local support up there."

"We'll ask the South African intelligence officer Dirk Lange to come along," Stone said.

"I don't know about—"

"Do you two trust him?" Colonel Frederick asked.

Both Stone and Sandra nodded.

"Make it happen." Frederick looked around. "That's it for the time being. Let's see what kind of game the ambassador has cooking on the grill."

Stone watched the people file out of the room and head for the patio area where the ambassador was hosting his function. Fleming held back at the doorway, directing his question to Frederick. "Bringing in this South African, Dirk Lange, can create problems. I know he helped Sandra save Farley Durrell's life, but it's best to vet his background before we let him in on our operation."

"Stone dealt with him in Freetown," Colonel Frederick said, pointing his thumb in Stone's direction. "He trusts him, and we need someone with local knowledge to help us."

"I'm sorry, Stone," Fleming said, "but when you get Lange, you get his security service. That's a little dicey now with the turnover in the South African Security Service. The old hands are bailing out and the new people are political appointees."

"You've a point," Colonel Frederick said. "How soon can you get a decent vet on him?"

"By tomorrow morning," Fleming said, heading for the door.

Colonel Frederick turned to Stone. "A moment of your time. You too, Sandra."

They moved to a corner of the room, and Colonel Frederick asked, "Have you seen Jacob?"

Stone told him about the meeting on Victoria and Albert's Wharf and how Jacob expressed concern about Wahab and Nabeel Asuty. Jacob knew Van Wartt wanted to sell them arms. "We know now that it's a nuclear bomb he wants to peddle."

"We have to contact Jacob," Colonel Frederick said. "I want to talk with him while you're up in the desert." He touched Sandra's arm. "Get in touch with Dirk Lange. Ask him to contact Jacob, in case Stone can't. Ask Lange if he can accompany you two to Namibia. I'm going to assume Fleming doesn't find anything too negative on him."

"I'll have to tell Lange about the nuclear device. So far, we haven't discussed it."

Frederick thought a moment, and Stone knew he might change his mind. "Colonel, I wouldn't doubt that he knows something about it already."

"All right. Just tell him we know about the bomb. That it's up in Namibia and Van Wartt wants to sell it to Wahab." Frederick pointed his finger at Sandra. "Don't divulge our sources."

"I'll see if I can meet with him tonight," Sandra said. She hurried out the room, calling back to Stone, "I'll be in touch."

Stone felt charged. The mission was straightforward. He'd be flying to a fascinating part of the world, the Kalahari. The orders were clear-cut. Keep the bomb out of the hands of the bad guys. He'd be working with two trusted, competent individuals. What could be better? *Stone, you're back in business.*

Stone made his way through the living and dining rooms to the patio where guests had gathered. All wore coats or sweaters against the early evening chill. He stopped, looked around, and saw Patience St. John Smythe heading in his direction.

"Hi there, sport," she said, affecting an Afrikaner accent. "Let's sink some tinnies and whack some steaks on the grill."

"I see you've gone native."

"I am sort of a native. Now about the last time we saw each other." She moved close and whispered, "Appreciate you not mentioning our meeting in front of my beau. He's the jealous type."

"Gotcha."

"Thank you. Now when we met last I mentioned a surprise was coming to town." Her eyes had that mischievous look that was absent when they talked at the cheetah sanctuary. "Come with me." She took his hand.

They passed two open grills emitting heat from the charcoal embers and stepped up to the bar, behind which sat stacks of game meat ready for cooking.

"You better have a stiff one," she motioned to the bartender. "An Irish whiskey for this gentleman." Her eyes softened. "Heard about the incident on the road. You okay?"

"Yes. Thanks for asking, and thanks for remembering my drink of choice. I can use it."

Handing him his drink, she said, "Save your thanks for the time being. Let's walk over there."

As they walked toward a group of four people, Stone's attention was directed to a woman whose back was turned. Dressed in a stylish gray pants suit, with a beige cashmere ruana draped over her shoulders, something about the way she stood looked familiar. The woman's auburn hair was identical to—

"Hayden," Patience said. "May I introduce a friend of yours?"

The woman turned. Stone froze.

Contessa Lucinda Avoscani.

Patience tugged at his sleeve. "Hayden? Say something."

With his face flushed, and now tongue-tied, he knew he looked foolish in front of the other guests. Before him stood his former lover, whose last words to him were she never wanted to see, nor speak to him again. Ever. What was she about to do?

The answer came when Lucinda took his face in both hands and kissed him gently, not on the cheek, but full on the mouth. She stepped back. No look of hate that he'd expected. Her emerald green eyes had a touch of mystery he'd never seen before.

She broke the silence. "Hello, Hayden. I have missed you."

CHAPTER TWENTY-THREE

CAPE TOWN—AUGUST 18, 2002

Standing in front of the ambassador's guests, Hayden Stone remained speechless. Contessa Lucinda stood next to him with her hand on his sleeve. Patience was enjoying her little game. She hugged Lucinda and babbled about how wonderful it was to play a surprise on two old friends.

Ambassador Bunting's sudden appearance gave Stone time to regroup. "Time to eat," Bunting said. The chefs are taking orders." He gave Stone a curious look. "Don't believe we've met socially."

"Marshall, this is Hayden Stone, an old friend of Lucinda's. We've gotten these two together after some absence."

"A pleasure, Ambassador." Bunting had a strong handshake. Did he suspect about Patience and his past relationship?

Bunting held the handshake a second too long. "Ready for your trip tomorrow?"

Both women said, "Oh!" simultaneously.

"Just for a few days," Stone said.

"We'd better give you two some time together." As Patience led Bunting away, she threw a glance back. "Don't forget to give your orders to the chefs."

Stone and Lucinda faced each other. Her eyes searched his. He sensed an awkward pause coming, so he began telling Lucinda how nice it was to see her again, but stopped. "Lucinda. I'm sorry about what happened on the Riviera last May. Your palace being wrecked. And about us." He stopped when he realized she wanted to speak.

"Hayden. A lot has happened in the last three months since we last spoke." She adjusted the cashmere ruana, revealing a diamond broach on her jacket. "The prince from Saudi Arabia has proved himself a perfect gentleman. He has taken all responsibility for the damage done to my home. After all, it was his man Abdul Wahab who arranged for those terrorists to lease it. The prince is not only making restitution, but is contributing to its renovation."

"The plumbing could use an upgrade."

Lucinda didn't smile. In fact, her expression announced that he was on thin ice. Just as quickly, the warmth returned. She moved close and continued, speaking in that husky voice he had missed. "You knew I was in a financial bind. That is why I rented out the palace for two months." She sighed. "Thanks to the prince's largesse, I have a few extra euros, and while my palace is being repaired I decided to come down here and look at real estate."

"How do you know Patience? I don't recall you ever mentioning her."

"In Villefranche we didn't have that much time to talk about things." She looked over at the guests gathered around the sizzling meats. "Shall we?" She motioned. "What do you suggest we have?"

The grills were lined close to the residence's brick wall. Other guests formed a queue, and the couple ahead asked the chef to identify the meats. He pointed out bratwursts, gazelle on skewers, rock lobster, and kudu steaks. On a side table he had placed creamy potatoes and an assortment of salads to accompany the meats.

"The *braai* is a tradition in southern Africa," Stone explained. "Men do the cooking, and in the bush it's done over an open fire." He pointed to the steaks on the left side. "That kudu is very lean. One of the tastiest game meats I've had. I suggest asking for it cooked medium rare."

"My, Hayden, you seem to know your way around Africa." She removed her ruana and handed it to him. "I don't recall you mentioning that you spent time here."

Both said simultaneously, "But we didn't have that much time." They laughed.

Their plates holding kudu and lobster, they took seats at a table set with white linen and silverware with Patience, Ambassador Bunting, and Gus Frederick. Stone introduced Lucinda to Colonel Frederick.

"Oh. Colonel," said Lucinda. "I do recall a friend back home speaking about you recently. A French gentleman who is with the French police, or he is with the security service. No matter."

Frederick squirmed. "Ah yes. I miss the South of France."

Stone smiled. *You certainly do, Gus Frederick, and will for a while before the French allow you back*. Lucinda was still the contessa, at ease in the international social circuit and well aware of Frederick's predicament with the French authorities.

She then asked Stone when he was departing on his trip.

Colonel Frederick frowned and answered for him. "He and Sandra will be leaving early tomorrow morning." He shot a look toward Ambassador Bunting.

Sensing the ambassador had spoken out of turn in revealing the secret trip to Namibia and could use some help, Stone offered, "We have some people to meet on business. Like I told you, we'll return in a few days." He asked Lucinda, "How long will you be here?"

"I have business also. Looking at some properties. A week, perhaps."

"I'll take care of her until you get back," Patience said.

Ambassador Bunting remained quiet but at the same time listened intently to the conversation. Then he excused himself, saying he had to check on the other guests. Patience followed.

"Hosts and hostesses on the diplomatic circuit rarely get to finish their meals." Frederick looked at his watch. "Excuse me. I have to make a phone call."

Stone and Lucinda remained seated. A slight breeze whispered through the tall gum trees. Stars peeked behind the leaves. He refreshed her wine glass, and before he could ask again how she knew Patience, Lucinda placed her hand on his arm.

"I met Patience about two, three years ago at a Canadian Embassy function in Rome. We just, as you Americans say, clicked. We've been friends ever since."

"She and the ambassador get along quite well, don't they?"

"Are you jealous?" Lucinda said with a laugh.

"So you know about our past. I'm not jealous, especially with you here." Stone took a deep breath while studying her face. He had missed her more than he thought. "I'm really glad to see you again. Happier that you're not angry with me."

"Oh, I'm still angry with you. But more about that at a later time." She folded her arms. "Who is Sandra?"

"She's a colleague. We work together." Stone knew he had to be careful. "I hope you two can meet."

Lucinda said nothing. She eyed him with those green eyes, then looked off at the other guests. Her Mediterranean tan blended perfectly with the color of her suit. Her long fingers stroked her wine glass, and he expected her to say something important, but she remained silent.

Some guests had finished their meals and had begun to move toward the exit. The time approached when he would have to leave, and he wanted to reach some form of understanding with her.

Again, she spoke first. "I trust you are still in the same line of business?" She paused. "And this woman, Sandra, is also in the same work?"

He took his time answering. "Yes, I am. My intentions are to make this is my last assignment." He stopped and let her digest his words and make sure she understood what he said next. "I had planned to go to California, to be near my children. Live by the Pacific Ocean." He hesitated. "Have I picked the wrong body of water? Would the Mediterranean be a better choice?"

"We can talk about it when and if you return." She reached over and traced her finger along the scar on his right cheek. He had missed her doing that, along with hearing her husky voice. Her touch sent sensations down his body.

Patience popped back and asked them to join her in mingling with the few remaining guests. As they did, Stone saw Frederick from across the patio give him the high sign. It was time to depart. Stone took Lucinda aside and told her he'd see her again in a few days.

"Lucinda. Tonight you kissed me when we first met." He took her in his arms. "I want to kiss you good-bye."

"I would rather you not." She joined Patience, talking with an Asian couple.

SOUTH OF CAPE TOWN

The sun hung just above the horizon, shooting dull golden shafts from behind the winter clouds. Standing in the driveway of his villa, Abdul Wahab glanced at the black ocean, then turned his attention to Nabeel Asuty, who was getting out of a white sedan parked in front of the portico. Three men remained in the car as Asuty walked up.

Wahab intercepted him and directed him to the garage. "Come, Nabeel. I'll show you my car. The Jaguar XK-150—you have seen it before. It's been repaired." Keeping an eye on his visitor, Wahab led the way to the three-car garage that stood separate from the main house. He wanted to see if this man displayed any reaction to seeing the Jaguar, the one that Dingane suspected had been vandalized by Asuty's men. Had it been due to some pique, or a subtle threat on this loathsome man's part? No matter. Soon Wahab would be rid of him.

Asuty's eyes became wary. He followed Wahab to the garage, mumbling something about the chill from the sea.

"It's warmer in here." Inside, Wahab positioned himself by a window to keep an eye on the men in the car. "I had an expert do the paint job. The color is British racing green," he said in Arabic. "What do you think?"

"Very nice," Asuty said, looking away from the car. "I have news. Three men have come from Sierra Leone. That makes six for the mission, including you and me." He pulled his jacket tighter. "We can manage to move that bomb if all of us go."

"You're missing one man. The one you brought the last time you visited."

"Mohammed is no longer with us. However, he learned the location of the nuclear bomb."

Wahab wanted to ask how and why Mohammed had departed, but let him continue with his report.

"I had Mohammed watch the house of Dawid van Wartt. Yesterday a South African man, who appeared very upset, visited Van Wartt. When this man left the residence, Mohammed followed him to an airport." Asuty paused and smiled broadly. "He learned from a Lebanese woman working at the ticket counter that this man flew north to a town called Bruin Karas. It is in the Kalahari Desert."

Wahab felt perspiration form under his armpits. He drew out a handkerchief and touched his forehead. Without consulting him, this imbecile had been watching Van Wartt, Wahab's contact.

"Where is Mohammed?"

Asuty shrugged and held his hands skyward.

"Please. Be more specific."

Asuty went to an adjacent window and peered out. In almost a whisper, he said, "He was shot." Then swinging toward Wahab, said, "That *ibn el-kalb*, the son of a bitch, Hayden Stone killed him." He folded his arms and glared.

Abdul turned away and felt for the Colt snub-nosed pistol in the pocket of his tweed jacket. This piece of *khara* had attacked Hayden Stone after he had ordered him not to. Wahab debated putting a bullet in the head of this idiot, but what would he do with the body? What would he do with the three men still in the car?

"I know you are displeased to hear this news." Asuty gave him a coy smile. "But matters have progressed. I suggest we take action at once. We do not need this Afrikaner, Van Wartt. We will head north to this Bruin Karas and find the bomb and take it."

"Did we get the money to pay Van Wartt?"

Asuty appeared confused with the question. "I repeat. Van Wartt is not needed."

"You do not have the money?"

"Yes. I have it. It's in the car. But no matter. The plan moves on without your Mr. Van Wartt." Asuty opened his windbreaker. "Or, for that matter, you. Perhaps it's best you stay here in

Cape Town."

Wahab's eyes settled on the butt of an automatic pistol protruding from Asuty's belt. Wahab clicked his tongue as if he was about to admonish an errant child. He pointed out the window. Beyond the car containing Asuty's three henchmen, a silver Bentley coupe accompanied by a black van had parked at the top of the long driveway.

"Mr. Van Wartt wants his money. I do believe his people are about to take us for a trip to … Is the name of the town Bruin Karas?"

For a moment Asuty appeared confused. He moved toward Wahab. "We are armed and if Van Wartt—"

Wahab pointed again. Van Wartt had exited his Bentley. From the passenger side a very large man with a bushy moustache got out and accompanied Van Wartt as he hurried down the drive toward the garage. The van doors opened and four men, equally as large as Van Wartt's companion, showed themselves.

Van Wartt walked past the white sedan and when the driver's door inched open Van Wartt's man kicked it shut, and not looking back, followed his boss. The four men from the van jogged down the drive and stopped, two men on each side of the sedan. Before Van Wartt entered the garage, he glanced at a second-floor window of the villa. Wahab peered out the garage door window and turned his eyes in the same direction. He caught a brief glimpse of his wife, Lady Beatrice.

"Good evening, Abdul," Van Wartt said, walking through the garage door. "So happy to catch you before dinnertime."

"Dawid, your visit is an unexpected pleasure." Wahab tried for panache. "May I introduce my colleague?"

"I know who he is." Van Wartt motioned to his man to stand next to Asuty. "Nabeel Asuty. Formerly from Alexandria, Egypt. Am I correct?"

Asuty looked out at his car. His three men were being pulled out and slammed against the doors. He tensed, moved toward Van Wartt, but in one motion the man standing next to him placed a large hand on his neck, tightened the grip, and as Asuty gasped, removed the automatic from inside his waistband.

"Please, excuse me, Abdul. We don't have time for debates, no matter how much you people from the Middle East love to talk." Van Wartt rested his arm on Wahab's shoulder. "Do you have the money?"

"Yes. It's in that car."

"It had better be all there," Van Wartt said to Wahab.

"Take that matter up with Nabeel Asuty here."

"If it's not, I shall."

Asuty threw his head back as if he'd regained his composure, but for the first time in Wahab's memory, he stammered. "I ... I believe we have all the money that was agreed upon." Then appearing confident, stated, "It is urgent that this plan commence. Are you prepared to take us north to Bruin Karas?"

Van Wartt froze, then walked behind Asuty, pulled out a pistol, and rapped the back of his head. Asuty dropped down on his knees for a second, but immediately was back up. Wahab recognized in Asuty's face the hate of a killer, but what surprised Wahab was that Van Wartt exhibited the same look. Truly, Van Wartt was no stranger to violence.

Wahab tried to speak, but Van Wartt raised his hand. "Abdul. Your man here needs lessons in manners." Now he spoke in Asuty's ear. "The South African authorities are searching for you, Nabeel Asuty. One doesn't attempt to shoot American agents in Cape Town's more respectable neighborhoods. In addition, you did a bad job disposing of the body of your comrade. It's now lying on a slab at the city morgue. Your picture and the pictures of those three goons out there are on the evening television news."

"What do you suggest we do, Mr. Van Wartt?" Wahab said. "We're at your disposal. Are we not, Nabeel?" Out the window he saw two of Asuty's men forced to the van and the other one shoved back into the white sedan.

Van Wartt moved close. "Abdul. We must act fast. My men will take Asuty and his thugs to the airport that is an hour's drive from here. You will ride with me. Arrangements have been made for us to fly tonight to Namibia."

The manner in which Van Wartt's men whisked Asuty and

the three others away impressed Wahab, who after watching the vehicles speed off, invited Van Wartt into his home. The two found Lady Beatrice standing in the living room.

She wasted no time. "Do you two have time for a drink before taking off?"

Van Wartt switched on his charm. "We must be going. An unexpected opportunity arose for an unusual safari. I do hope you don't mind me taking Abdul away for a few days."

Wahab suggested to his wife that Van Wartt might care for a drink while he went and packed some clothes. In his bedroom closet he found khaki shirts, trousers, and a pair of boots, which he threw in a travel bag. He headed for the door, then went back to his chest and traded his Colt for a new 9mm Beretta M9 pistol. He loaded it and slipped it in a shoulder holster. As he turned, placing two full magazines in his jacket pocket, he was startled to find his wife standing next to him.

Beatrice looked him up and down and sighed. She placed her hand on his jacket where it covered his automatic. "You are coming back, aren't you?"

"I'm planning to."

"When you return, you'll cease this nonsense, won't you?"

She surprised him by kissing him on the cheek and again on the lips.

CHAPTER TWENTY-FOUR

SOUTH OF CAPE TOWN—AUGUST 18, 2002

The late afternoon crowd had gathered at the seaside hotel's lounge. Sandra Harrington spotted Dirk Lange sitting at the far end of the bar, nursing a Castle beer. He was smoking a cigarette, something new. The entire time she had known him, she never even caught a whiff of tobacco on his clothes. She took a seat on the barstool next to him, blocking the view of a redhead in a tight green sweater a couple of seats away, who was leaning provocatively toward Lange.

"That's a dirty habit, sport."

"The lady over there glaring at you offered it to me." With his eyes Lange indicated the redhead, who in a huff moved to the far end of the bar. "But it's not a habit."

"Cigarettes or redheads?"

Lange gave her the same boyish grin that she remembered from back in Freetown, Sierra Leone. In many ways, he reminded her of boys she knew in high school before they lost their virginity. However, Lange's clothes sense betrayed a degree of sophistication not consistent with shy men.

"When you called, you said you had something important to tell me." He looked around the bar filled with guests of the hotel and what appeared to be locals from the nearby seaside town. "You came alone?"

"Yes. Hayden is attending a function at my ambassador's residence. I would have liked to have attended. Never been to one of your barbecues." He grinned. "I said something funny?" she asked.

"Tonight our mate Hayden Stone, according to my sources, will have a big surprise."

Sandra stiffened.

"No," Lange said. "Nothing unpleasant. Just that an old friend from France flew down to see him."

She let a few seconds go by, wondering what friend he was referring to. "You seem to know an awful lot about us."

"You know my profession. You forget this is my country. My job is to know what's going on." He touched her fingers. "It's almost sundown. Let's move to that table I reserved. We can watch the sunset."

"First I'd like to ask a question. Back in Freetown, we heard that you and a gal from our embassy were, shall we say, quite close." She watched pain come to his eyes. "It ended badly?"

"Thanks to your people in Washington." His voice held an edge. "The lady, her name was Marsha, decided she'd had enough of Africa, and so she'd departed Freetown, never to be seen again." He looked away. "In the end she believed what they had told her. That I was merely recruiting her. Using her, that I didn't love her."

Sandra looked across the bar. "And both she and her superiors in Washington were wrong."

"I'm sure our table is ready."

Their table provided a view of the rough coastline with long, wide breakers coming in from the South Atlantic, the foam tinted red from the setting sun. Sharp angled mountains sat back inland looking down on homes scattered in both directions along the shore.

Although her companion ordered another beer and some chips, Sandra ordered a soft drink. For the foreseeable future she needed a clear head. It was her turn to surprise Mr. Lange.

"How would you like to come with Stone and me to Namibia?" she asked.

His eyes flickered. She waited.

"That's a big country." He looked at his beer but pushed it away. "Are we going on safari?"

"One could say that." She was pleased that he had been caught off guard. "The three of us will go up to the Kalahari and find an abandoned railroad car sitting out in the desert."

Lange came close, putting his elbows on the table. "I met with our Mossad friend Jacob this afternoon. He said that a …"

Sandra whispered, "A big explosive device."

"Yes. Your old friend Abdul Wahab desires such a device. And Dawid van Wartt is the person furnishing it." He turned and looked at the sunset. "For years, this, what you Yanks call an 'urban legend,' has been tossed about in our circles. The missing atomic bomb." He tapped his knuckles on the tabletop. "So that's where it is. Not surprising. We should have realized that Van Wartt and his crowd had stolen it."

"Did Jacob have anything else to say?"

"He wants to meet with Stone."

"I don't think that's possible, but Stone's boss, Colonel Frederick, will be in touch with him." She spoke softly. "We want to get the bomb before it falls in the hands of those madmen. We don't have much time. People we can't identify have been snooping around the boxcar."

"I'm not sure I can tell anyone at my home office about this. Things are a bit confused there nowadays." Lange tapped her hand. "There are some people in the new government who would go *befok* to have this thing. For the prestige and power, if you understand what I mean."

"We need your knowledge of the area. Is there anyone you can trust in your organization?"

"Of course, but it would take time to tell them." Lange said as if making a formal declaration, "I'll come with you."

"We leave tomorrow."

"I suggest we travel there as if we were on safari," he said. "Ever been on safari?"

"No, but my people will be able to round up the necessary guns and gear." She rose. "Thanks for the drink. I'll be in touch."

She hesitated and remained seated on the edge of the chair. "By the way. What was that big surprise for Hayden?"

"Some baroness is in town to see him."

"Do you mean a contessa?"

"Pardon. That's it, a contessa. I'm told she has a thing for him."

"I believe you're right." Sandra strode out of the bar. Last thing she wanted at this time was for Hayden Stone to have distractions.

The fire in the bedroom's brick hearth eased to crumbling red embers. Ambassador Marshall Bunting relaxed on the bed, his head propped on the pillow, wondering if he should or should not get up and add a log or two. Patience solved the quandary.

Lying close to him, she stretched, moved her face toward his, and asked, "Shall I add a log?" Without waiting for an answer, she slipped out of bed and went over to the fire. She bent over and took two small logs from the bin and carefully placed them on top of the embers. Within seconds, both logs were blazing. She remained crouched by the fireplace, looking into the flames.

Bunting admired her, wearing his white dress shirt, which didn't quite cover her firm, delicious ass. She pulled her hair back with both hands; the motion opened the front of the unbuttoned shirt, and when she turned sideways, allowed him to see her breasts glowing in the gold light of the fire.

She rose quickly, took three quick steps toward the bed, jumped in, and made one more leap, landing on top of him. "That'll keep us warm for a while," she said, giving him a wet kiss.

The last hour had been all lovemaking, and Bunting was exhausted. The last stragglers hadn't left the *braai* until after midnight. They were businessmen and their wives from Austin, Texas, who obviously didn't know diplomatic functions ended before eleven. That is, Bunting's functions did.

"What shall we talk about?" she asked, running her hand down along his side, then stroking the inside of his thigh.

"Interesting group of people tonight, wouldn't you say?"

She took a deep breath. "Yes. Quite fun." Her eyes glistened in the firelight. "What did you think of the contessa?" Without waiting for an answer, she said, "I think she's just great."

She hugged him, and after a second, gave an exaggerated sigh. "You didn't like Hayden Stone?"

"How well do you know him?"

Ignoring the question, she continued. "My plan to reunite Lucinda and Hayden worked. Don't you think? I'm like cupid shooting an arrow. Hmm. I'm a bit hazy on my mythology. Was cupid male?"

"In some pictures, Cupid looks somewhat androgynous," Bunting said. "Where do you know Hayden Stone from?"

"We knew each other in New York City. Years ago."

Bunting ran his fingers through her hair, looking directly into her wary eyes. The sleeve of his shirt she was wearing had lipstick on it. Why did women do that? Marking their territory? He let her answer hang before he continued, "You know he's heading to Namibia on a trip. That region has very interesting birds." He stopped stroking her hair. "I'm thinking of going up to Botswana next month to do some bird-watching. You might find it interesting. Want to join me?" He waited for a response.

"Sounds like fun. Let me know the dates."

"Someone told me that you and Hayden Stone met the other day."

She stiffened. "As I said, we're old friends. We met ... For one thing, I was seeing if he was ready to meet the contessa again." She moved away from him and placed two pillows behind her head. "Please don't tell me your people are watching me?"

"Are you aware of his line of work?"

"Yes. He's a spy."

Bunting was taken back by her candor. "To be more precise, he's a counterspy. A similar but quite separate vocation."

"How interesting."

"And you, dear." He touched her shoulder, and she withdrew. "Are you also in the trade?"

She rolled out of bed and stood in front of the fireplace. "You know I am. If you didn't, I'd bloody well say that you are incompetent. Or your people are." His white shirt came off and she rolled it into a ball. She threw the shirt in his direction. "Time for me to depart."

Bunting sat up. "I'm curious. Who do you work for?"

She straightened her back and stood naked, in silhouette by the bright firelight. "Who do you think?"

"The Brits. MI6."

"That's what your people told you?"

Bunting nodded. "We're on the same side, you know. Colleagues. The Five Eyes program and all that. Now come back to bed."

"I'm off." Patience picked up her clothes and headed for the bathroom, but stopped and walked back. "I'm glad I drove myself here tonight." She carefully laid her clothes on the foot of the bed and slowly dressed in front of him.

"Sweetheart. It's late. You shouldn't be driving on the roads at night. What with the crime."

"Bugger off." Taking her time, she put on her lace pants, started with her brassiere, then threw it down, and put on her blouse, leaving the top three buttons open.

"Please, dear, reconsider." *How dramatic. How bitchy. God, she is wonderful.*

"You had me followed. You didn't think enough of me to ask me directly if I worked for MI6, or if I was meeting Hayden. No trust on your part!"

"I am, or was, a bit jealous." He patted the bed with his hand to return.

"For your information, Hayden and I were never lovers. We were just in love."

"See. That answers everything." Bunting clapped once. "We can get back to normal."

She headed for the door. "When I report this episode to my people, I don't think they'll like it one bit."

"For God's sake. You're not going to tell your people at MI6 everything we've done?" He waved his hand around. "Are you?"

Patience came back to the end of the bed. "No. I'm not telling MI6. They are the people that I've been loaned to." She smiled. "You didn't know?" She waited for a response but he didn't give one. "I'm telling my organization, the CSIC. The Canadian Security Intelligence Service."

For a moment, Bunting said nothing, then muttered, "I didn't know Canada had spies."

"Few people do. Precisely the reason we're so good." She walked to the door. "Cheers, Mr. Ambassador."

CHAPTER TWENTY-FIVE

BRUIN KARAS, NAMIBIA—AUGUST 19, 2002

Hayden Stone watched the pilot and copilot of the twin-engine Otter search for a clear landing space in the semi-arid savanna one hundred feet below. The sun had yet to rise, but first light revealed rolling hills and arroyos. Dirk Lange leaned over and told him they were called *dongas* in Zulu. Through the square window, Stone saw a dirt road undulating through tall brown grass and thorn bushes. Finally, the pilot used the road as a landing strip.

When the plane hit the ground, it bounced once and then pitched forward to a stop. Outside the plane dust swirled from the rotating propellers. Across the aisle Colonel Frederick gave orders to the two CIA logistics officers sitting next to him. Stone signaled thumbs up to Sandra Harrington and Dirk Lange, who in turn released their seat harnesses. The tail door of the plane lowered and the two CIA officers, a man and a woman, jumped up, unstrapped the three miniature motorcycles, and wheeled them down the ramp.

Stone and his two companions carried their gear off the plane while the pilot eased up on the throttle, which helped lessen the noise level.

Stone surveyed the surrounding terrain. Sunrise was still a half hour away and the desert had yet to reveal its colors. The morning temperature had to be in the low 40s and by noon they could expect it to reach the high 70s. Not bad for winter.

Stone called out to Frederick in a raised voice, "How much time do we have?"

"Only five minutes on deck. Then we're wheels up." Turning to Sandra and Lange, he yelled, "Important thing is to make sure your radios are working. After that, get these bikes ready." Frederick held a satellite phone to his ear.

The front and back fenders of three Suzuki DS80s were loaded with packs containing water and provisions. The female CIA technician quickly went over the specifications of the dirt bikes used by the special operations units. They learned the motorcycles could hit fifty miles per hour but had limited range.

"They're easy to handle." The technician proceeded to show them how to brake and shift gears. "We fabricated special mufflers. They sound like the wind on a blustery day in Chicago."

The other CIA technician handed them rifles with shoulder straps—Browning BARs to Stone and Lange, a Browning BLR Stalker to Sandra. "They're all .308 calibers, so you can exchange rounds if necessary."

Stone examined one of the .308 Winchester rounds knowing it to be effective, but the bullet had more drop at long range than the .30-06 Springfield he was accustomed to.

"They look like the 7.62 NATO rounds I'm familiar with," Lange remarked as he loaded a box magazine and inserted it into his rifle.

Frederick, still holding the phone to his ear, shouted over the plane's engines, "Remember. If you meet any locals, you're on safari. That's why we gave you hunting rifles."

"What are we hunting for?" Sandra asked as she strapped the rifle across her back.

Colonel Frederick shrugged. "Don't know. Maybe elephants?"

Dirk Lange said, "No. The desert elephants are farther north. We'll say antelope or gemsbok. We have a lot of game here," Lange continued. "Lions and cheetahs. Watch out for the hyenas. They're nasty."

"You said we'd be here two days max?" Stone asked.

"No more," Colonel Frederick said. "In a nearby country, which for the time being shall remain anonymous, we're preparing to stage a takeout of the bomb." Frederick held up the phone. "One thing I just learned that might complicate things. Last night the satellite people back in Virginia detected activity at the Bruin Karas airport. A plane landed and they saw a number of people on the airstrip."

"What's unusual about that?" Sandra asked.

"Planes don't normally land there at night," Lange said. "The airport is just a dirt strip with a windsock. No airport lights."

"We have company," Stone said.

"Yes," Colonel Frederick shouted as he rubbed some dust from his eye. "We're flying up to Windhoek. I'm bringing in people from the station in Pretoria and the base in Cape Town. By tonight we'll be able to provide backup if you need it." He slapped Stone's shoulder. "Meantime, keep low and avoid contact with strangers."

The technicians and Colonel Frederick climbed back into the plane and as the tailgate rose, Frederick yelled, "Good hunting."

The plane took off, and at the moment the sun broke over the horizon, it dipped its wing to the east, and staying low to the ground, disappeared.

Following the last sounds of the plane's engines, Stone took in the quiet of the surrounding land. The clear, dry air allowed an unobstructed view of nearly fifty miles to distant blue-tinted mountains. Even in the morning, an almost full moon bright in the hard blue sky prepared to drop below the horizon.

Stone and his two companions took a gray gravel road that ran to the base of a six-hundred-foot ridge. After a half hour their programmed GPS beeped the alert to turn. They left the road and proceeded cautiously over the countryside toward the ridge, and began a careful climb. At one point they had to dismount and push their motorcycles up the hill over boulders and rock ledges. An hour later, exhausted, Stone and his companions reached the crest and rested, cautious to remain out of sight.

On the other side of the ridge, in the valley below, Stone saw the hamlet of Bruin Karas scattered along a paved road and a parallel railroad track. Further searching through their binoculars, they found to the right the airstrip with a twin-engine plane parked off to the side. Turning to the far left, he spotted a lone brown boxcar sitting on an isolated rail siding about two miles from the main road.

"Pretty quiet down there," Stone said. "No signs of activity."

"Got a *bakkie* along the road to the right." Lange pointed.

Sandra said, "Excuse me."

"That pickup truck kicking up dust." Lange touched her shoulder. "Hello. Look over at the landing strip. We have some people walking around that two-engine plane. Dark clothes and beards. Can't quite see what they're doing."

"The plane Colonel Frederick talked about coming in last night."

The three continued to scope the valley and saw another truck drive away from what resembled a general store. A lone Wahlberg's eagle hovered below them, using the currents rising from the warming air.

Stone asked the question that always came to mind when passing through isolated towns and villages: "What do people do around this godforsaken place?"

Lange answered him. "A bit of mining. Mostly farming. Farmers drive in to buy petrol and goods." He lowered his binoculars. "They enjoy the place like their fathers before them. Afrikaners have a need to plant things."

"Where are the Bushmen?" Sandra asked.

"You mean the San people. They have settlements all about." Lange searched again with his field glasses. "Can't see any. Their villages look like clumps of thatched haystacks. Only rectangular in shape. They blend in with the countryside." He stretched and looked at Stone. "What's the plan, mate?"

"If we go down into the valley now, we may be spotted. Maybe we should wait for dusk. Just enough light to make our way without breaking our necks."

After a moment, Lange said, "A suggestion. The locals hereabouts have sharp eyes. They can pick up movement in the hills because they hunt, but strangers like Wahab and Asuty probably wouldn't. I would suspect that plane brought in those two along with Mr. Van Wartt."

"If so, they'll make a move on that boxcar," Sandra said. "I haven't seen any activity there, but we're too far away."

The breeze had become a light wind. The cloudless sky warmed Stone's head. "If we walk our bikes down slowly and don't kick up dust, we have a chance of not being seen," Stone said. "I'd like to get closer to that boxcar."

The others agreed and they started their descent using shrubs and boulders as cover. An hour later they were on the valley floor with line of sight to the settlement and airport gone, but with the advantage of using the low hills and vegetation as concealment. They drove the mini-motorcycles toward the railroad siding where the boxcar sat.

About a half mile away from their target, Stone signaled to make camp. "From here we have sight of the railcar and to the right, part of the village. We should be able to see anyone approaching."

After settling in and checking their rifles, they opened MREs and ate. Lange laughed. "You Yanks certainly know how to do field rations. The South African Army's rations are a bit less elegant."

"Were you in the military?" Stone asked.

"*Ja*. Of course. I still hold a captain's rank."

"My God! What's that?" Sandra said. An ugly piglike creature scrambled out of the brush, stopped when it saw them, then ran off.

"That's a bushpig. You see a lot of them now that the leopard population is down." Lange threw a rock in the bush where the animal had emerged, and a minute later three piglets scurried out and followed their mother. "No worry unless she thinks you'll harm the kids." He looked around. "Just be on the lookout for snakes. Some bad ones about here, I'll wager."

"I don't especially care for snakes." Stone eyed the nearby thornbushes. "Let's set up a watch schedule on the boxcar. I'll take the first one. How about an hour at a time?"

Stone positioned himself on top of a rise behind grasses where he could use his binoculars. He spent the first few minutes scanning the horizon, pausing on the hamlet's buildings.

Two figures, a man and woman, sat on a bench in front of what appeared to be the general store. From the looks of his shorts and her sundress, they appeared to be locals. A pickup truck passed them and they waved. Focused back on the boxcar, only an occasional bird broke the stillness. The smell of dry grass and brush drifted in with the intermittent breeze.

Stone kept up his visual routine while going through a mental checklist of things to do after his watch: recheck his rifle, make sure all magazines were loaded with .308 cartridges, check his Sig Sauer. He had to sharpen his knife. Also, check his radio. *Odd. Frederick hasn't checked in with us.*

Having gone over the checklist twice, his mind wandered to the place he'd avoided since he left Cape Town. His renewed relationship with Contessa Lucinda.

Three months ago she had made it clear that she never wanted to see him again. Now, she flies down from the French Riviera and arranges with Patience, of all people, to reunite with him. What was he missing?

What resembled a hat or a head moved in the grass a hundred yards away from the boxcar. Stone wasn't certain. He called to Lange and Sandra, who dropped on the ground next to him.

They remained still for a few moments. "Could have been an animal. It's late afternoon. They start moving this time of day," Lange said. "I'll take over the watch."

Sandra followed Stone down the slope to their campsite. The two sat with their backs against the motorcycles. She remarked that when the sun went down it would get really dark. "Pitch black."

"Ah, but we got a moon tonight, kid. Almost a full moon."

Stone's phone buzzed and he saw Frederick's number displayed on the screen. "Stone here. What's up?"

Colonel Frederick advised that personnel and equipment had arrived at the staging area. "We're waiting for Department of Energy people to arrive. When they do, we'll bring in two C-130s. That'll provide some entertainment for the local folks."

"What about our competition? Pick up any traffic on what

they're up to?"

"Why ask me? That's your job to keep track of them. Our reports indicate they're on the ground there."

Stone looked at Sandra and mouthed a curse. Colonel Frederick could be a pain in the ass at times. Especially when he was right. "A plane is parked off the dirt runway. We saw a couple of men walking around it. Probably our bad guys. They appear to be waiting for something or someone. No activity at the boxcar."

"That's the runway we're landing on. You saw only two men?"

"Thought you'd known that. Has the satellite spotted any others?"

"No. Keep me posted." After a pause, he asked, "No activity around the boxcar. Right?"

"Affirmative."

"I'll get back to you with any updates." The line went dead.

Sandra moved closer. "What's wrong?"

"Let's join Lange."

Again lying prone next to each other, they searched the surrounding area with binoculars as Stone gave Lange the gist of the conversation with Frederick. While talking, they now observed four bearded men in dark pants and jackets walking around the parked airplane.

"What's your take on the situation, Hayden?" Sandra asked.

"I think Colonel Frederick thinks we're behind the curve. Van Wartt is about to hand over the bomb in that boxcar to Wahab and his buddies. Frederick's worried he's not going to get here in time."

"So where does that leave us?" Lange asked.

"That leaves us hanging."

They lay silent for a time, continuing to scope their targets. A light breeze rustled the grasses and bushes around them. Stone broke the silence. "I'm going to take a look inside that boxcar."

"No. Hayden," Sandra said.

"They may have already taken the bomb to the landing strip." Stone rubbed his eyes. "We've got to know if it's still there."

"Think it over," Lange said.

"We'll leave the bikes here," Stone said. "You two cover me."

Sandra and Lange made sure their weapons were loaded. All three began crouching toward the railcar.

Sandra and Lange held back a few yards behind Stone. Their task was to provide cover. The three would communicate using their radios. At the spot where Sandra and Lange would station themselves, Stone paused for a couple of minutes.

The sun dropped fast and long shadows streaked the landscape. All appeared calm.

As Stone signaled he was advancing, Lange whispered over the air, "It's too quiet. No animals. No birds."

Stone hesitated. Lange was a hunter. He knew this land. Again in the fast-dimming light, he scoped the boxcar with his binoculars. The side door was open about two inches. Back at the original site, he had been too far away to detect this.

"Shit. Door's open. We may have an empty boxcar," Stone said to his companions.

He moved fast in a crab-like fashion toward the clearing that circled the railcar. Once he reached the open ground surrounding the boxcar, he stopped.

Still no movement. He raised his rifle to ready position, stood, and raced forward.

He slid to a stop, hitting his back against the boxcar. Rifle raised, he searched the surrounding bush over the gun sight.

Inching toward the open door, and without looking, he pushed open the door with his left hand.

As he did, from the open door the hard barrel of a pistol jammed the back of his head.

CHAPTER TWENTY-SIX

Two of Nabeel Asuty's men jumped out of the boxcar and threw Stone to the ground. They bound his arms behind his back with duct tape. Kneeling on one knee at the open door of the boxcar, Asuty waved his AK-47 in the direction where Sandra and Dirk Lange lay hidden in the underbrush.

"Come out with your guns lowered," Asuty shouted, "or Stone is a dead man."

As Stone lay pinned to the ground, he knew odds were he was already a dead man. Before the tape could be placed over his mouth, he managed to yell, "Stay there. Open fire." Stone knew the Browning rifles with telescopic scopes Sandra and Lange carried could easily take out Asuty.

Both Sandra and Lange opened fire. Thuds came from bullets penetrating the wooden side of the boxcar. Asuty leaped from the boxcar, rushed over to Stone, and had his men yank him up by his hair. He held the AK-47's barrel under Stone's chin.

"Surrender and Mr. Stone just might live," Asuty shouted in a panic. "If you don't, I kill him."

Stone's companions continued firing, and then the skull of the man on his left exploded from one of their shots. Bone and blood splattered on Stone.

Asuty and the other man now held him up as a shield. Asuty let off a few rounds from his machine gun.

Two bearded men jumped out of the brush behind Dirk Lange, guns drawn. Stone watched Lange curse and slowly stand, raising his arms. Asuty yelled at his men in Arabic to find the woman.

"Your choice," Asuty hollered. "Lay down your gun or he dies."

Sandra rose from the tall grass and swung her rifle back and forth from Asuty to the two men holding Lange. "Take as many out as you can," Stone growled under his taped mouth. *Do it. Do it.*

Seconds passed. Finally, she tossed the Browning rifle in the grass and came forward. Stone hoped she had a trick up her sleeve, like shooting them with a hidden Glock, but she continued to walk, hands now raised, toward where Lange was held. She had her hands bound and both were marched to the boxcar.

As the three were pushed to the ground next to the wheels of the railcar, Asuty growled. "That was easier than I thought it would be. You CIA are not much of a threat after all."

For a half hour the beatings continued until the sun had dropped below the horizon and the savanna colors faded. The blows were administered not to gain information or to avenge their dead comrade—merely for sport. Stone had read accounts from victims of jihadist torture. Always at some point the punishment administered shifted from a religious connotation—and this was from the victims' recollections—to a sensual, even sexual enjoyment.

Stone took most of the abuse and he felt himself weakening from the assault. He tried to shift his consciousness to another realm as his Tibetan friend in Lhasa had taught him. Thank goodness he had met her and she had shared her wisdom.

No broken bones yet, but a good deal of torn flesh. Stone's capturers repeated the blows to areas where blood appeared. Asuty enjoyed head kicks, but his attention turned to Sandra.

"Hit her stomach and legs. Do not mark her face," Asuty ordered. "We will have fun before we kill them."

His men became excited. Stone saw from Sandra's expression that she understood what Asuty meant. He also knew if the opportunity arose, she would kill him.

"Remove her pants," Asuty ordered. "And carry her over to the back of the truck."

Stone saw the flatbed truck that had pulled up during the beatings. The jihadists lost interest in hitting him and moved over for the show. Stone flipped over on his stomach and went into a kneeling position. His feet were bound at the ankles, his hands behind his back. With his fingers he searched for the release switch on the heel of his boot. He found it and the inserted knife blade snapped out. He easily slit the duct tape around his wrists and ankles, got to his feet, and lunged toward the men carrying Sandra's prone body.

Stone used his body as a ramming device. He and three of the assailants tumbled to the ground. The other men seized Stone and dragged him toward the boxcar. Asuty tossed Sandra aside and yelled a long succession of Arabic curses, approaching Stone with a knife.

Stone's pants were yanked down and as Asuty placed a knife to his genitals, two gunshots stopped him. Asuty and his men froze.

"Don't we have more important tasks at hand, Nabeel?" came a hard voice speaking in Arabic.

Another voice in English sneered, "Bloody lowlifes your men are, Abdul."

Stone twisted his head around and through swollen eyelids saw Abdul Wahab and Dawid van Wartt standing a few feet away. Wahab had a Beretta pistol leveled at Asuty's stomach.

Van Wartt and his companion, Bull Rhyton, took little time gathering the guns from Asuty and his men. Bull threw them in the backseat of an old Land Rover.

"Nabeel, dear friend," Wahab said, still pointing his automatic, "you may have these back when you leave with the bomb. For now, your hands will be full moving the bomb to the truck."

Asuty stood expressionless and Stone wondered what he was thinking. What was more interesting, months before on the Riviera, Stone had seen Wahab at a party but never heard his voice—it was deeper and had more authority than he had expected.

Wahab continued, "Shall we look at what we've paid for?"

He motioned with the gun toward the open door of the boxcar.

Bull came over to Stone and motioned for him to stand up. When he did, he yanked up Stone's trousers and told him to go and sit next to Lange and Sandra. Bull cradled his submachine gun and used it to wave Asuty's men over to their flatbed truck. He knelt down next to Sandra and closed her shirt, cursing low in Afrikaans. At that point Dirk Lange made a loud sound under his taped mouth and nodded his head.

The Afrikaner rose and asked Lange if he was a *Landsman*. Again, Lange nodded vigorously. Stone watched the wide-shouldered man glare at Asuty's men milling about the truck, now guarded by two of Van Wartt's men.

Wahab, Van Wartt, and Asuty had climbed into the boxcar and were examining the bomb, which Stone now saw for the first time. Bull interrupted Stone's attention when he reached down and carefully pulled back the tape from Lange's mouth. Dirk's right eye was swollen, and blood ran down his ear. He whispered a few minutes to Bull, who partially replaced the tape so that it drooped.

Interesting and encouraging, Stone thought and noted the same impression in Sandra's eyes. His attention went back to the nuclear weapon inside the boxcar. The terrorists held flashlights that illuminated the same fat, brutish bomb that had appeared in the photographs he studied a day before in the CIA safe house. Stone had never been in the presence of a nuclear bomb. As he studied it, he tried to fathom the awesome destruction contained within the bronze-colored metal casing. Then there was the radiation leakage. How bad was it?

Wahab, Van Wartt, and Asuty seemed to be perplexed about how they were going to move the heavy object onto the flatbed truck.

Bull jumped from the boxcar and walked in the direction of Asuty's men, who had assembled by the truck, speaking quietly. He stopped, placed the submachine gun on his shoulder, and shot a worried glanced back at Lange.

Van Wartt ordered the truck to be pulled alongside the boxcar and instructed Asuty to position his men to move the bomb while Van Wartt's two men watched with guns ready. The makeshift crane on the flatbed truck didn't look capable of lifting the heavy metal mass, but it could drag it. Bull climbed on the back of the truck and directed the maneuver. The crane pulled rather than lifted the bulk resting on a wooden pallet onto the flatbed, straining the truck's suspension and flattening its rear tires. After securing the bomb with ropes, a ragged canvas tarp was thrown over it. They were ready to move to the airstrip, and Stone knew the next order of business was the disposition of him and his two companions. Would Abdul Wahab do the killing?

Asuty leaped from the truck and shouted in Arabic to two jihadists. They walked purposefully in Stone's direction. At the same time, Stone saw that Bull was talking to Van Wartt and pointing to Dirk Lange. Bull knew that Lange was a South African and an Afrikaner. Did he suspect Lange was an intelligence officer? Van Wartt turned away, but Bull continued to speak, now gesturing with his hands.

The two henchmen approaching with Asuty had large grins. Asuty spoke as if addressing a classroom of students. "Time to die." He waved back to the truck, enjoyment in his eyes. "This bomb is a message to your corrupt world."

"We don't have time for this nonsense." It was Van Wartt speaking, aiming an automatic at Asuty's head. Bull and Van Wartt's men covered the jihadists standing on the truck. "Get your bloody asses on the truck. Now!"

Asuty straightened and lifted his chin. "They will die. Then we leave." He motioned to the man next to him, who drew an automatic pistol from inside his shirt.

Van Wartt turned his head, keeping his eyes on Asuty and the man with the gun. In Afrikaans he spoke to Bull, standing behind him. Bull said, "*Ja*," and raised his gun to eye level, aiming at the man.

"*Enough*," Abdul Wahab shouted from the side. He pointed his Beretta at Asuty. "Tell him to drop the gun."

Asuty's face contorted, and then he motioned to his henchmen to drop their weapons.

"Get in the truck."

Wahab's actions confused Stone. Why did he stop Asuty from killing them? Did he fear Van Wartt? Stone looked over at Sandra, who also appeared perplexed.

At this, a plane roared past a hundred feet overhead, landing lights on, heading for the Bruin Karas airstrip. Stone looked up, not believing what he saw. An ancient twin-engine Fairchild C-119, Flying Boxcar, a Korean War-era military cargo plane. Probably the only remaining aircraft of its kind not in a museum. He detected a faint trail of black smoke coming from its starboard engine.

Asuty's men began shouting. One started the truck and switched on the truck's headlights. Amid the commotion, Wahab took Asuty's arm firmly. "Let's go!"

Van Wartt and Bull looked down at the three lying on the ground. "We'll put them in the boxcar for the time being. If the need arises, we can use them as hostages," Van Wartt said while studying Lange.

Stone and the other two were dragged across the hard-packed dirt to the boxcar and lifted inside. When all three were in, Van Wartt looked at them for a moment, but again said nothing. The door closed and someone slid the bolt shut. The straining groan of the overloaded truck's motor grew fainter as it headed for the airfield. The Land Rover could be heard following.

A moment of quiet passed in the darkness, and then, as if on cue, all squirmed next to each other. Stone and Sandra with their free fingers attempted to pull off the duct tape, first from their hands, then when free, their feet. Lange freed his mouth from the loose tape and whispered words of encouragement. The two carefully peeled the duct tape from their mouths and took deep breaths.

"Do you see any way out of here?" Stone asked, finding the closed door with his hands.

"This might help." Sandra switched on a miniature LED flashlight attached to a key ring.

The interior of the wooden boxcar smelled of dust and age from years sitting in a relentless sun. They found the doors on either side locked from the outside.

"Shine the light up on the roof," Lange said. "Should be hatches up there."

"There," Sandra said. "Either of you two gents care to give me a boost?"

Both Stone and Lange lifted Sandra up to the hatch. She pushed and banged, but the hatch wouldn't open. While holding her, Stone's legs, groin, and arms ached. His face, he knew, was bruised, but neither eye was closed like Lange's. Sandra hadn't complained of any injuries. "Tough gal," he wanted to tell her, but knew she would consider the remark condescending.

They sat, or rather collapsed to the floor, with the flashlight's thin light pointing in the center of their circle. Exhausted, Stone wanted to close his eyes and sleep, but knew they had to come up with a plan of escape.

"Nothing in the realm of possibility would allow for one of us to still have a radio?" Lange asked.

"They used mine to put this gash in my head," Stone said.

"I threw mine out in the bush along with my Glock before I surrendered."

Stone stretched, but stopped when a pain shot along his back. He closed his eyes and reviewed what could be the sequence of future events. "Our terrorists are now loading an ancient atomic bomb in the hold of an equally ancient Fairchild C-119, named by airmen years ago without affection as 'The Flying Coffin' for its shape as well as its propensity to crash."

"Hayden, how do you come up with that stuff?" Sandra sounded annoyed.

"I had a ride on one when I was in college ROTC."

"Considering your age, I imagine it would have been in one of those World War I biplanes, mate." Lange laughed. "By the way, I want to thank you two for inviting me along on this little picnic."

Remembering that the man called Bull had a private conversation with Lange, Stone asked, "What was up with you and your fellow Boer?"

"Agh. To take a turn on one of your expressions, Boers are

thicker than water."

Stone explained. "Dirk. Knowing you were an Afrikaner saved us ... for the time being. I still can't believe Wahab let us live."

"Any ideas where they're taking the bomb?" Sandra asked, but no one answered.

Sandra turned off the light to save the battery. They sat silently in the dark. Colonel Gustave Frederick would soon fly in with the bomb removal team, late for the show. Chances were good they'd come to the boxcar and release them. Then they'd make plans to intercept the C-119 carrying the bomb.

Stone began thinking about how radioactive the boxcar could be when Lange whispered, "Hello. I believe one of our motorcycles has returned."

"Hope your buddy Bull has come to release us," Stone said.

They waited for someone to release the latch on one of the doors. Stone and his companions got to their feet and heard an unwelcomed voice.

"Well, CIA spies. The time has come. You did not truly believe you would live?"

It was Nabeel Asuty's voice, and they soon learned what he had in mind. A hissing sound came from below the wooden floor, and through the cracks in the planks he saw a crimson glow. Smoke started creeping into the boxcar.

"Would have preferred to saw off your head, Mr. Stone. You too, blonde slut."

As the motorcycle took off, Sandra growled, "Let's make a pact. If anyone lives, that asshole dies."

A second flare had been placed at the opposite end of the car. It took no time for the dry planks to catch fire and burn hot. The smoke proved the immediate problem—they would be asphyxiated before they burned to death. The two red glowing areas lit the inside of the car, and through the smoke, Stone watched Lange place both arms around Sandra. He should be the one doing that.

One of the hot spots burst into flames and the heat became oppressive. Stone wondered if he could jump through one of the flaming holes to the outside, but quickly realized the choking smoke would not allow them the time to wait for a hole to form.

"Our only chance is to break open this door," Stone yelled. "Let's hit it. All at once!"

They repeatedly slammed their bodies against the door. Stone knew he ached from the beatings he received and knew his companions hurt. Their determination to open the door despite their pain impressed him.

The flames came from both sides, and all coughed from the smoke. Finally the aged planking holding the latch gave. They yanked the door open and cool air rushed in. All three leaped from the boxcar, landing and rolling on the ground.

Not long after, as they sat on the dirt and coughed, Bull and a youngster drove up, came over, and passed around a water jug. The railcar roared in flames. All lifted their heads as the old plane lumbered above them.

"There goes the bomb," Bull said.

The flames reflected off the plane's gray undercarriage. There were no aircraft identification markings. Just as they heard the last of the C-119's engines, another smaller twin-engine propjet flew overhead and turned south in the opposite direction.

"Mr. Van Wartt and Abdul Wahab returning to Cape Town." Bull searched their faces and asked, "Would have expected any competent military operation to have a backup, aye Mr. Dirk Lange?"

"Our backup must have stopped for coffee," Stone said.

"Quite the joker, Yank," Bull said. "But there is a bit of Armageddon on that plane."

Stone wanted to thank him for his part in having the bomb get into the hands of the terrorists, but considering he held a submachine gun, thought better of it.

"I'll try to find my phone," Sandra said, groaning as she raised herself. "I ditched it before surrendering. Do you mind?"

"Take this torch, miss," Bull said, handing her a flashlight. "Watch out for the creatures."

Stone offered to go with her, and they walked carefully toward the spot where she had hidden. In short time they found her phone and the Glock she had left there.

"Hide it under your shirt," Stone said. "Our friend Bull would more likely suspect me of having it."

"*Really?*"

"Sweetheart, you know me better than to be chauvinistic, but Bull's world is a few years behind."

"Don't give me that 'Sweetheart' shit."

"Sandra. Did you notice the friction between Abdul Wahab and his man Asuty?"

"Yeah. Trouble in paradise."

"Might have saved our lives."

"And how about that Bull and his buddy Van Wartt?" Sandra whispered as they neared Bull and Lange.

"Lucky for us Bull has a mind of his own."

When they came up to the two Afrikaners, it was apparent they had established some sort of bond. The two men conversed as they walked to the Land Rover. At the same time, Lange motioned for Stone and Sandra to follow. They passed the burning hulk of railcar throwing a trail of sparks to the star-crowded sky.

Sandra phoned Colonel Frederick. "Colonel, I have some news. Asuty has taken off flying north with the nuclear bomb in an unmarked C-119." Pause. "We couldn't stop him ... We were captured—" She stopped and swirled around toward the boxcar fire. Stone saw from her body movements that Frederick was doing all the talking and from her nervous "Yeses" and "Rights" that he was pissed. At one point she suggested he talk with Stone, but when Sandra threw up her free hand, Stone knew he was not going to speak with him.

The conversation ended with her saying she'd wait for further instructions. She whispered to Stone, "Frederick was only an hour from landing here. He's decided to return to the staging area. Someone will come and pick us up. I think he said early morning." She put her phone in her pocket. Touching his shoulder, she added, "He suggested I tell you something."

"Oh?"

"Retire."

• • •

Bull Rhyton's homestead was a mile away from the town of Bruin Karas and a quarter mile off the paved road. Dinner consisted of leftover breakfast *putu* porridge, venison sausage, and fresh oven-baked biscuits, hard on the outside, soft inside. Bull passed around jerky, called *biltong*.

Mrs. Rhyton, a stout woman with graying hair and weather-worn features, did not conceal her dislike for the Americans, but Stone watched Bull pull her aside and point to Sandra. She bent over and touched her bruised face, and tenderly led her toward the bedroom. In between tut-tuts, Stone heard her tell Sandra she had medicines for the cuts. The children, barefoot and bronzed, wandered through the kitchen, and even the youngest, not much over six years old, wasn't hesitant to look Stone straight in the eye.

At the kitchen table huddled over their meals, Dirk Lange and Bull spoke in low tones peppered with *ja-nee*, the non-committal Afrikaner phrase for "yes, no," and used when nothing else comes to mind. Stone took his plate out to the front porch open to the sky. He sat on a wooden crate and gazed up, remembering Sandra's words on how dark it got in places like this, in the middle of nowhere. Dark it was, except for stars so many and so bright that it was impossible for him to make out their constellations. The moon's mountain ranges etched its brilliant surface.

Hayden Stone knew his impatience had led to a bad decision. He should have stayed with his group and not approached the boxcar. It had been a trap and he fell into it—like a greenhorn. The blame for the terrorists escaping with the bomb rested on his shoulders. Colonel Frederick had reason to be disgusted. He had screwed up before, but never with such potential consequences.

Bad situations had been turned around in the past. He'd do so again, he was certain. Still. Flying somewhere over the vastness of Africa, jihadists had a nuclear weapon and planned to use it against the West. Maybe if the gods were on the right side that relic of an airplane wouldn't make it to its destination.

Bull came out the screen door and sat next to him. He held two mason jars with clear liquid. "I gave your comrades pain pills. Do you want one?"

"No. Thank you." Stone looked down at the drinks.

Bull huffed. "You were the one who took the worst beating. Maybe this is more to your liking." He handed Stone a jar. "Not a very fancy glass for an American."

"This is how we drink our moonshine back home." Stone took a good gulp and, as expected, felt the burning slide down his throat. "Nice and mild."

Bull grunted.

"If you knew where that plane was headed, would you tell me?"

"I wouldn't tell you."

Therefore, Bull would tell Dirk, not me the Yank. "Would Van Wartt tell me?"

"Dawie van Wartt doesn't talk to your kind." Bull leaned his elbows on his knees. "Dawie is happy to be rid of the whole mess."

"Did you hear Abdul Wahab mention where Asuty was headed?"

"Wahab. Now there's a slippery devil. I don't think you'd have a problem getting the information from him. For the right price."

There it was again. The black-and-white image of Abdul Wahab as an adversary fogged. Stone took another drink and let the alcohol seep down into his body, dulling the pain.

Bull said as he got up, "Guess you have to ask Nabeel Asuty where the bomb is."

"When I meet Asuty again, a conversation is not on the agenda."

The next day, Stone waited on the side of the red-dirt runway, taking in the sweet liquid of an African morning. Sandra's phone buzzed. From the speaker Stone heard a familiar voice he hadn't expected—Jacob, his Mossad friend. Minutes later a large helicopter made a wide sweep around the airfield. The three miniature motorcycles and the equipment that Asuty's jihadists hadn't pilfered were staged for loading. As if not to have guilty knowledge, Stone turned away when Lange handed one of the Browning rifles to Bull. A token of appreciation from Lange for saving their lives.

Stone watched Bull's nephew, Corneliu, whisper to his uncle. Bull came up to Stone. "My nephew says the same copter landed here some days ago. People who were in it got out and inspected the boxcar."

The helicopter landed, blowing dust and gravel over everyone. Stone watched Jacob hop out the door. He wasn't smiling.

Over the noise of the rotors winding down, Jacob yelled, "You fucked up, Stone. Big time."

"Any idea where the jihadists are?" Stone asked.

Jacob now had a coughing spell and motioned for them to move away from swirling dust. Given his cough, Stone was surprised to see that Jacob looked healthier than the last time they had met.

"They were heading north," Jacob said. "I suspect toward Libya."

"They'd have to stop for fuel a couple of times," Stone said. "Probably near Luanda, Angola first."

The pilot cut the engines and dust sank silently around them. Stone had a few questions for Jacob—first, what Frederick was up to.

"He's in Windhoek with the two planes. He's waiting to get a fix on the C-119 carrying the bomb," Jacob said. "Your satellites lost contact with it."

Stone thought a moment. "My guess is Asuty brought in a nuclear engineer, and he discovered the bomb was leaking radiation. Somehow they masked or patched the bomb, or whatever those nuclear people do. Our satellites probably can't detect any emission signatures." He watched the miniature motorcycles being loaded aboard the helicopter. "Where are we going?"

"I'm taking you back to South Africa." Jacob looked away. "Just as well. Colonel Frederick is in a foul mood. Best you not meet with him now."

"Any word on Wahab or Van Wartt?"

"I have it on good authority that Mr. Dawid van Wartt is headed for some extensive legal problems in his country," Jacob said. "As far as Abdul Wahab is concerned, he may have lucked out."

"How's that?"

Jacob spat. "You'll have to bring the matter up with your Colonel Frederick when you see him next."

CHAPTER TWENTY-SEVEN

CIA HEADQUARTERS—AUGUST 20, 2002

Elizabeth Kerr stopped in front of the metal security door and tapped five numbers on the keypad. The lock clicked open and she walked into the special task force office space. In more than a week the fourteen-person group gave the appearance of having been together for months. Maps and posters were pinned to the off-white walls; piles of files and books lay scattered on desks along with various-shaped coffee mugs.

As she started for John Matterhorn's glass-enclosed office in the corner of the expansive space, flashing yellow warning lights suspended from the dull white ceiling startled her. They served to alert the office staff that non-CIA or non-cleared visitors were present in the office space, so safeguard classified material.

Kerr halted. Furious. This was the third time it happened. Everyone on the staff knew she was from the National Imagery and Mapping Agency, with security clearances on her dossier that matched theirs and a few additional accesses most of them hadn't heard of. These people knew she was the reason for their existence as a task force. She had seen the blip on her computer indicating a nuclear emission originating in southern Africa. Because of her perseverance, her superiors followed up on the discovery and notified the CIA. Clutching her folder, she turned to leave when the chief, John Matterhorn, ran out of his office toward her.

"Elizabeth." He led her to his office. "I'm sorry. It won't happen again."

If it weren't for their family connections, she would have told John to take his task force and his surly, insular people and stick them all up his ass. She had calmed a bit by the time she entered his office and settled in a chair across from him. John began sorting out the photographs and data sheets she laid before him. Lost in studying the material, it appeared he had let the earlier flashing light incident pass—she hadn't.

"John, before we start analyzing this data, please explain what happened in Namibia yesterday."

He removed his glasses and cleaned them with an ironed handkerchief he pulled from his back pocket. A heavy sigh followed. Carefully he replaced them, avoiding her gaze. "Things did not go as planned."

"Yes, I know. The plane flew off with the bomb." She let the words hang.

"Our people were captured, tortured. Thank goodness, they're alive." He avoided her gaze. "We have alerted CIA stations in Angola and the Congo. We're setting up an interception in the Chad region."

"Interception?"

"We're looking for an asset in one of the foreign air forces. Force the plane down, you know?"

Kerr looked out John's office and saw his people on the phones, walking back and forth with papers in their hands. These people with all their sources and analysis hadn't a clue where the plane was now, or was headed. She did.

"John. Look at this map and this readout." She slid them in front of him. "Five hours ago we identified what we believe is our target aircraft flying over the northern region of Angola. The direction of the flight was still due north."

"How?" John looked up. "Is the bomb leaking again? Is that how you found it again?"

"No. It's not leaking."

Then how …?"

"We have a new satellite. Polyphemus."

John moved close to her. "Really?"

"Not to get overly specific, the satellite …" She searched for words not too technical and not too revealing of her agency's sensitive information. "The satellite took an image of the plane while it was parked on the Bruin Karas runway. Sort of a three-dimensional fingerprint. The image is in the satellite's computer memory, and it can search for the plane using the stored criteria."

"So you know where it is all the time?"

"No. The technology's not perfected. Weather, clouds play havoc with the input." She folded her hands on the table. "You can imagine the problems with the tropical storms."

John studied the map and the data in front of him. "It was here five hours ago. Looks like the intended destination is Libya."

"Maybe."

"I know what you're thinking. We're fixated on Libya."

"What really happened on the ground in Namibia? I thought you had your top man there."

John raised his hands. "We did. Gus Frederick told me his people fell into a trap. He's very irritated with Hayden Stone."

"John, you can say it. He's damn pissed off. As he should be."

"Yes, Gus is disappointed."

"So get a new man."

John Matterhorn studied her. "We all make mistakes. All have setbacks." He looked down at the report as he spoke. "For years Gus and Stone have had running battles. Sort of like an ongoing Kabuki dance."

"This is no time for dancing."

"Hayden Stone always comes through."

Kerr murmured, "Yeah."

Matterhorn's assistant knocked on the door. "Miss Kerr. You have a call on the Green Phone."

Kerr left the office and went to the long table by the far wall holding a bank of secure phones. When she left his office, she heard John instruct his assistant to pass the word that the warning lights were not to be turned on when Kerr came in.

A few minutes later Kerr returned and sat waiting for John to finish his own phone call. When he hung up, he said, "Latest position we have for our target is over the Congo River. Moving faster than we thought it would. Wonder where the next refuel stop will be," "Another bit of information. One of its two engines is giving it some problems," Kerr said.

"Polyphemus can see that? Amazing." He thought a second. "Good news. That'll slow them down or force them to land."

"Something else. The direction of flight is shifting slightly to the west."

"Ah. North by northwest."

"Sorry, John. That's only a movie title. On a compass rose the direction is north-northwest."

He looked up on the map of Africa on his wall. "That is not in the direction of Libya, is it? Unless they were blown off course."

"More in the direction of Gabon or Cameroon," Kerr said. "We should know in a little while. Unfortunately, Polyphemus is down right now."

CAPE TOWN

At the CIA safe house, Hayden Stone tried to relax on the wooden deck overlooking a gloomy False Bay. The gray, overcast sky accompanied a wintry wind from the beach. A doctor and nurse from the American Consulate were examining Sandra's and Dirk Lange's multiple injuries. Stone volunteered to be treated after them. He knew none of his bones were broken, although he had large welts and bruises on his chest and legs. The two gashes in his scalp might need stitches.

That morning they had flown back on Jacob's helicopter and were dropped off at a nearby airport. The Mossad agent had fidgeted and huffed the entire flight. Jacob kept saying, "Shouldn't have let them take it."

An hour out of Cape Town, Stone leaned close to him and said he knew that the same helicopter they were in had landed a few days ago near the boxcar and the occupants had inspected the bomb.

"Were you one of the people the CIA satellite saw?"

Jacob answered with one of his token sour looks. Before they parted, he handed Stone a phone number. "Contact me if you hear anything," Jacob said. "Contact me if you don't."

The nurse came out on the deck and told Stone it was his turn to be checked. "Your friend Sandra Harrington will need X-rays," she said. "We're worried about her. She's on the way to the clinic."

Lange came out of the bedroom being used as an examining room. "Thanks for having your people look me over. No broken bones, just this eye, which they advised I have a specialist look at." He bit his lip. "Worried about Sandra. She may have a cracked rib or two."

Stone found Lange's concern for Sandra annoying. "Suppose you'll report back to your service," he said. "I wonder how they'll react when you tell them what you've been up to." "I've been informed that your embassy has notified my government about the bomb. Officials in Pretoria must be in turmoil. Can you imagine when they hear that one of their nuclear bombs was stolen? And by a leading member of the white community? They'll want to know why I didn't inform them about our trip to Namibia."

"So they didn't know anything about Van Wartt or Abdul Wahab? They had no idea what they were up to?"

"Not exactly. Let's just say our intelligence services are covering their activities."

Stone decided to remain silent. Let Lange reveal as much as he thought he could.

Lange touched his swollen eye. "My home office is in disarray. I've been telling the friends I trust about what's been happening. My service may be taken over by the politicos, the crowd who made up the ANC's infamous secret service, *Mbokodo,* during apartheid. If the politicos take over, my friends and I are out of work." He laughed. "Lack of job security, as you Yanks would say."

"Stay in touch," Stone said. "We might put you on our rolls."

"Two things before I go. I ... we've come up with some information that may help in knowing where that plane is headed." Lange sat on the edge of a folding chair. Stone did likewise. "Nabeel Asuty went to Abdul Wahab's villa immediately after Sandra shot her former, uh, friend, Farley Durrell."

Interesting. Did Dirk see Farley as a rival? Things were close between Lange and Sandra, and he didn't quite approve.

Lange continued, "Asuty told Wahab that Farley was an infiltrator. They planned to kill him, but his plans were thwarted when gunfire erupted on the Victoria and Alfred pier. When Farley got shot in the leg."

"Really?" Stone leaned back on the doorjamb. *Sounds like they listened in on the conversation. Should have known the South Africans had a bug or an informant in Wahab's villa.*

"I remember one bit of interesting information. A mention was made that Farley was working with some shipping company in Cameroon. Douala, I believe."

"Douala is north on the way to Libya." Stone said.

"Exactly. No doubt, the CIA analysts debriefed Farley before they sent him back to the States."

"It's worth checking."

Lange leaned forward. "The second matter involves Sandra and me." He looked down. "We're fond of each other. We both know this may cause problems with her employers and mine. I'm sure both organizations will take a hard look at our relationship."

"This comes as a complete surprise to me," Stone said with a straight face.

"Do you have problems with me being involved with Sandra? I mean, have you ever had ideas about her ...?"

Stone took his time in answering. "Dirk. Sandra and I are business partners. We work well together. We like each other, but more important, we trust each other. When I was in the FBI, at times you needed a partner, and if you were lucky, they were good like Sandra. If so, you could count on them and they could count on you, especially when crunch time came. Adding romance to the equation brings complications."

"Thanks. That's a relief." Lange got up and they shook hands.

Stone watched Lange carry out his gear and get in a car with a CIA staffer. He hoped Sandra wasn't getting herself into another romantic mess. More than that, he resented Lange moving in on Sandra. What would that do to his relationship with her? Nothing positive. From the window, Stone watched the car depart for Cape Town.

He found the doctor waiting in the room—a man with a

Pakistani accent. As Stone suspected, he had no broken bones and didn't need stitches for the two gashes in his scalp. The doctor handed him a bottle of pills for his headaches. The pain came from a slight concussion, he was told.

One of the CIA technicians looked in the door and said, "Colonel Frederick wants to speak with you ... on the computer."

Stone went to the communications room and sat before a laptop. The last message on the screen read:

> *Get me Stone. NOW.*

Fredrick was still pissed. He would have to be diplomatic. He typed:

> *Hi, Colonel. We all made it back. Sandra is having her ribs x-rayed for fractures. Dirk's eye may give him problems. I've a concussion. Any leads on the plane?*

Stone waited for over five minutes. Frederick responded, and Stone watched the letters form into words across the screen.

> *The plane with the package you let get out of your hands is somewhere over the Congo River. What did Jacob say? Did he have anything important to give us?*

Stone let out a whistle. Frederick's anger bounced from the computer screen. Couldn't exactly blame him.

> *Plan to meet with Jacob later today. Confident he will have something of value to give us.*

A few minutes passed.

> *Stone. My confidence in you is very low today. Give me something.*

What Lange said about the meeting of Asuty at Wahab's villa came to mind. Not much, but it was something.

> *Reason to believe Farley Durrell was working at a shipping company in Douala, Cameroon, before Asuty learned he was an informant. Did anyone look at Durrell's debrief after he left?*

Another two-minute pause before Frederick responded.

We will look into that when we have time.

Stone typed quickly.

I can do it. What about Abdul Wahab? He may know where they are going. He may be receptive if the approach is right.

The answer came quick.

No, on both suggestions. Out.

Stone stared at the screen. It appeared Colonel Frederick no longer required his services. The colonel could be difficult at times. No matter. Stone would ignore him. He'd continue on the case. Colonel Frederick would have to accept it.

He left the computer and took a throwaway cell phone from his jacket pocket. At the ambassador's function, Lucinda had given him her telephone number. She answered on the third ring.

"Hi, Lucinda. I'm back."

She immediately responded. "Oh good. I hoped you would not be gone long." Noise came over the phone as if she dropped something.

"I'd like to see you tonight," he said. He told her he was out of town but planned to be in the city later that day. "What hotel are you staying in?"

"I am Patience's guest at her apartment in Newlands," she said. "Where are you staying?"

"I have to find a room."

A long pause. "Patience is staying with a friend overnight. I don't think she'd mind you staying here." Another pause. "In fact, I know she wouldn't. You and I have a lot to talk about."

Ringing off, Stone wondered what Lucinda wanted to "talk" about? However, Jacob was next on his call list. Surely the Mossad agent had come up with something from his many sources. What his friend learned could prove crucial in finding the nuclear bomb. Time was running out. Jacob answered on the first ring.

When he heard Stone's voice, he skipped pleasantries. "Meet me at the South African National Gallery in an hour."

CHAPTER TWENTY-EIGHT

CAPE TOWN

On the way downtown, Hayden Stone encountered heavy traffic and had trouble finding a parking spot, all of which accounted for being almost a half hour late. Inside the white one-story South African National Gallery, he found Jacob in the African wing studying a tall standing figure made of dried grass and feathers.

The only other visitor in the room was a middle-aged, well-dressed black woman who left the room, her high heels clicking on the polished oak floor. The skylights in the high ceilings softened Jacob's features, but not the tension around his eyes.

"You're late," he said, turning toward a foot-high ebony figure standing on a pedestal. "You should wear a hat to cover those bandages."

Stone remained silent, pretending to be interested in the sculpture. Jacob would voice his concerns, afterward Stone would see if they could find a solution to the problem of the bomb.

"Time is not on our side, Stone. These people are an unknown quantity. They've split from al Qaeda." Jacob turned his attention to the cream-colored walls as if he was about to comment on the choice of color. "This Nabeel Asuty wants to be the new idol of the worldwide jihadist movement. So he wants to outdo them."

"The plane is somewhere over the Congo River," Stone said in a low voice. He noticed an echo in the gallery. "Frederick and others assume Asuty is headed for Libya, but I'm not convinced."

"Neither are my superiors in Tel Aviv." Jacob started moving to the far end of the gallery. "What does Frederick have you doing now?"

"Nothing. I think I've been dumped, but that's not stopping me from making amends, as it were." Stone looked around to see if they were still alone, and then he related what Lange had told him about Cameroon. "My hunch is that's where they're headed."

Jacob nodded. "Good choice. Ever been to Douala?"

"Yes. A steamy, dirty, dangerous seaport. It's the end of the line. A perfect place to find some tramp steamer to take on cargo with no questions asked." A thought occurred to Stone. "Let's go talk to Abdul Wahab if he hasn't already disappeared. By the way, the South Africans have him under surveillance."

"I know, and he's not disappearing." Jacob smiled for the first time. "He's about to see the light."

Stone let that statement settle. "He's being pitched by your side and the South Africans?"

"Both, and also your side."

"The agency wants to recruit Wahab? The man instrumental in the deaths of two young CIA officers three months ago?" Stone knew his anger showed. "I can't believe it."

"Hayden. Try to understand."

"The FBI doesn't rest until it nails those who kill one of its own."

Jacob held up his hand to calm him down. "You must learn that this is a different ball game. You're in the spy business. You are no longer someone trying to *catch* spies like the FBI does."

"It takes a thief to catch a thief. It takes a spy to catch a spy."

"Abdul Wahab is more valuable alive than dead," Jacob said. "At this time he has information and contacts we can use long term."

Stone paced the wooden floor. Two college-aged girls with notepads stood at the entrance to the room studying the paintings on the walls. He let what Jacob said sink in. Evidently Abdul Wahab had offered his services, and the way the world had evolved since 9/11, the intelligence community couldn't pass up the opportunity.

"Do you plan to go to Douala, and if you do, who will go with you?" Jacob whispered as the two girls made their way into the room.

"I'll hold off going there until I hear something from Frederick, but I'm not waiting too long," Stone said in a low voice. "Sandra would want to come, but she's hurting. There's Dirk Lange—"

"Lange is about to part from the secret service. In fact, he has a position with the Scorpions."

Stone gave him a quizzical look.

As Jacob motioned they should leave, he explained, "The Directorate of Special Operations. It's a unit formed to fight the South African crime syndicates."

"So he's no longer in the business?"

"No one ever leaves our business," Jacob said. When they reached the gallery's foyer, he tugged Stone's sleeve. "I guess it's just the two of us. Have any contacts in Douala?"

"This should be interesting, the two of us working together." Descending the entrance stairs, Stone said, "We have a CIA station in Yaoundé. Surely they'll be in the loop." He thought a moment. "France has a close connection with Cameroon. Three months ago on the French Riviera, I met a guy in French intelligence. He might help us. Tonight I'll get his number from a friend."

The late afternoon sun came in through the louvered blinds and brightened the library in soft yellow light. Abdul Wahab always felt at peace here, even when he entertained difficult guests. Lady Beatrice and he sat patiently for the arrival of two individuals who would determine his future.

"When did you say they would be here?" Wahab asked.

"Momentarily. Dingane has been told to show them in."

"I know this Dirk Lange fellow. He's a South African intelligence agent, but Patience St. John Smythe. Why is she coming? She was at the Van Wartts' party we attended recently, wasn't she?" Wahab felt warm. Maybe he should remove his jacket. No, he must give a dignified appearance to these people. "She's involved with the American ambassador."

Lady Beatrice closed her eyes. "Patience is an old friend of mine from London. Her family belongs to our club. We sail together. Surely, I've mentioned it to you."

Wahab gave a weary sigh. Nothing had gone as planned, but now that he looked back, he had lost control of this foolish endeavor a month ago. When that lowlife Nabeel Asuty came on the scene.

"I'm sorry, dear, you may very well have mentioned her name. She is an attractive woman." Then remembering his original question Wahab asked, "So why is she coming?"

"She's in the same business as Dirk Lange. She'll be part of the ... bargain."

"Interesting."

They heard Dingane at the front door bring people into the vestibule. A moment later there was a knock on the library door. Wahab opened it and led Patience and Lange into the room, offering them armchairs.

Wahab sat next to Beatrice on the leather settee. Should he ask how Lange felt? He looked at the man's swollen eye and thought better of it, even though he had helped save his life. There was the matter of his being the original cause of Lange and his companions' capture and subsequent beatings. He'd let them begin the negotiations.

"Mr. Wahab, you have a big problem." Dirk Lange began. "You are a guest in South Africa and you assisted in the sale of a stolen nuclear weapon to foreign terrorists. The authorities are thirsty for blood."

Beatrice touched Wahab's arm as he leaned forward to rest his elbows on his knees.

"Some people have suggested that if you enter into an arrangement, you could avoid considerable unpleasantness," Lange said. "Like imprisonment for the rest of your life in our Pollsmoor prison facility."

The last statement made an impression on Wahab. "What are your terms?"

Patience now spoke. "You have vast knowledge and contacts with terrorist organizations. You will provide us a continuing stream of information on individual terrorists, terrorist cells, and when needed, will assist our people in any counterterrorist operation. We understand you have important contacts in Yemen. That is of particular interest to us."

Wahab turned to Beatrice, who nodded. He did the same. "Who are these 'people'? CIA?"

"It doesn't really matter," Lange said. "If you agree to our terms, and it will be in writing, we'll arrange for your safe transport to another country."

"I see." Wahab looked at the ceiling. "I suppose I have no choice. Yes, I agree to your terms."

"Good. We'll begin to put matters into motion when these papers are signed." Patience handed Wahab four official-looking memoranda. "You may want to sit over there at your desk and read them before signing."

Taking the papers, Wahab read the top one while slowly walking to his desk. He looked up. "Canada? These are official Canadian documents! I would have sworn you were CIA. Oh well, I have no quarrel with Canada."

Wahab went back to the forms and carefully signed each while the other three waited in silence. He looked up at Beatrice, but her eyes were looking off in the distance. He signed the last one and handed them to Patience.

"Have a seat over there, Mr. Wahab. We have some questions that demand immediate answers."

Wahab obliged and noted his wife sat expressionless except for the downward curve of her mouth that appeared when she was distressed.

"We must know where Asuty is taking the bomb," Lange said.

"He never told me. Not directly, that is. The deal was once he took possession our association ended. He never said what he was going to do with it, but it is assumed ..."

"You assumed he intended to kill a lot of innocent people." At Dirk Lange's words, Beatrice jerked. "Think, Wahab. Give us something to go on. If you do, then those papers Patience is holding will become official. Otherwise ..."

"I remember him saying something about a seaport and a shipping company. Oh, yes, Cameroon was mentioned, but so was Sierra Leone. Asuty's group was infiltrated by a British agent. They tried to kill him but bungled it somehow." Wahab looked at both his interrogators. "Ask MI6 what they know."

"What about Libya? Could he be taking it there?" Patience asked.

"Definitely not. The Libyan intelligence service is at odds with Asuty's group. He's Egyptian, you know. Some bad blood there. Don't know why."

"We better get this to the right people," Lange said to Patience.

This was the time to ask a question nagging Wahab since the morning. "Where is Dawid van Wartt?"

"He's under arrest," Lange said. "Very serious charges, you may imagine."

"Knowing Dawid, he'll buy his way out of this mess. A real blackguard. He talked me into this stupid idea." *Not quite fair.* Since they were receptive to that question, what about the most important one. Why isn't the CIA, and more importantly why isn't his nemesis, Hayden Stone, present? He'd need to go about it obliquely. "I'm surprised Hayden Stone isn't with us."

Patience waved off the question and said, "I'm surprised you haven't asked where we're taking you."

Wahab thought a moment. "Yemen?"

"Not yet. You're heading for a colder climate. Pack your wools." Patience rose. "Lady Beatrice, may I speak with you privately?"

"Before you leave," Wahab said, " I want to say I truly regret my actions. They were not at all thought out on my part."

"Please," Lange said. "No more of that bullshit."

The absence of Hayden Stone concerned Wahab. If the CIA was not part of the deal, then dues were unpaid. Like the deaths of those two young CIA officers in the South of France. Another stupid mistake on his part.

"I have reason to believe that Hayden Stone still holds some grudge against me. Even though in Namibia I was instrumental in the saving of your life, Mr. Lange, and Stone's life. Have you any idea what his thinking is about all this?"

"It's always difficult to say what Mr. Stone is thinking or what he will do, for that matter," Lange said.

"I'll second that," Patience said.

Wahab detected something in Patience's aside that he couldn't quite grasp, but it made him uncomfortable.

CHAPTER TWENTY-NINE

CAPE TOWN—AUGUST 21, 2002

Rain pelted against the sliding glass doors that opened to the apartment's third-floor balcony. Hayden Stone moved the sheet aside and, with half-closed eyes, peered out at the dim early dawn. He lay naked next to Lucinda, listening and feeling her slow, quiet breathing. She had put on a short chemise "To keep my shoulders warm," she told him after their last lovemaking.

The wind accompanying the steady downpour rattled one of the sliding doors, and Stone, in that state of half awake, debated whether he should rise and check the latch. He waited a few moments, it rattled again, this time louder, and he slipped from under the covers and made his way to the door. It was secure.

He looked out at the gray winter storm coming off the South Atlantic. In the last minutes it had gained strength. He returned to the warmth on the sheet where he had been sleeping and eased closer to Lucinda. She stirred, stretched without opening her eyes, reached over, and squeezed his thigh. As if reassured he hadn't left her, she went back to a hushed slumber. His face touching her back, his fingers roamed over her soft skin from waist to bottom and settled on her smooth buttocks.

Stone floated in a comfortable haze, allowing his mind to drift back to the events of the night before. He had picked up Lucinda here at Patience's apartment in the Newlands, a district south of Cape Town's that spread along the base of Table Mountain. They drove to a bistro Patience had recommended and gone to the trouble to make a reservation. Stone found the décor woody and dark, but in a way welcoming after coming in from the cold evening air. The lighting as well as the atmosphere was subdued. Most of the patrons consisted of young professional Cape Towners, and thankfully the noise and music level was low enough for conversation.

From the moment she'd entered the car, Lucinda had been concerned with Stone's bruised face. After they were seated in the restaurant, she continued, "Is the rest of your body … discolored and cut?"

He told her it was, and now reminded of his injuries began to feel the aches that come as the body repaired itself. "I'll live," he joked.

She took a deep serious breath and placed her hand on his. "You wonder why I came down here to see you?"

He told her he hadn't expected to ever see her again, but he was glad she had come.

"Last May we parted on bad terms. I told you I never wanted to see you again." She shrugged. "Of course, I was upset about how things went … with us, with my palace wrecked by those Arabs. I blamed you, but our mutual friend, Inspector Maurice Colmont, told me that the French intelligence learned that it was the Arabs who were responsible. Not you."

Stone considered it a stroke of luck that the waiter came for their order, giving him time to rethink his initial impulse to admit part of the responsibility. In fact, he had led a commando team into the palace, and they had done most of the shooting and damage. Oh well.

Lucinda leaned forward and asked if he minded her ordering for both of them. "Patience gave me some hints on the food here," she said, looking pleased.

Tonight her auburn hair was pulled back and fastened with a silver filigree clasp. It looked Egyptian, probably a family heirloom. Her face, a mix Italian and Coptic-Egyptian blood, exuded an exoticism in the candlelight. Using the candle to read the menu, her green eyes studied the selections, and with authority she ordered the guinea fowl paupiette and smoked breast with wild rice and Kalahari truffles for him. For herself she chose the blue wildebeest with braised red cabbage, turnip puree, and red currant jus.

"Have you ever seen a wildebeest?" Stone asked. "They don't look very mouthwatering. They're quite ugly."

"Out on the plains, lions find them most appetizing," she said. "Besides, tonight I feel adventuresome."

Stone suggested a bottle of red wine, she agreed, and he chose a Stellenbosch Shiraz.

"I am fortunate that the Saudi prince who rented my palace agreed to pay for the damages." She sighed. "It turns out he is quite the gentleman. To change the subject, the reason why I am here is because I want to tell you that I still ... love you." She let out a deep breath as if in relief. "I always have loved you. However, sometimes, the way you act, I don't trust you. I'm not sure you still love me."

"I always loved you. It's just that you scare me."

Her eyebrow arched.

"In many ways you're almost, well, unattainable."

"I know. But you're the only man I know who can—" she thought a moment, and then laughed. "Attain me."

Their dinners arrived. The portions were modest, which pleased Stone, as the meal was rich in flavor, satisfying his appetite after only a few mouthfuls. The wine was adequate. He kept looking at Lucinda, wondering how it would be to live with her, permanently.

After the waiter removed their plates, both declined dessert but decided to share a cheese plate. "We were talking about the Saudi prince who reimbursed you for the damage to your place. His son-in-law, Abdul Wahab, lives here," Stone said. "He's behind the terrorist plot I tried to stop."

"That *cochon*, that pig was the reason I agreed to rent the palace to those Arabs. Maurice Colmont told me that Wahab is on the French police wanted list. He can't return to France."

"He also may have outlived his welcome here."

Lucinda touched his face. "Was he responsible for this?"

"Indirectly." Stone thought a moment. "Ironic, I'm alive and so are my colleagues because Wahab prevented the other terrorists from killing us."

"Where are your colleagues? Where is, what is her name, Sandra?"

"Yes, Sandra. Neither one came out as well as me. Both are in bad shape."

"Is this mission over?" Lucinda asked.

"No, it's not. However, my part in the operation may be over."

Lucinda looked puzzled.

"I screwed up. Botched the case," Stone said. "Gus Frederick, who you met at Ambassador Bunting's function, has lost confidence in me."

"So you will be leaving Cape Town?" She placed a blue cheese on a cracker.

"I should know tomorrow. By the way, do you have Colmont's telephone number? I'd like to call him and ask a favor."

After dinner they drove back to the apartment. The moment Lucinda led Stone into the flat, he knew from the modern Italian décor that this was Patience's home. Her signature was everywhere. He had little time to admire the furnishings, as Lucinda had taken his hand and pulled him to her bedroom.

Again rain hit hard on the glass doors, bringing Stone out of his semi-dream. The sheet tightened over his body and he sensed Lucinda stir, throw off the blanket, and go to the bathroom. The wind pounded against the glass, and even though daybreak had arrived, the sky remained gloomy. After a while, she slipped back in bed and snuggled close.

Stone let himself drift again into that world of partial consciousness. Lucinda appeared in the dream, but as the girl he first met long ago in Nice, France. Her hair was shorter, her figure trim, and her white blouse brought out her tan from hours sailing on her father's ketch. The boat's name was *La Claire*, and the two of them sailed the dark Mediterranean.

The dream shifted to a dinner dance during the Christmas holiday season. She in a long black gown, he in his naval officer's uniform. They danced very close. Later that night she sneaked into his bedroom and they made love for the first time.

Startled, Stone was awake and back in the present. Lucinda yanked off the covers and sat on top of him. She held a mug of hot coffee in her hand, the rich aroma rising with the steam.

"Good morning, my dear," she said. "What first? Coffee or me?"

"No contest," he said, taking the cup from her hand and placing it on the nightstand.

Slowly and dramatically, she lifted her white satin chemise over her head and discarded it. She came down hard, kissing and biting his neck. She laughed and tightened her legs around his body. He had no idea where her body would twist next, but intended to enjoy the ride.

Exhausted, Stone stared at the ceiling, waiting for his breathing to slow. She had collapsed on him after giving out that sharp cry he remembered from past times. Shifting her head on his arm so their eyes met, she whispered, "As good as ever, no?"

"*Oui, mon contessa.*"

Now giggling, she said, "Come back with me to France and we can do this all the time."

He reached over for the coffee mug. "Want some?"

She sat up and shook her head. From her serious demeanor, Stone knew a heavy conversation was about to commence. Probably something about making their relationship permanent. He would have liked a little more time, at least to finish his coffee, before committing to a long-term relationship.

He fought back a smile. How could she possibly expect him to pay attention, sitting there with her beautiful breasts displayed in their firmness—and yes, that mole was still there below the left nipple. A sculptor would love to spend time with her.

"Are you paying attention to me?" she asked, nose uplifted.

"Of course."

"I have something to ask you."

"Can't wait to hear." The coffee was perfect, dark, and strong, with a touch of nut.

"Come live with me in Villefranche. Perhaps we could …"

She slipped out of bed. "You think about it. Yes?"

"Yes." He'd think about it.

During the following hour, while they showered together, dressed, and had breakfast that, to his surprise, she prepared, Hayden Stone carefully watched every word and gesture he made. *Don't do or say anything wrong.*

He let the realization of the two of them sharing their lives in the South of France slowly sink in. It was not an unpleasant notion, no matter how he had to adjust the view of his new future.

Watching her place the dishes in the sink, he remembered he had to call Jacob. How life had just changed for him since he and Jacob had met in the museum. He searched for his cell phone.

"Who are you calling?"

"A colleague. I'm traveling with him to Cameroon."

"What is this job? Why is it so important to all of you?"

He stopped dialing. "Patience didn't tell you?" He watched her return to the kitchen table and sit, waiting for him to explain. He gave her a thumbnail version of the terrorist plot and how he screwed up in Namibia.

"An atomic bomb! You must stop them!"

Stone stood, went to the window, and watched raindrops form on the glass. The tall blue gum trees and pines swayed in the wind. "My superiors think the bad guys are headed north for the country of Chad. Jacob, my old Israeli friend, and I believe they're heading for the seaport of Douala in Cameroon."

"Your other colleagues are recovering from their wounds. So you and Jacob must go alone." Her gaze was fixed on him.

"I would expect you to tell me not to go."

Lucinda rose and came up next to him. "Do you think I want you to go and possibly get killed?"

"You think I should go?"

"This is not the case of a … a petty matter." She rested her head on his shoulder. "You had a failure, made a mistake. So, who does not from time to time? Do you still want Maurice Colmont's telephone number? Perhaps, he can help you."

She took him by the hand, led him to the living room, and

turned the gas on in the fireplace. "Sit," she commanded and stood in front of him, arms crossed. "My family line is long and involved. On the Italian side, we go back to the Middle Ages, when the Moors attacked our villages and castles. We fought back. On my father's side, we are Coptic Christians who have lived in Egypt for two thousand years, most of those years under persecution. My family does not bend. We are survivors, because we do not walk away." She sat in front of him on a footstool. "If you don't go, you will never forgive yourself. In time you will place all the blame on me."

Contessa Lucinda Avoscani arched her back and pronounced, "I will not have that."

A brief moment passed and Stone said, "You said you had Colmont's number? I have to call him before I meet with Jacob."

She went to the bedroom and returned with the number. After he made the call to Colmont and got the name of a contact in Cameroon, he started to dial Jacob. She held her hand on the phone while leaning her head over to kiss him. She placed a gold object in his hand. "Take this with you for good luck. It is a family talisman."

He looked down at the small Coptic cross on a gold chain.

CHAPTER THIRTY

DOUALA, CAMEROON—AUGUST 22, 2002

The Douala International Airport was how Hayden Stone remembered it fours years before. Courtesy of the French, it was an impressive complex for West Africa, but had had little routine preventive maintenance from the day it opened. It smelled rank and looked shabby. Few people walked the high-ceilinged terminal. If arriving passengers were lucky enough to find their luggage after paying a bribe, they had to pass through a gauntlet of a screaming, pushing mob outside the door, wanting to carry your bags, sell you a flashlight, take you to their taxi, or just demand money.

Jacob cursed and shoved his way through the crowd with Stone following in his wake, holding his backpack with one hand, the other on his money belt beneath his shirt. Beyond the throng, two tall men with short haircuts waved to them.

"They're our contacts," Jacob shouted. "They have a car waiting for us."

The two pushed their way through the crowd and reached the SUV. As Stone closed the door, he discovered that somewhere between the airport and the SUV someone had managed to slip his cheap watch off his wrist. They were practiced in their art.

With all four men inside the vehicle, the driver inched away from the curb while remnants of the besiegers attempted one last effort to extract money from those whom they considered well-heeled foreigners.

"Now that's what I call a welcome reception," Stone said, removing his jacket and wiping the sweat from his face. He hoped his departure from Douala would be soon and a bit easier. When he flew out, he'd remember to have a fistful of local CFA francs to grease the palms at the airport.

Jacob spoke at length in rapid Hebrew with the two Mossad men in the front seat. Jacob's organization definitely had a presence here in Cameroon, which he had neglected to tell Stone. Jacob sat back, deep in thought, and then turned to Stone.

"Here's the rundown. My boys here are in contact with the CIA station at your embassy in Yaoundé. Colonel Frederick and his people are having trouble getting visas, but should be here tomorrow."

"That leaves only us to find the bomb."

"No. A man and a CIA woman will arrive from Cape Town later today. I assume Sandra Harrington and Dirk Lange. I have four more men at the safe house."

"Sandra and Dirk either had quick physical recoveries or can't bear being out of the action," Stone said. "Any leads on Nabeel Asuty and his men?"

"Six hours ago your satellite found that C-119 at an abandoned French airfield ten miles outside the city. No further word on the terrorists or the bomb. My embassy and your people in Yaoundé are in contact and will keep us updated."

Stone asked if the man in front would turn up the air conditioning. The additional cool air blowing in from the vent brought some relief from the humid air. He turned to Jacob. "I have the name and telephone number of a contact that Maurice Colmont, my friend in Paris, gave me. Do we have a clean cell phone?"

The man in the passenger seat passed back a cell phone to Stone. Stone held up the phone to Jacob, who waved a "go ahead and call."

The male voice on the other end of the line identified himself in French as being a member of the Cameroon police. In French, Stone asked for Reynard Abdulyale. When he came on the line, Stone gave him the parole Colmont had provided to identify him to Abdulyale as a trusted agent.

Abdulyale paused, then asked when they could get together.

"Today. Lunch in two hours?"

A name and address of a restaurant was given to Stone,

who repeated out loud to Jacob. The driver motioned he knew where it was.

When Stone hung up, Jacob suggested only the two of them meet with Abdulyale. "My boys will stay outside and cover our meeting with this fellow."

"Where is the restaurant?" Stone asked the driver.

In English with a Brooklyn accent, he told him it was near the port area. "In the Lebanese district. Rough area. We have pistols for you."

At that, the man in the passenger seat turned and handed them 9mm Glocks along with two magazines each, first to Jacob, then Stone. Not Stone's favorite caliber.

They drove toward the city using back roads, alert for surveillance, but as the driver informed them, the intelligence service was underpaid and ill supplied with resources. "They are only interested in Nigerians and the opposing political party."

Stone looked out the window at the usual parade of women in tie-dyed kaftans with baskets balanced on their heads, children walking holding each others hands, and men on bicycles. As they entered the edge of town, open sewers flowed on either side of the road.

"I think I'll contact a guy I know. If he's still here," Stone said. "Don't know his telephone number, but do know the name of his business and the street where he's located."

Jacob had him give the information to the man sitting in the passenger seat. The man called the safe house and had another agent find the firm's telephone number in the Douala city directory.

Carl Cardinale answered Stone's call and happily agreed to meet him. A half hour later, Stone stood in front of a two-story complex in a mixed residential and commercial area, which looked clean and safe. Before exiting, Jacob told him he would run a trace on Abdulyale. Like all Douala, Stone knew that because of its relative wealth this neighborhood had to experience high crime. He remained alert.

Carl buzzed him in the entrance door, and he climbed to the second floor to another locked door, this one identified it as the Regional Transportation Office. Carl quickly opened the door and welcomed him into his one-man cluttered office. The RTO handled all the shipping and logistics for the American diplomatic establishments throughout central Africa.

He was genuinely happy to see Stone, not because they were good friends, but being one of the few Americans in town, his social life was nil. There was little entertainment in Douala to speak of except for a few sorry restaurants and nightclubs offering cheap liquor and expensive women.

"May I ask what happened?" He pointed to the bruises on Stone's face.

"Bad fall."

"What brings you to this hellhole? Or shouldn't I ask?

"Looking for bad guys. Know any in this town?"

"You got it ass-backwards. Ask me if I know any good guys."

Carl was on contract with the US State Department. His two-year tour had been extended one year, which he confided was a double-edged sword. "I miss my family, but the pay is great. You may want to take over for me when I leave. I'll give you a recommendation."

Stone thanked him, but said that he planned to retire. "I have an appointment in an hour, and a friend is picking me up. I know you have good contacts on the waterfront and with shipping companies."

"Yeah. I do." Carl looked disappointed that Stone's visit would be short.

"Right now, I don't exactly know what I want to ask you. I should know later in the day. Maybe we can get together for dinner?"

At the suggestion for dinner, Carl perked up. "Sure. What else can you tell me?"

"The people I'm looking for are from the Middle East. They're in possession of some bad-shit contraband. This is a seaport, and it's logical to assume they're going to ship it out of here. That's it so far."

Carl thought a moment. "Most of the non-Africans here are French and Lebanese. Both groups are tight and wary of outsiders."

"Some of the people I'm looking for are Egyptian. The leader's name is Nabeel Asuty, and he has at least five people with him. Maybe more now. They landed here today with their *goods* at the old French airbase a couple of miles out of town. We have no idea where they're headed."

"They're terrorists. Correct?" Carl asked, and when Stone nodded, said, "So, we're not talking drugs?" When Stone shook his head, he said, "I'll make some discreet inquiries."

Stone waited outside under the roof to the doorway, and when the SUV stopped at the curb, he jumped in and was greeted with Jacob's sour look.

"This contact of yours, Reynard Abdulyale, is a relatively honest man who lives very well. He must receive a big stipend from your French friends to afford his lifestyle. He's from the north of Cameroon, a Fulani and Moslem. We have to be careful what we say."

Obviously, Jacob wasn't impressed with Stone's selection of a source. Stone put on his sunglasses. "Any news?" he asked.

"Dirk and Sandra arrived with two other CIA people," Jacob said. "Our safe house is getting crowded."

"Hope our stay won't be long. Any word from Colonel Frederick?"

"He wants to talk with you after the meeting with Abdulyale." Jacob asked the driver how soon they would arrive at the restaurant and was told five minutes. "Your satellites have seen no recent activity at the airfield." Jacob leaned closer. "How good are these satellites?"

"As good as the people who interpret the data. Technology can't replace us here on the ground. And we on the ground have to get to that field pronto."

"Are you suggesting we conduct an assault?" Jacob asked. "Before Colonel Frederick and his team arrive?"

"Let's discuss it at the safe house after lunch."

* * *

Outside the restaurant Stone and Jacob spotted two parked Peugeot sedans. Men wearing glares and dark glasses slouched inside.

"I don't like this," was Jacob's only comment as they entered the establishment.

Stone felt the same but trusted Maurice Colmont. His friend in Paris would not lead him into a lion's den; however, the presence of the Glock in his waistband was more of a reassurance. Reynard Abdulyale wore a tailored brown suit, white monogrammed shirt, and a silk tie. His skin was light tan and his short-cut hair had traces of gray throughout. Tribal scars marked his cheeks. He sat with his back to the wall. The restaurant was empty, and the staff stood erect at a respectable distance waiting to be beckoned.

The big man rose and extended his hand to Stone. "I was only expecting you, Mr. Hayden Stone. You've brought along an associate?"

How had he recognized Stone? Had Colmont sent him a photograph? On the other hand, Abdulyale's men might have taken photographs of him at the airport.

"It is wise to travel in strange lands with friends," Stone said.

"Sounds like a phrase in Arabic." Abdulyale smiled broadly, revealing a gold tooth. "I assure you this is not that strange a land." He motioned for them to take a place at his table. He clapped his hand and in French ordered that another place be set for Jacob.

Seated, Abdulyale directed his attention to Jacob with eyes that lacked warmth. "I didn't catch your name." He looked back at Stone and laughed. "An American phrase that our mutual friend in Paris taught me the last time I visited Nice."

"It's Bjorn Anderson," said Jacob, using the alias Stone knew was on his passport. "Norwegian."

"And your business, sir?"

"Oil and fishing."

Abdulyale showed his gold tooth again, but the eyes

remained unfriendly. *Christ*, Stone thought. I should have come alone. He cursed himself for not thinking this meeting out. He might as well get to the point, hope to get some information, and leave.

"Mr. Abdulyale. Pardon, do people use your rank when addressing you?"

"Mister will do, Mr. Stone. And before we start our talk, would you care for refreshments?" Abdulyale called the waiters over and ordered light food and non-alcoholic drinks. "Now. What can I do for you?"

Stone saw the irony of the question. Here was a man whose usual mind-set was: What could one do for *him*? The waiter brought the drinks, giving him time to respond. "The US is still recovering from the 9/11 attack. We and the French government are interested in any information we can gather about terrorists in this region who might be planning another attack."

"It seems to me that your government has located the culprits far from here. In Afghanistan. Are you saying they are also here in my country?"

"We suspect some are in the region. It would be appreciated if you had any information to help us."

Abdulyale waited as the waiters set down the plates of grilled meats and yogurts. The silence had approached awkwardness when he finally said, "If anything of a terrorist nature comes to my attention and I believe it threatens your country or France, your governments will be informed."

"Thank you, sir. Sorry for taking up your time." Stone reached for his wallet. "May I?"

"I can't allow that. You are my guest." Abdulyale stood, and when he shook Stone's hand, he palmed a business card. He merely smiled at Jacob.

In the SUV, Jacob immediately told his men they had to switch cars before they went to the safe house. He turned to Stone. "That character knew about us. Knows we're on to something big."

"It didn't go as well as I expected," Stone said. "I should have gone alone."

"I should have insisted you did. He got more out of that meet than we did."

"I'm not sure about that," Stone said, fingering the business card in his pocket. "He was expecting us. He covered us at the airport, which, by the way, we didn't pick up. He probably thinks we're here on an 'extraordinary rendition.' Snatching a high-level terrorist to take to another country for interrogation. He wants to be part of the action."

"Ha! You have it all figured out." Jacob reached for a pack of cigarettes, seemed to think twice about it, and put them back in his pocket.

Stone knew from the past that when Jacob got edgy he went back to smoking. Time was running out to get that nuclear device before Nabeel Asuty fled the country with it. He thought about the words written on the business card passed to him.

URGENT THAT I SPEAK WITH YOU ALONE.

CHAPTER THIRTY-ONE

DOUALA, CAMEROON

No sooner had Hayden Stone walked into the safe house than Sandra Harrington handed him a satellite phone. No time for small talk, like how she and Dirk Lange, standing next to her, were recovering from their wounds. The flesh around Dirk's swollen eye had now turned a yellowish black. Sandra's face had a drawn, tired look.

"Colonel Frederick is on the phone," she whispered. "He wants to speak with you."

Stone took the phone while surveying his surroundings. The two-bedroom safe house felt crowded, with only a noisy air conditioner blowing out warm air. He knew Frederick would give him a hard time.

"Hi, Colonel. Where are you?" From past experience Stone knew that immediately asking Frederick a question put him off balance.

"A half day's trip from your location," he mumbled. "What have you been doing? Do you have the nuclear bomb located?"

"Checking with sources here in Douala. We've been told the plane is sitting at an abandoned airfield ten miles out of town."

"*Told!* Why the hell aren't you there?"

Jacob stood close enough to hear Frederick's voice coming from the speaker. "Hayden." Jacob spoke loudly enough for Frederick to overhear. "We have eyes on the target. The plane is still in the hangar. There are four armed terrorists guarding it."

"Did you hear that, Colonel?"

"Who's that with you?"

Stone told him and asked, "When did you say you'd get here to join the party?"

243

"We'll be there in less than three hours. I'm looking at satellite photos of the airfield." His voice lowered as he talked with people near him, then came back online. "Our assault team will land at the airfield. We still have two planes. I want you and your people to clear the target area for our landing."

"Will do," Stone said, and the line went dead.

Stone told Jacob what Frederick had planned. Sandra spread photographs of the target sent by CIA headquarters on the kitchen table. They showed a high chain-link fence enclosing the site. Two hangars and three other buildings sat alongside a weeded runway.

Stone studied the photographs. "They have a wide-open field of vision from the hangar." He looked at the people gathered around him. "And we can't wait for dark."

"We'll be ready to head for the airfield in five minutes," Jacob said.

Taking Sandra by the arm, Stone led her outside onto the balcony and closed the door. He wanted the others to think it was a private conversation, but his real intent was to phone Reynard Abdulyale at the number written on the business card he had given him.

Sandra came close and whispered, even though no one inside the apartment could hear her. "You know about Dirk and me?"

Stone pulled out the business card and started punching the telephone number into his cell phone. "Yes. I hope you two will be happy."

"Do you mean that? I mean … do you have any strong feelings about us?" She bit her lip. "About you and me?"

The phone rang at the other end, and he tried to think fast before someone came on the line. "Sandra. You and I are close. Very close." The phone continued to ring. "But Lucinda was there before you and I met. She'll always be—"

"*Bonjour*," Reynard Abdulyale said in Stone's ear.

Stone touched Sandra's cheek and spoke into the phone, "Mr. Reynard Abdulyale. This is Hayden Stone." Sandra moved to go back inside, but he took her hand.

"Yes, Mr. Stone. I had a call from our friend in Paris." Abdulyale sneezed. "His office is concerned about a terrorist group that has come here. I also am concerned. He said this group might have a weapon of mass destruction. These are the terrorists you are seeking?"

Stone didn't want to give him any more information than necessary. "Possibly. It will be best if we act fast. Have you heard anything about people from the Middle East contacting shipping companies?"

"People from the Middle East ship goods out of Douala every day, but I will ask our sources." Abdulyale sneezed again. "You must keep me informed of your whereabouts and actions." He wanted Stone's number. "Our friend in Paris said that he was sending men to Douala. This is my country. This apparently is a serious matter, and I must be kept informed." His last words were not a request.

"Who was that?" Sandra asked.

Stone explained that the man he talked with was a source of Maurice Colmont, the French intelligence office who both knew from working on what they referred to as "the Riviera contract." He kept holding her hand. "This mission has a shorter time schedule than we thought. Colmont is sending French agents here. Abdulyale is concerned we're going to shoot up the place."

"We better get to that airfield and take possession of the bomb ASAP," Sandra said.

"Before we go back in, Sandra, I want you to know—"

"We'll always be buddies, right?"

"No." He searched for the words. "I always thought we were more than good friends."

"What are you trying to say?"

"Don't laugh." He squeezed her hand. "I'm jealous of Lange."

She took a deep breath. "Thought so."

As they hurried back inside the apartment, Stone caught Dirk Lange watching them from through the glass door.

. . . .

The four SUVs pulled off the dirt road in a position where scrub trees hid them from the airfield's buildings. Stone and Jacob exited their vehicle and crept up to the rusty eight-foot chain-link fence. They searched their objective with binoculars.

"Two men at the open door to the hangar. Probably where the plane is," Jacob said. "Neither one is Nabeel Asuty."

"I see a panel truck with the back door open. A guy just pulled out a piece of machinery. They may be repairing the plane's engine." Stone lowered the glasses. "Mr. Asuty may be covering his bases. If they can't get that bomb out by ship, they'll fly it out of here."

Jacob grunted. "Like you said back in the safe house, we can't wait until dark to move."

"Don't see any guys walking out in the field assigned as lookouts." Stone thought a moment. "I say we go as planned. Use wire cutters to make an opening in that section of fence." He pointed. "We'll drive on the runway. Two SUVs go to the hangar. One vehicle moves toward the outbuildings. One SUV hangs back to fill in where necessary."

"Still don't want to send in one or two men as scouts?"

Stone shook his head. "We've got an open field with very little cover. Chances are someone would spot them."

"Let's go for it."

The moment the fence was cut, the SUVs moved into position and tore through the short stretch of bush and grass, pulled onto the runway, then sped at maximum speed to their assigned positions. The attack unfolded fast.

Stone was surprised they didn't take on gunfire until they pulled in front of the hangar, and that was from a lone man at the hanger entrance holding an AK-47.

The SUVs screeched to a halt, and the teams rolled out of the vehicles, shooting their way inside the hangers. Stone led one contingent into the hanger where the C-119 was parked.

Stone raced with a Mossad agent to the rear of the plane and scrambled up its opened ramp. Two men not older than twenty emerged from the flight deck firing automatic weapons. Stone aimed at the man on the right and hit him with two bursts from his Glock, then fired at the man on the left. Neither dropped, so he repeated two shots to the right, two to the left until both collapsed. He looked down and saw the Mossad agent groaning on the ground.

Stone reached down, felt the man's throat. "I'm still alive," the agent yelled and pushed his hand away. Stone reloaded and looked inside the flight deck. Situation under control.

Someone outside blew the all-clear whistle, and Stone ran out of the plane yelling, "Man down! Man down!"

Sandra and Lange ran back to an SUV and found a medical kit.

"Jacob! What's the situation?" Stone shouted.

"We're secure here," Jacob called from out on the tarmac. He indicated with his fingers. "Six of them dead. The other buildings are being searched."

Stone let the adrenaline work its way off. He drank a full bottle of water as he searched throughout the hangar for the bomb using the Geiger counter Dirk Lange had handed him. Trash, old rusty equipment, and crates were scattered in the hangar. Sunlight shone down through holes in the ceiling. Not finding the nuclear device, he raced to the other hangar and again found nothing.

When he went out onto the tarmac, Sandra ran up to Stone. "We better get that man some medical attention."

Jacob shouted from the plane, "We arranged for a clinic in the event this happened. Let's get him into one of the SUVs. Stone, did you find what we're looking for?"

"No. They've moved it. They've still got a lead on us."

When Hayden Stone left for Douala, Jacob said he'd stay with his wounded Mossad agent. The two CIA operatives who had flown in with Sandra also stayed at the airfield to facilitate the arrival of Colonel Frederick's team.

In the backseat of the SUV, Stone sat with Sandra and Lange

as the two Mossad agents in front chatted between themselves. As the SUV bounced in a manhole-sized pothole, Stone guessed Nabeel Asuty and his fellow terrorists were in Douala by now and loading the bomb aboard a ship. Dozens of ships went in and out of the port daily. He debated calling Carl Cardinale when his cell phone rang, and saw that Carl beat him to it.

"Hey, pal," Carl said. "Got some information that may help you." He sounded out of breath. "You said one of the guys you're looking for is Egyptian. This morning a big bearded guy screaming Arabic, his pants all bloody, ran out of a flophouse near the wharfs and down a street with two of his buddies following him. Shortly after, a well-known Russian prostitute was found in her room in the same flophouse with her head almost chopped off."

"Do the police have a lead on the guy?"

"Listen to this. The Middle East guy and his buddies ended up going to a Catholic dispensary where he had his cock sewn up."

"How do you know all this?"

"It's the talk of the town." Carl laughed. "This Arab is going to get more than he paid for. The Russian gal was a favorite of the local Russian drug lord, and he's pissed."

"Shit," Stone said. "Sounds like the guy we want. He killed a South African gal in Sierra Leone. Give me the name of the clinic. We have to find him before that Russian mobster does."

Carl gave Stone the address of the dispensary. "Ask for Sister Margaret. Tell her you're a friend of mine."

On arrival at the Catholic dispensary, an ageless Sister Margaret in a white habit and speaking French informed Stone that she couldn't give him the name or particulars of the man who visited with a bleeding groin area. She did identify Nabeel Asuty's photograph when Stone showed it to her.

"I didn't ask his name," she said. "He had a gun and so did his two companions."

Stone and Sandra walked out the dispensary door onto the crowded street and heard a woman's voice in pidgin French. Sitting next to the stoop, an uplifted face without a nose or ears spoke, "I know where they went." Her palm lifted for an offering. The fingers of the hand were absent.

Sandra squeezed his arm and took a deep breath. At that, Sister Margaret called from the open door, "Isabelle!" She admonished her with a wave of her finger.

"That's all right, Sister," Stone said, taking a handful of CFA francs from his pocket and placing them in the still-outreached palm. "Where did they go, madame?" he asked.

"Only a few blocks away. There's a truck parked outside. Many men with beards and guns under their coats stand around."

"How long ago did you see them?"

Isabelle looked up at Sister Margaret with questioning eyes, then looked up and down the street.

"They may return. I don't want trouble at my clinic," the nun said. She leaned down to Isabelle. They both whispered before she stood erect. "The men were cruel in their speech to this poor thing. One accused her of sins, and that is why God cursed her with leprosy." Stone recognized fury in Sister Margaret's eyes. "Isabelle followed them and saw where they went. It had to be two hours ago when all this happened. If you have a map, I'll show you the location."

Back inside the SUV, Stone called Jacob to update him. "I figure we're an hour and half behind Asuty."

Jacob snorted. "Just follow the trail of that prick's blood. Pun intended. Colonel Frederick is due to land in forty-five minutes. He's bringing reinforcements."

"We're going to check out the building Asuty was seen entering."

"Be careful. Don't get either of my boys hurt." Jacob rang off.

Stone suggested that Sandra stay with the parked SUV and act as support while the four men broke into two teams and scouted the target. She bristled and clenched her fists. Seeing this, Lange leaned over and told Stone he'd stay with the vehicle, as his eye was hurting. They exited and Stone gave him a "thank you" pat on the shoulder.

He and Sandra began searching for the address given to

them. Being white in an African town, Stone felt the curious eyes. He didn't want the word to spread that non-Africans were wandering around the vicinity. Rumors might reach Asuty or his men.

Sandra tied a light blue scarf over her hair and put on sunglasses. They passed single-story homes set back from the road, surrounded by hard, flat dirt. Short palm trees and overgrown bushes waved in the light breeze. They stopped when Stone spotted a water-stained, two-story concrete building with a red tin roof.

"That must be it. Let's move in until we see someone who doesn't look African," Stone said.

"Wait. I've got one of the boys on the other team calling," Sandra said. She listened on her cell phone a moment. "They're on the other side of the building. No activity."

"Tell them to move in cautiously. We will too."

They were approaching the building when they stopped, seeing no one outside or looking out the open windows. Birds chirping and wind blowing through the palm trees were the only sounds.

Stone's cell phone vibrated. Abdulyale's number appeared.

"Hello. Mr. Abdulyale."

"No need to whisper, Mr. Stone. Nabeel Asuty and his men have left. Headed for their ship."

Stone tugged Sandra's sleeve and said, "Careful."

"Keep walking, Mr. Stone," Abdulyale said, "and you'll see my black Peugeot sedan."

CHAPTER THIRTY-TWO

After Sandra returned to the SUV with the two Mossad agents, Hayden Stone got into Abdulyale's car and headed for the waterfront. He and Reynard Abdulyale talked in the backseat until the driver parked within sight of the Douala piers. Cries of seagulls came through the open windows.

"That is the ship Nabeel Asuty has chartered." Abdulyale pointed to a ship tied up along the quay. "It is registered in Panama and my office found some irregularities in the ship's paperwork. Most of these tramp steamers do." Looking at his gold watch, he said, "Asuty's men loaded a large crate into the forward hold of the ship exactly one hour and forty-seven minutes ago. The ship, the *SS Natal Bay*, is set to sail at six o'clock this evening. Destination is Montevideo, Uruguay."

"It's three o'clock now," Stone said, "Not much time to get the ..."

"The weapon of mass destruction." Abdulyale flicked his cigarette out the window. "Mr. Stone, hear me. You and your people will not board that vessel while it's in the harbor. I will not chance having those jihadists blowing up my city."

Stone said he understood. He studied the lines of the vessel. Like many ships plying the African coast, it was an ancient freighter, needing a good coat of paint. It resembled a WWII Victory ship, except it was smaller—he judged about 250 feet in length. The engine room, he guessed, would be toward the stern.

"Do you know the size of the crew?" Stone asked.

After Abdulyale spoke at length with his driver in an unfamiliar language, possibly the Fulani lingua franca, *Fulfulde*, he said, "The normal complement is around twenty men, but we saw crew members leaving the ship with their belongings. Asuty's men are replacing them."

"Damn!" Stone pulled out a handkerchief and wiped his face. The car's interior had become hot with the air conditioning turned off. "If terrorists can learn to fly commercial jets, they certainly can learn how to handle a ship." However, Stone knew a crew unfamiliar with the port and littoral needed help to sail twenty miles downstream to open water.

Stone thanked him for the information and asked to be taken back to his companions. During the ride, Abdulyale emphasized that he and his people would closely watch Stone and the ship until it set sail.

Returning to the SUV, Stone told Sandra and Dirk Lange they had less than three hours to come up with a plan. "That's when the ship is scheduled to leave for South America. Abdulyale won't allow an assault on the ship while it's in port. He's afraid Asuty will detonate the bomb."

"Reasonable position," Dirk said. "Why not let it sail, and when it reaches mid-Atlantic have one of your submarines torpedo it?"

"Great idea," Sandra said, "but the Washington lawyers and bleeding-heart environmentalists would have a heyday. A nuclear bomb lying on the bottom of the ocean."

Sandra's secure satellite phone rang and she whispered that Colonel Frederick was on the line. She held her hand over the handset and said Frederic and the team had landed at the airfield. He wanted to talk with Stone. Taking the phone, Stone gave him a rundown on the location of the ship and Abdulyale's position regarding any plan of assault.

"Screw him!" Frederick said. "We know where Asuty and the bomb are. We're not letting either get out of our hands *again*."

Stone got the message. "Colonel. I've cased the area. A raid would be very difficult. The ship is tied up on a quay with nothing around it. Absolutely no concealment to hide our approach. Abdulyale's people have the area under surveillance.

If Asuty has a nuclear engineer with him, they could set the damn thing off before we could get to it."

"I'm running this show, correct, Stone?"

"Absolutely."

"My decision is we board the ship. So get prepared," Frederick ordered. "We're leaving the airfield shortly. Have an attack plan ready."

Stone handed the phone back to Sandra. "Even after I explained the situation, Frederick wants to launch an assault."

Both Sandra and Dirk shrugged. Sandra said, "This whole operation could get real melancholy."

"Maybe not, if we come up with an alternative plan." Stone dialed Carl Cardinale. When he answered, Stone asked, "Could you get the name of the harbor pilot who's taking the *SS Natal Bay* out of port at six o'clock?"

Carl said he could and told him to hold on, saying he'd phone somebody on his landline. Two minutes later, he gave Stone a name, adding, "This guy is real slime. He's a big shot at a local charity that sends money to the jihadists in Palestine."

"Shit!" Stone said after hanging up. He told his companions what he learned. As he spoke to them, an idea came to him, and he called Abdulyale.

"Mr. Abdulyale. A harbor pilot has to take the ship out to open water beyond Cameroon's jurisdiction. Then a pilot boat comes alongside the ship, and he is taken off and brought back to port." Stone paused. "We could be on that pilot boat. As the pilot leaves the ship, we could get on."

"Very risky, but that would be your problem," Abdulyale said. "Not mine."

"I have another problem." Stone gave him the pilot's name and explained he could ruin the plan.

"That particular individual is on my organization's list for questioning on smuggling matters. I'll see that a more reasonable person will be assigned."

Stone's mind was racing. "Another thing. Is it possible that we can lease three fast motor boats, large enough to operate on open seas?"

Another pause at the end of the line. Finally, Abdulyale said, "Of course. It so happens I have a cousin in the boating business. This can be arranged. Unfortunately, he charges extremely high rates for his boats."

"Under the circumstances. I'm certain my organization will see no problem."

After he rang off, Stone took a deep breath. His companions stared at him. Sandra laughed. "I want to be there when you explain all this to Colonel Frederick."

"Ah. The colonel admires initiative."

In the cramped safe house, Colonel Gustave Frederick arched his back, threw out his chest, looked down his aquiline nose, and began pacing back and forth. Stone pictured Gus in full-dress Army uniform, similar to General George Patton, wearing khaki jodhpurs, riding boots, and slapping a swagger stick on his leg. He wished he would get over his theatrics, so they could get on with business.

Frederick surprised everyone. "Stone, with reservations, I say we set this plan of yours in motion."

"I need some volunteers to come with me on the pilot boat," Stone said.

Sandra, Dirk, and Jacob came forward. They were asked to decide on the choice of weapons and communication gear. "We want to take control of the bridge," Stone said. "Once we do that, Colonel Frederick and the assault team can come alongside in the power boats and board. Then we'll go down into the engine room."

"How many of the enemy will we face?" a CIA operative asked.

"Eighteen or nineteen," Jacob said. "We'll have them outnumbered once we get all our people aboard the ship."

"Our objective is to seize the nuclear bomb," Frederick said. "After that we wait for a US Navy amphibious ship that's just entered the Bay of Biscay. It will take a while for them to meet us."

"Any other help nearby?" Stone asked Frederick.

"There's a submarine in the vicinity," he answered, "but it can't be much help in an operation like this."

Stone asked Sandra what time it was.

"We have less than an hour."

"Not much time," Stone said. "Let's get cracking."

The pilot boat trailed in the wake of the *SS Natal Bay* steaming down the river toward the Gulf of Guinea. The sun had dipped below the horizon, leaving traces of a saffron-yellow glow on the cloud layer overhead.

Stone crouched in the bow section of the pilot boat and peered out at the ship ahead. His three companions sat next to him, checking their arms and extra ammunition. The brackish air coming in the open porthole relieved some of the oil and diesel fuel stench hanging inside the cabin. He calculated that in less than five minutes they'd board the ship. Sitting back, he followed his companions' routine and made sure his weapons and communication gear were in working order.

The freighter slowed as it entered the open estuary leading to deep water. The pilot would be leaving the ship. From behind a half-opened hatch, Stone looked up at the ship's deck. Crew members above lowered the accommodation ladder for the pilot to climb down from the ship. The boat pulled alongside the ship, bumping against the hull with its row of huge old truck tires lining the gunwale.

The pilot made his way down and jumped aboard the boat. He said to Stone, who emerged from the cabin, "Three armed men on the bridge, four on deck with machine guns. Good luck!"

Stone yelled to Sandra, "Now!"

The crew on the deck above prepared to hoist the accommodation ladder. Sandra raised her rifle, put the scope to her eye, and commenced firing. Stone jumped from the boat onto the ladder and scurried up while Jacob and Dirk followed. He saw two terrorists go down from Sandra's accurate shots.

Stone reached the deck and found two more men kneeling

over the bodies of the dead terrorists. The jihadists raised their weapons and fired. Stone sprayed them with his MP7 submachine gun, then ducked.

"Hand me a grenade," Stone shouted.

Dirk handed him a grenade and Stone pulled the pin. Waiting a few seconds, he tossed the grenade over the railing onto the deck. Screams followed the blast.

All three scrambled on deck, and Stone looked down to see Sandra climbing the ladder.

"Up to the bridge," Stone ordered and pointed to an open hatch. "That way."

Stone entered the passageway and the others followed. The plan called for a quick takeover of the bridge. Once there, they could control the ship, allowing Frederick and his team in the three speedboats to come alongside and board.

Stone came to a connecting passageway and stairs leading up to the next deck. Checking around the corner before going up, he almost hit a terrorist running with a pistol in his hand. Again, a short, quick ripping from the MP7 downed him. Jacob took the gun from the man's dead hand.

Up two more decks and the four raced down the passageway to the open door of the bridge. Stone rushed in and went to the right. Sandra followed and went to the left. They surprised only two of the expected three. Both were neutralized, their bodies thrown overboard.

The first part of the plan had gone well. The command center of the ship had been taken. All four were out of breath. Down below on the forward cargo deck, they watched armed men running for cover. Stone went to the ship's controls, which resembled those he knew from his navy days on a destroyer. He pulled the brass handle of the ship's engine order telegraph down to full stop.

Meantime, Sandra was on the radio with Frederick. Stone didn't like the way she said, "Oh." He also didn't like the fact the ship's engines continued to rumble on.

"One of the boats won't start," Sandra said. "They're in the remaining two, but they're barely able to keep up, let alone overtake us." She looked at the ship's controls. "Can't we stop this thing?"

"I've signaled the engine room to stop." Stone pointed to the telegraph. "Either no one is there to shut down the engines or the order has been countermanded." Stone ran out to the flying bridge and looked back at the two speedboats a thousand yards behind. Below, on the aft cargo deck, Stone watched Nabeel Asuty lead three men to the fantail of the ship, where they began shooting at the two speedboats.

Stone hurried back inside. "Two of us have to find our way down to the engine room to stop this ship. Two of you stay here and keep in contact with Frederick."

"Let's go, mate," Dirk said. "We're wasting time."

Stone guessed the engine room would be below them or farther back toward the stern of the ship. The noise and heat from the engine compartment would draw them to its location. The two encountered only one adversary, who popped out a door firing his machine gun. Dirk made short work of him and took the dead man's AK-47. "Never know when you could use an extra weapon," he said.

They went down the stairs, passed the empty galley, and reached the hatch leading down into the heat and smell of oil in the engine room. Stone indicated halt.

He couldn't see the control panel or where the attendant was stationed. Therefore, he'd have to race down the ladder, exposed to gunfire before he hit the deck below. They had eliminated six of the enemy, leaving at least twelve, including Nabeel Asuty. Stone had seen four on the forward deck and an equal number on the stern with Asuty. That left up to four who could be assigned to the engine room.

"Wait until I jump down before you follow," Stone said, speaking close to Lange's ear. "If they get me, toss these two grenades down in the engine pit and hope for the best."

With that, Stone slid down the ladder, and when he hit the metal deck saw two men pointing pistols at him. Before he could fire, they did. Their bullets clanged on the metal bulkheads and machinery around him. Raising his MP7, a bullet hit the gun's barrel, knocking it out of his hand. A piece of metal from the damaged submachine gun tore into Stone's left forearm.

Stone had managed only a "Motherf—" when Dirk Lange landed beside him, threw him the AK-47, and with one hand pointed and squeezed the trigger. The two men went down, but with difficulty. They fought the inevitable, continuing to shoot until it was apparent that all was lost. Stone had emptied his magazine.

"Bastards were tough, ay, mate?" Lange shouted over the nose of the engines.

"They should have accepted they were dead," Stone said, studying the control panel. "Waste of valuable ammunition." Thinking back to his days on a navy destroyer, he studied the series of switches and lights, then disengaged the engines' gearboxes. The two propeller shafts stopped turning.

Stone debated placing a grenade in the control panel, but wanted to leave the option of a sailable ship. "Let's get back to our companions. They may need us." As Stone reached for the handrail on the ladder, he winced in pain. He'd bother with the arm later.

Back on the bridge, they found Jacob and Sandra under fire from a terrorist sniper who had climbed one of the forward masts. The windows of the bridge were shattered. The two speedboats were moving up to the accommodation ladder that still hung down the side of the ship.

Sandra rolled up Stone's left sleeve and examined his wound. She opened the medical kit on her belt and wrapped the gash, stemming the flow of blood. "Now what?" she asked when finished.

"Get that sniper. When the team is aboard, we find the bomb. And Asuty."

Stone met Colonel Frederick standing at the head of the accommodation ladder ordering half his team aft to clear the jihadists who had positioned themselves on the fantail. Sunset had long passed, and from the bridge Jacob had turned on the ship's deck lighting.

Frederick wanted to know how many terrorists they had taken out, and Stone told him nine.

"Leaves about eight or nine. Shouldn't take long to complete the mission." Frederick stared hard. "Find the bomb?"

Stone shook his head. "Not enough time to look for it, but the Cameroon intelligence chief had told me he saw it being loaded in the forward cargo hold."

"Let's search that area. We'll probably find Asuty there."

Sandra partnered with Stone as Frederick led the second half of his team down numerous passageways until they all reached the three-story-high cargo hold. Stone and Sandra inched past and crawled over stacked machinery and crates. They came to an open area where, under an overhead spotlight, they saw the bronze-colored casing of the atomic bomb secured to a wooden pallet.

Nabeel Asuty and two men with AK-47s watched a man with a long scraggly beard standing by the nuclear weapon. A section of the casing had been removed, and the man's hands were inside using a tool on a mechanism.

"He's planning to set that thing off," Stone whispered and looked around for Frederick and his team.

At that, Sandra shouldered her MP7, set it to single-shot, and fired once, then again. Two bloody holes appeared on the back of the engineer's shirt. He fell to the side.

"Good shooting," Stone said.

Asuty was the first to return fire. He didn't retreat, instead advancing along with the other two men. Stone fired bursts from his Glock, and Sandra had gone to full automatic with her submachine gun. One of the men went down. Asuty turned left and ran behind a tall crate.

Stone chased him while Sandra continued to trade fire with the remaining terrorist, using stacked containers as cover.

Asuty scrambled across the cargo hold, packed goods acting as a shield, but Stone saw he was heading into a blind corner. Finally he reached the bulkhead with nowhere to go. Stone heard him reloading and did likewise, putting a fresh magazine into his Glock.

"Remember me, Nabeel Asuty?" Stone yelled. "You should have killed me when you had the chance."

The response came from Asuty firing a burst from his AK-47. Stone hit the deck and crouched as bullets buzzed around him.

Firing from the AK-47 stopped and Stone heard Asuty reloading. He leaped up and ran forward. From twenty feet away, Stone began shooting at Asuty's midsection and continued to fire until his gun clicked empty. Asuty hadn't had the opportunity to raise his gun.

Stone rested on a box, breathing hard. Without taking his eyes off Asuty's lifeless form, he inserted his last fresh magazine into his Glock.

"Thanks for nothing, Stone," came Sandra's voice from behind. "I wanted the pleasure of killing that son-of-a-bitch."

Stone and Sandra joined the assault team that had assembled on deck. Frederick seemed pleased with the results, saying they had only two casualties.

"Three," Jacob said, holding up Stone's injured arm.

Frederick sniffed. "Only two. That's just a scratch." He shouted to everyone, "We have seven minutes to get off this ship before it goes down."

"What?" Stone asked. "When and who set the explosive charges?"

"No explosive charges, Stone," Frederick growled. "Remember, I told you that I was running this show, not you. That is, most of the show."

"What happens next?"

"Change of plans. I've arranged for that submarine lying off the beam to torpedo this tub. They've been told to aim for the stern to avoid the bomb. With the stern blown off, she'll sink, leaving the forward section intact."

Stone took Frederick's arm and walked him over to the rail. "Gus," he said. "The navy's surface ships are only a day away.

Let's wait for them."

"Meanwhile we just sit here with that bomb?"

"No. We can get this ship underway. I can handle her."

"How long's it been since you've been in the navy? It's a very sound decision to torpedo this thing." Frederick pointed downward. "The bomb could go off any time. We don't know what those bastards did to it. Maybe placed a timing device on it."

"Hey, there's a nuclear sub out there with people who know all about nukes. Let's get them aboard to look at it."

Frederick looked out to sea. "Makes sense."

"We can also get someone who can navigate. If we steam toward those navy amphibious ships, we might meet in less than a day."

Frederick turned and spoke into Stone's ear. "All right. You win this one, but it's the last one."

Stone thought he detected a smile. "Don't worry, Gus. Once you send me that fat bonus check, I'll be out of your hair."

EPILOGUE

LANGLEY, VIRGINIA— SEPTEMBER 2002

Elizabeth Kerr sat behind her desk at the CIA's Task Force 21. Her boss, John Matterhorn, came in the office and took a seat. How funny life is, she thought. Only a month ago, she detested this motley collection of misfits, but now not only was she a member of the group, but also one of their bosses.

"So happy you decided to come over to the agency," John said. "This task force has a bright future. The agency is gearing up for a major push against international terrorism, and because of you our group will be a major player. It may even become a CIA Center!"

Elizabeth played with some paper clips on her desk. They had been instrumental in thwarting that threat, but they hadn't been on the ground. In the thick of things.

"Any more news on the situation there?" she asked.

"We've recovered the bomb. The Republic of South Africa wanted it back, but realized how embarrassing it would be if it were known they lost track of a nuclear weapon they said had been destroyed. Worse, one of their own people sold it to jihadists."

"What's become of Dawid van Wartt?"

"Charges were dropped for political or other reasons. He hasn't been seen lately."

"What about Hayden Stone?"

"Came through like a trooper. Retired now. Living somewhere along the Riviera. Villefranche, I believe."

"I'd like to meet him someday," Kerr said.

VILLEFRANCHE-SUR-MER

Hayden Stone sat on the open veranda enjoying a cold beer, watching sailboats on the Bay of Villefranche. He kicked off his boat shoes, lifted his feet onto the wood railing, and tried to relax. He had spent a whole morning sailing on the ketch, *La Claire*, and when he returned washed down the craft, stowed the sails, and tended to the rigging. Still, he felt restless. Perhaps it had to do with reading the articles on the one-year anniversary of the attack on the World Trade Center.

"There you are." Lucinda came up and stroked his hair. She eased into the chair next to him. "I've been over to Nice shopping."

They had been living together for almost a month, and things were working fairly well. Weeks before, when he had suggested he sell his home in Virginia, she surprised him. "Don't you dare," she protested. "I love to visit America."

"Are you bored? What do you plan to do with your days here in the South of France?"

Stone thought a moment. "I might grow flowers like that retired jewel thief in the Alfred Hitchcock film."

"What kind of flowers?"

"Pretty ones."

"I'd rather you work on managing my investments. I need someone I can trust. Also, you might like to look over the repairs to the palace roof, and while you're up there on the mountain check on the landscaping along the patio." She took a sip from his beer glass. "We might also go shopping for you. You need a new sweater for the winter." She reached over and pulled up the pant leg of his jeans. "Where on earth did you get those socks?"

Stone found the contessa bossy. This came as a surprise. He took her hand and kissed it. They watched a motorboat pull up to the slip.

"Are we expecting guests?" she asked.

"No," Stone said. Jacob waved from the boat, his white fisherman's sweater bright against the sky.

"Do I know that man?"

"He's a colleague. I mentioned him to you our last morning in Cape Town. We were together in Cameroon."

"Oh."

Stone went down to the boat. Two other men stood on the open deck. Stone didn't recognize their hard faces.

"Can we talk?" Jacob asked, stepping onto the pier.

Stone invited him up to the house to meet Lucinda, but he begged off. "Best we make this a chat between ourselves."

"Let's take a stroll along the waterfront."

He put his arm on Stone's shoulder. "Did anyone thank you for Africa?"

"A handsome bonus was sent to my bank in Switzerland." Stone was touched by Jacob's unexpected visit. "What brings you here to the Riviera?"

"Passing through. Have some diamond business to conduct. Dirk Lange returned to Sierra Leone. He's still deciding whether he'll join the new South African anti-corruption organization. When I was there he told me your mutual friend Jonathan benefited from your generous donation to Doctors Without Borders."

"Guess Jonathan will get his prosthetics after all."

"Some more news. Your adversary, Abdul Wahab, has managed to make himself indispensable to the intelligence community. They've taken him to Yemen to help counter al Qaeda activities there."

"Abdul Wahab lands on his feet like a cat."

"You've landed well too, my friend." Jacob directed his gaze at the seaside villa and the yacht, then pointed to the mountain. "Is that Lucinda's palace up there?"

"Yes."

After what seemed like a long moment, Jacob said without looking at him, "Hayden, everyone we know is getting into the fight. Afghanistan is going to be a protracted campaign. There's talk about going into Iraq. The jihadists are spreading their influence throughout the Horn of Africa." Jacob moved his face close to Stone's. "You've chosen the soft life."

"I've put in my years of service. I've done my part."

"I suppose there's no getting you back?" Jacob asked.

They didn't speak as they returned to the motorboat. Jacob said he'd stop by occasionally. The motorboat left as quickly as it came.

Lucinda insisted they drive into town and shop at a men's store. "Why did Jacob drop by?"

"He wanted closure on the African affair."

She slowed the Maserati. "Isn't the matter closed? You were instrumental in preventing a catastrophe, and now you are retired here." She took a deep breath. "With me."

He leaned over and kissed her cheek. Was she hinting he'd miss the intrigue, the danger?

After a relaxing dinner in the village of Èze, Stone changed into his pajamas and then heard a buzzing sound. He thought it was a faulty electrical circuit, then guessed he'd left his electric razor on. On his way to check, he saw the secure cell phone he'd neglected to return to the CIA when he departed Cameroon. Colonel Frederick's name appeared on the caller ID.

"Hello, Gus."

"Stone. What other CIA equipment haven't you handed back?"

"Pay me a visit and I'll personally turn the phone over to you."

"Right now, Hayden, I'm on a plane above you, looking at the lights of Nice. We're headed for Yemen." A pause. "You live well, my friend."

"Yes. I do."

"Have to sign off. Oh, Sandra Harrington is sitting next to me. She says, 'Get off your ass, Stone.'" The line went dead.

Hayden Stone went out to the balcony and peered at the sky. Among the many stars he was certain he spotted the lights of the plane carrying his comrades southeast to the Arabian Peninsula, to Yemen, the land he knew so well.

Turning, he looked back into the bedroom, where Lucinda was slipping on her negligee. No other woman was like her. If he left and joined his colleagues, would she welcome him back?

He shook his head in disbelief at what he was about to do. He looked down at the cell phone and redialed the last number.

THE END

GLOSSARY OF TERMS

Agent/Asset - Person obtaining intelligence for an intelligence agency, under control of a case officer

Blown/Burnt - Spy who has been exposed

Brush Pass - Momentary person-to-person contact to pass intelligence

Bug - Covert listening or recording device

Canadian Security Intelligence Service - Canada's foreign intel service

Case Officer - Staff officer of an intelligence agency

COS - Chief of a CIA station posted to a US Embassy

Counterspy - Intelligence officers charged with uncovering spies. FBI. MI5.

Double Agent - An agent believed to be working against a target country but is actually loyal to that country

Dry Clean - To evade surveillance

Extraordinary Rendition - Kidnapping of spies or terrorists for interrogation

LEGAT - Legal attaché, FBI agent attached to a US embassy

Legend - Life story created for a covert agent

Mossad - Israel's spy agency

MI6 - British Secret Intelligence Service (external)

NOC - Non-official cover, CIA equivalent of Russian illegal agent

Parole - Password used to confirm identity between agents

RSO - A US Embassy's regional security officer

Safe House - Place where spies can hide from hostile security services

Sleeper - Deep cover agent

Target - Person, place of intelligence interest

Tradecraft - Mechanics of/proficiency in espionage

ACKNOWLEDGEMENTS

I want to thank the members of my writing group, especially Betty Webb, for their support over the years. My ongoing thanks goes to my readers Judy Starbuck, Deb Ledford, and Virginia Nosky, who read and critiqued every page of the completed manuscript.

This book would not have been written without help from my publisher, Diversion Books, in particular Mary Cummings, Sarah Masterson Hally, Brielle Benton, and especially my editor Randall Klein, whose patience and assistance with the manuscript was invaluable.

My associates in the Desert Sleuths chapter of Sisters in Crime, Society of Southwestern Authors, and the International Thriller Writers have been most supportive of my writing. Special thanks to Nate Deason of the Phoenix Herpetological Society, in Scottsdale, Arizona for extending to me his knowledge of African reptiles.

Of course, thanks to my agent, Elizabeth Kracht of Kimberley Cameron & Associates, who works so hard on my behalf.

Finally, I want to express my gratitude to my wife, Donna, for her love and support.